INTRODUCTION

In the great tradition of beloved magical literature, like Peter Pan, Alice in Wonderland and Harry Potter, you are sure to fall in love with Mrs. Chubbly and her tribe! In a fantastic tale that transverses space, time and species, we are awakening. Mice, humans and all creatures struggle together valiantly to create a world of love and peace from one gone mad with greed and spiritual separation. The Secret Tales of Mrs. Chubbly awaits. If you believe that the good-hearted will prevail, then come with us now and save our world!

Ready? Our adventure begins…

Praise for the Author

Cindy LeBow weaves a world of incredible detail and warmth with the tales of Mrs. Chubbly. My first impression upon reading the manuscript was delight in discovering what felt like "Little Mouse on the Prairie", transporting one to a place and time long gone from this earth. There hasn't been a mouse this inspiring since Mickey, nor a nanny this magical since Mary Poppins.   —Roger Scot, Creative Consultant

I am amazed by Cindy LeBow's vivid imagination!!! This book is like Wind in the Willows meets Mary Poppins meets Watership

Down. Looking forward to more adventures with Mrs. Chubbly. —Tessa Lucas

The Tales of Mrs. Chubbly will touch the innermost sanctum of your heart. It will remind you of when you were young and small, relying upon a larger world to protect you, with an open heart and a full imagination. It will transport you to the present to your highest and best self, your expression of your compassion, your nascent and ongoing evolution, and the desire to become who we can be. Not preachy or even teachy, but through kindness and empathy one cannot escape the recognition of the essence of Mrs. Chubbly in each of us who have experienced -- not just waltzed through -- life. Read it and enjoy being present. —Jordan glass Esq

Flippin' fantastic book. A page-turner. Charming, very well-written, perfect adorable character names and development, and likable personalities. I can visualize each scene in my head, and I love the use of new words in this new world. —Keri Bowers, Author

Cindy LeBow's novel is definitely a page-turner. From the beginning, there is feeling of being handed a cup of tea and told to sit back, relax, and prepare for an adventure. Each chapter leaves a longing to visit the warm nest in Chelsea and to meet Mrs. Chubbly and her charming company. I'm waiting for the amazing sequel! —Zac Gilbert, Author

Copyright © 1986 & 2020 Cindy LeBow

Mother Tree Publishing
264 1st Street
Brooklyn, NY 11215
www.mothertreepublishing.com

Ordering Information:
Quantity sales. Special discounts are available on quantity purchases by corporations, associations, and others. For details, contact the publisher at the address above.
Orders by U.S. trade bookstores and wholesalers. Please contact us at Tel: 718-369-9000; Fax: 718-369-9011 or visit
www.mothertreepublishing.com
Printed in the United States of America

The Secret Tales of Mrs. Chubbly

(How one small mouse saved the world.)

By

Cindy LeBow

Dedication

For David the Relentless Adventurer.

You inspire me.

And for the Kilby Book Club, I am grateful.

Acknowledgements

Thank you, Roger Scott and Wendalyn Wolf for artwork, encouragement and editorial support during this creative process, some pieces of your art have been used in this special edition. Thank you to everyone who encouraged me along the way. Thank you, James K. for my first good pen. Thanks to all of my children (in order of appearance) Wendy, David, Ben, Lucas, Daniel and Robert for relentlessly encouraging me to write, and do what I love. You guys never let up on me, and never stopped pressing me forward. You all know what you did. Myra Sonnenblum and Natalie Goldberg, for encouraging me to write and read and love the written word. Gratitude to Mallory Loehr for reading an early manuscript and encouraging me to publish (even though I wasn't ready yet). Thank you to each person who read Mrs. Chubbly and laughed and cried and asked me when they could have the next book. Gratitude to all of my spiritual teachers, writing teachers, and to all of my students, and to everyone who has walked this amazing path beside me.

May the Great Creator Bless your lives in all the ways you have blessed mine, and more.

Aho-Maste

Table of Contents

1. The Interview

Every tale has a time to be told and now the time has come to tell this one. It began one cool autumn morning as I was seeking employment. I answered an advertisement for a full charge nanny. I think it was the Rodent Herald Record. The ad read simply:

FULL CHARGE NANNY TO CARE FOR TWINS AND A NEWBORN. MUST KNOW HOW TO DEAL WITH CATS.

ROOM AND BOARD AND A STIPEND.

START IMMEDIATELY! 22 North Chelsea Lane

Well, I've had a lot of experience with cats and the thought of twins was challenging to my abilities as a nanny, so I packed my bag and hurried over for a look.

The house was lovely, tall and white with lots of gingerbread trim and pale blue shutters on all of the windows. The front gate was wrought iron, freshly painted white and a well manicured lawn led up to the large oak doors. A brass lion head stood as guardian and door knocker, with a thick brass ring hanging from his mouth. Below him, close to the white marble stoop, was an extremely ornate brass mail slot—ah!—with a nice wide opening. I climbed through the mail slot and slid down the other side coming to a perfectly soft landing on the rose coloured hall carpet.

I was immediately greeted by a fat, furry, black and white cat with gleaming green eyes. He looked down at me hungrily and licked his lips. I looked around and quickly spied a large crack in the entry wall; it was a short dash from where I stood. Even an elder like myself could make it in time, so I distracted the beast with a hard blow on the tip of his pink nose. I always carry a walking stick; they're terribly handy! He retreated quite surprised that any creature would ever challenge his authority and I realized he would need a few lessons in good manners. Before he got over his surprise, I slipped quietly into the crack and found myself in a richly furnished nest.

No sooner had I entered, then I was met by a frail-looking young mother who was clearly in need of my assistance. She carried a basket lined with her own soft grey fur and nestled in it was the cutest four-month mouseling I had ever seen. Right behind the mother scurried two energetic young mice, both of them bright eyed and curious—but they stood behind her shyly, as if they were unused to strangers.

"Hello, I'm Mrs. Twingle," she extended her paw as she greeted me in a charming, soft-spoken voice. "And you are?"

"Mrs. Chubbly, at your service." I took her paw in my own and patted it comfortingly. "I've come in answer to your advertisement for a nanny."

She looked me over and her tail twitched nervously. Good nannies are difficult to find, and one doesn't leave young mouselings with just any creature. I smiled at her warmly and gave her my letter of reference. She read it quickly, nodding her head as she read, then smiled up at me with approval.

"How impressive! Thank you for coming, Mrs. Chubbly. As you can see, I've got my hands quite full with the twins running around and a quarter-old to care for."

The twins were peering out shyly from the protective folds of her floor length purple satin dress. They were dressed in good fabrics, immaculately groomed and well behaved. I guessed them to be eight or nine years old. The entry to the nest was also immaculate, tastefully decorated in several shades of blue. This would be a nice place to call home for a while.

"I suppose you'll be needing somecreature to start immediately?" I asked.

"Oh yes! That would be extremely helpful, you see," she went on confidentially, "Herbert, I mean, Mr. Twingle has been doing all the gathering and with a family of five mouths to feed, he really does need my help. Why don't I show you to the nursery."

I picked up my bag, smoothed my apron and followed Mrs. Twingle through the walls, feeling pleasantly employed as she led me to the nursery, mouselings in tow.

And what a nursery it was! No expense was spared. The mouselings seemed to have the best of everything. The wooden blocks were pawmade and brightly paw painted with alphabets and charming pictures of many creatures, and there were dolls and animals of every sort. The beds were lovely and overstuffed with the fluffiest sparrowdown, and the bedclothes were made from the finest scraps of fabric a mouse could gather. But what impressed me the most were the books. There were shelves and shelves, floor to ceiling, of the loveliest pawmade books I had ever seen, and I have been in many fine nurseries. There was a full set of mouse encyclopedias, the full history of rodents, and all of the human classics copied into mouse size. It was truly a nest filled with the love of knowledge.

How lucky these mousekins were until the paw of providence reached down and suddenly changed all of our lives.

"Here we are, Mrs. Chubbly, these are the twins Weency and Eency." Weency curtsied in a fine, well-mannered way. Eency bowed self-consciously, still behind his mother.. "And this is our new addition, little Mop," she said, smiling and tipping the basket toward me for a better look. I gazed into the basket of the angelic sleeping mousekin. It was obvious why they named her Mop, her full tuft of thick headfur, tied in a sliver of pink velvet ribbon, flopped back and forth between her ears as Mrs. Twingle passed the basket into my waiting arms.

"Hello mouselings, I am Mrs. Chubbly and if everything is satisfactory, I shall be your new nanny."

The mouselings looked surprised and I realized that they probably never had a nanny before. I was to be their first. Mrs. Twingle's face was all aglow, delighted that I would consider overseeing her brood. She sighed deeply, with long awaited relief.

"Oh, thank you, Mrs. Chubbly. Now, you just make yourself right at home and get to know the mouselings." She put her paw to her mouth and whispered to me, "they've never met an outsider before, I do hope you'll be patient if they appear to be a bit shy." Then in her normal voice she continued, "when I return, I'll show you to your quarters. Herbert and I are just going to step out for a bit of gathering, the cupboard is empty and it's been so long since I've been out. Oh, did I mention the cat? Chesterfield can be quite a nuisance if you have no experience with cats."

"No trouble, we met as I came in. I don't believe he'll be bothering me any further. You just run along and have fun, your brood is in good paws." I turned to the twins, "Would you like to hear a story, mouselings?"

The twins looked me over carefully then Weency nodded—more to Eency than to me, but that's the way it is with twins. I pulled a large ratskin volume down from the shelf and when I sat down and opened the book in my lap, the twins cautiously sat on either side of me, to better see the colourful illustrations. I placed Mop beside me, still napping quietly in her basket.

And I remember quite well the sense of foreboding I felt, as Mrs. Twingle waved goodbye and twittered gaily out of the nursery to join her waiting husband.

"Hurry, Jenny, we'll be just in time for the breakfast dishes if we get there before Mrs. Hammond clears," Herbert shouted from the crackway.

They were both unusually excited that day, as they had not been gathering together since the mouselings were born. And from their excitement, all the lessons every mouse learns from the time it is old enough to forage for itself flew from their heads.

I felt it in my bones as I sat quietly reading to the unsuspecting mouselings, and if we paid more attention to that warning voice within us that we hear from time to time (when we are listening), think of the events we could change. But I dismissed my fearful thoughts and continued the story in the safe and quiet nursery, while Jenny Twingle ran through the crackway, hurrying to catch up to her husband.

And then it happened: The hem of her lovely long satin dress caught on a carpet tack that some human had carelessly turned up on the hall rug. She grabbed at her skirt and pulled and tugged, trying in vain to set herself free, and when she turned to call Herbert for help, she found herself looking into the hungry mouth of Chesterfield Cat. She barely had time to squeal in fear. I'm sure it was over in an instant, but Herbert turned to the sound of her squeal and looked on in horror as his delicate wife was gobbled up. Throwing all caution aside, he ran bravely to her aid and fell into the clever, sharp claws of the cat. Chesterfield was so hungry, thank The Great Creator, he didn't even give a thought to playing with the second mouse, but also gobbled him up instantly.

The mouselings were (of course) now orphans—which is not unusual for young mice, as it is dangerous business being a mouse in a house that keeps a hungry cat. Lucky for everycreature, I was there, or I'm sure the little ones would have been the next to go.

That is how I came to be nanny to Weency, Eency and Mop—and from that day onward I was also mother, father, and nursemaid to them, teaching them the lessons that every smart mouse must learn, if it is to survive.

I stayed on to care for my new family, and also in time, to teach Chesterfield Cat that although cats will be cats and mice will be mice, there are some things that one just does not do!

2. Chesterfield's First Lesson

The twins sat silently leaning on my abundant lap, their large grey ears perked open, listening carefully to every word of the story I read aloud. Mop still slept peacefully in her fur-lined basket near my knee, but she awoke suddenly with a frightened squeal as we all heard the loud and familiar sound of a hungry "Meeeeoooow" and the ensuing struggle at the crackway to their once safe and quiet nest. Their eyes were as large as thimbles, trying to understand the meaning of the terrible noises they were now hearing and the familiar voices of their mother and father squealing for help, and then all was quiet.

"Mother! Father!" Eency and Weency screamed as they stood up like brave young mousekins to run to the sound of their parent's voices. They started toward the opening that led from the nursery but knowing my duty, I grabbed their long tails and stopped them in mid-step, not without first turning poor frightened Mop out of her basket and onto the nursery floor.

"Mouselings! Stop this instant!" I commanded. "Being a mouse, you must always think before you act. Eency, sit down at once—now you will be the elder male of the nest. Weency, sit right here next to Eency and don't either of you move a whisker until I return." I scooped Mop up off the floor, dried her tears and placed her in her older sister's arms.

"Now Weency, you will be the Momma and Mcp will be your mousekin, and you will all quietly play at nestkeeping while I examine the situation. Is that clear?"

"Yes, Mrs. Chubbly," they nodded in unison.

They were obviously frightened and confused but mouselings can be fickle, so I successfully distracted them from disaster long enough to slip away and discover the horrible truth. I straightened my spectacles, took hold of my walking stick, and headed for the crackway.

Peering cautiously out of the crack, it all became horribly clear. The overturned carpet tack stood like a monument next to the mousehole. It was covered with a torn piece of purple satin from Mother Twingle's dress, and by examining its barbed end, I could see exactly how it trapped her and brought her to an untimely end. Father Twingle's red velvet cap lay next to it on the hall rug, empty. Another awful clue that I loathed to find so easily. And here lay the culprit himself, fat and lazy, lolling on the drawing room rug in front of the fireplace, licking the innocent blood from his claws. I took a deep breath and put my own distress aside. I wouldn't stand for this type of behavior from a cat who was at least a year old and well out of kittenhood. Knowing that he already had quite a large meal and was temporarily rendered harmless from his barbaric feline instincts, I marched right up to his nose, my walking stick held high above my head as I charged forth.

"Chesterfield Cat!" I shouted, in my strictest nanny tone. I had him by surprise and he forgot the difference in our sizes and pulled himself into the stance of a kitten being scolded by its mother.

"Meow?" he cried in a small voice.

"You have done a terrible and ill-mannered thing, taking the lives of a mother and father mouse and leaving three innocent mouselings orphaned."

"Me? What?" Chesterfield cowered at the sight of my sharp walking stick raised not an inch from his tender nose.

"Don't play innocent with me, Chesterfield, facts are facts. And now you must take responsibility for your unforgivable actions." I brought my stick down hard on his nose, and the pain caused him to wince and pull back. His large green eyes became wide with surprise and he covered his sore nose with his paws.

"Why, you're just a mouse." he said rather uncertainly, as if he wasn't sure just who was the cat and who was the mouse anymore.

"That's where you're quite wrong. When I entered this house for my interview, I was just a mouse looking for a nanny position. But now that you have committed this terrible crime, you have caused me to become the sole caretaker, protector, and nanny to three very young mouselings."

"I see," said Chesterfield, not really seeing at all. He scratched at his pointed ear, trying hard to understand the strange situation he had created.

"Now, where is your mother?" I asked, my paws placed firmly on my hips in a most authoritative fashion. I tapped my foot loudly, waiting for his reply.

"My mother? Uh, I don't know." He looked down embarrassed by his reply. "I was brought in from the animal shelter to keep the pantry free from rodents. I... I never knew my mother." He groomed his paw nervously.

Of course this softened my heart and I better understood poor Chesterfield's situation.

"Aha, now I see. You were brought up by humans at an animal shelter, never nursed or licked properly. Well, that accounts for your lack of good breeding." Chesterfield was saddened by the truth of my remark, and put his face between his paws, listening for my next reproach. I stood silently watching him.

"I suppose, I mean, you're probably quite right, but don't my personal circumstances count for anything in this matter?"

"Why, of course, Chesterfield. All of these things will be taken into account when I decide your punishment." Chesterfield looked quite shocked and immediately stood up and puffed himself up into a full grown tom, ready to defend his territory.

"Punishment! Wait just a moment here. I'm the cat, aren't I? And you're the mouse, aren't you? And instincts are instincts. Well, I was just doing my job!" He growled at me, as cats often do when they're unsure of their position.

"Poppycock! Instincts are no excuse for barbaric ill-mannered behavior!" I countered loudly, still taping my foot. He unpuffed and sat down. I still had the upper paw, so I went on calmly.

"Of course you're a cat and we all understand that cats eat mice, that's your nature, however there are still certain rules of etiquette that everycreature must follow."

"Etiquette? rules? I don't quite understand." He cocked his head to one side and looked rather confounded.

"Oh, Chesterfield—of course you don't understand, you've never even been given the chance." I explained in a gentle voice. "Think about this for a moment, Chesterfield.

Perhaps your own mother had just birthed a litter of furry black and white kittens, yourself among them. Perhaps your father, doing his rightful duty, had gone out to hunt for food to feed his hungry mate who was busy nursing her litter."

Chesterfield looked dreamy eyed, watching visions of his kittenhood appear before him, and he listened entranced as I went on with my story.

"Perhaps, while your father was absent, a large hungry dog chased your mother down and had her and several of your brothers and sisters for his lunch." A horrified expression filled his large green eyes as I went on. "Now, that dog was just following his instincts but he showed terribly bad manners by leaving you as an orphan. The only decent thing would have been to eat you all or he could have found a cat under different circumstances. Do you see now?"

"Oh Mother," Chesterfield whispered mournfully, as he realized that my tale might very well have been the truth of his past. "What have I done? How can I ever make this up to the little orphans?" he said, hanging his head.

"That's a good kitty, Chesterfield—perhaps we will be able to help you, yet." He fetched a stuffed felt mouse that smelled strongly of catnip and offered me a seat. Though his lack of good breeding clearly showed by his choice of the seat, at least he was trying to make amends.

"Thank you," I said, as I sat cautiously on the back of the strange cushion. Chesterfield sat down next to me, moping and filled with self-pity.

"Listen to me carefully Chesterfield, the first thing you must always remember is: you must never, under any circumstances eat the mouselings. Is that clear?"

"Oh, I would never think of it, of course not!" He seemed appropriately taken aback, that I would even suggest that he would eat the little ones. He sat up tall, trying hard to look proud and well bred.

"Next, you must keep your hunting to the rats in the cellar and only those who do not have ratkins, do you understand?"

"Of course, I may not have a mother but I'm certainly not dimwitted." I stood up, smiled at him and reached out my paw. He just sat there looking at me quizzically.

"Chesterfield, when somecreature extends their paw to you, it is only polite to extend yours as well."

"My goodness, how silly of me for not knowing." He extended his paw awkwardly and touched it to mine for a moment.

"Good, now we have shook on it and have a gentlecreature's agreement." I brushed the cat fur off of my apron to keep from frightening the mousekins any further. "I must be running along now, the little ones have had a difficult day and need my full attention, I'm sure you understand."

"I hope to see you again soon," Chesterfield said, using his best tea manners. "Please, do apologize to the mouselings for me, I really don't know what else to say." He bowed his head at the thought of his reckless act.

"Well spoken, Chesterfield, like a good English house cat. I certainly will express your condolences regarding the untimely passing of their Mother and Father, and I'm sure we will see each other again very soon. Aho-maste" I finished with the commonly known greeting of peace and safe-passage. Aho-Maste means Peace and Truce to all creatures, I see The Great Creator in you and you see The Great Creator in me. Even natural predators who use this sacred greeting are assured of not being eaten or harmed so we can communicate safely and freely and work together for the highest good of Creaturedom.

I hurried off to the nest, certain that the mouselings must be wondering what had become of me and as I glanced back it seemed to me that Chesterfield Cat looked very pensive and soft, and certainly more mature.

3. The Cupboard is Bare

When I returned to the nest, the mouselings had given up the game of nestkeeping and were nervously peering out of the nursery.

"It's alright mouselings, Mrs. Chubbly is here."

"Oh, Mrs. Chubbly, we were so worried. It seems you have been gone for ages." Eency was speaking for all of them, and now Weency stood behind him clutching Mousekin Mop. My, how circumstances change one's plans! They followed me back into the nursery, the three of them looking at me through worried eyes. I began to pick up toys and books, straightening up the nursery, while thinking of the gentlest way to tell these innocents the awful truth.

"Where is Mother?" Weency asked in a frightened voice. Mousekin Mop began to fuss and Eency looked away from me. The young ones always seem to know the truth before you tell them, so I thought it best to just say it in the most straightforward manner.

"Mouselings, you must all be very brave when I tell you what I've discovered. First, let me assure you that I will be staying on to love you and care for you all—as if you were my very own." The words I chose to comfort them frightened them all the more and they huddled together near the bed.

"Where is Mother?" Eency demanded.

"I'm sorry, Eency, but your mother is gone. Your mother and father were eaten by Chesterfield Cat."

Weency screamed, and I took Mousekin Mop from her arms as she fell into a faint on the bed. I tucked Mop tightly into her fur-lined basket and dangled it from my arm as I had seen her mother do the same. It comforted her to be rocking that way as I sat down next to Weency on the bed. She came to and began crying pitifully. I put my arm around her and she sat there crying softly against my shoulder.

Eency was furiously storming about the room, too angry to allow himself to cry.

"I'm going to kill that cat. I'm going to go after him and kill him for eating my parents!"

"Now, Eency, I understand how you must feel," I said, trying to calm him.

"How could you? He didn't eat your parents!"

"I too have lost loved ones to a hungry cat. My parents in fact." I patted the bed next to me and he reluctantly came and sat down beside me.

"You did?"

"Yes, and I was angry and sad, as you are. I know this may seem very difficult for you to understand right now, but the answer to killing is never more killing. The answer is going on with life and living well. Sadness and grief are natural and important, and healing. But if you hold onto anger and rage and hatred, you will soon become like the very thing that you hate. And that's not what your parents want for you. Now we have the task of survival to contend with." I kissed Weency on top of her head and lay her down, tucking the bedclothes around her and placing the basket by her side. By the time I was finished, she and Mop had both fallen into an exhausted sleep.

Eency looked at his twin sister for a moment as she lay sleeping, and turned to me whispering, "You know, Mrs. Chubbly, I suspected the truth all along but I didn't say anything because I didn't want to frighten my sisters."

"Well, that was very good of you Eency. I'm glad you can behave in such a grown-up fashion, which brings to mind another important matter. Have you ever been gathering with your father?"

"Certainly! I'm no yearling, you know."

Weency must have been listening while she dozed, for she sat up suddenly and cried loudly.

"Mrs. Chubbly, don't let him go! He'll be eaten by the cat—he's never been out of the nest before!" The mouseling was terribly afraid of losing her twin brother after the sudden loss of her parents. I smoothed her headfur and lay her back down as I spoke in comforting tones.

"Dear sweet Weency, I have taken care of Chesterfield Cat, and as far as Eency's experience out of the nest, well, he's the head male of the nest now, and he has to learn sometime—why not today?"

Eency looked away, embarrassed at being caught so easily in his lie.

"Eency, you must never lie. It is in very bad form, and will only bring you more trouble than you can imagine, more trouble than facing the discomfort of telling a difficult truth."

He looked down at his lap and answered quietly, "Yes, Mrs. Chubbly, I'm sorry."

I checked on Mousekin Mop and took Eency's paw.

"Now we've got things to get on with, so first things first. Weency, you rest here and care for Mop if she awakens. Eency, come along and show me to the pantry, and we will see about provisions for dinner."

We scurried along the wallway to the pantry and the kitchen. Mrs. Twingle was a good mother and had everything fixed up just so. The kitchen was clean and cheerful, and was done very brightly in finger paint yellow. A nice large wire spool served as a table and the top of it was neatly finished by the cover of a cracker tin. There were six small thread spools, each with its own yellow cloth cushion, making up a nice matched set of kitchen chairs. And Mr. Twingle was innovative enough to put the kitchen on an exterior wall and had installed an old tin can as a stove pipe over a lovely red candy tin that served as fireplace and hearth. He must have been very handy, for over the tin on a bent pin hung a large thimble that was used as a stew pot. Being a well-trained nanny and gourmet cook, you can imagine my pleasure in discovering this wonderful kitchen where the mouselings and I would be taking our meals. But, to my disbelief, when I opened the pantry curtain—I found the cupboard was totally bare, except for a hunk of cracker that appeared as if it had been there for some time.

"Dear me! There isn't a thing to eat," I said, as Eency stood next to me on tippaw, peering into the empty cupboard, his stomach growled loudly.

"We haven't had any breakfast," he said, with the frightening realization one gets when one's parents are suddenly gone, and one discovers all the little things they've been doing for you that you now must do for yourself.

"Hmmm, and it's almost time for dinner. Weency and Mop will be most upset when they wake up and find nothing to eat. Eency, it's time for you to learn how to gather food. You are the head male of the nest now that Mr. Twingle is gone." Eency tried hard to look sure of himself and he stood up tall.

"I can do it, Mrs. Chubbly. I'll go get us dinner. I'll bring back enough food to fill the shelves!"

"Well your enthusiasm is good, but your lack of experience could send your running out of the nest into the steel jaws of a mousetrap, or perhaps the mouth of a hungry cat."

My speech gave Eency pause for thought, and he no longer seemed so ready to dash off without thinking.

"Gathering food is a big responsibility. You must be very brave and very smart not to get caught." Eency looked very young all of a sudden and neither of us were sure he was up to the task at hand. "I will help you get started, but first you must promise me that you will never lie. You must always be willing to admit that you don't know something. There's nothing wrong with not knowing, but no elder mouse will be able to teach you—until you are willing to be honest and admit your ignorance."

"I promise, Mrs. Chubbly, I promise to be honest.' His voice was quiet and serious. I believed him.

"Good, then let's see about getting dinner, shall we?"

"But, Mrs. Chubbly, I don't even know where to begin," he said nervously.

"The perfect place to begin is the beginning." I looked around the kitchen for the proper tools to help Eency with his gathering. "I've seen to it that Chesterfield Cat won't be bothering any of us, however, as all mice know, one must never trust a cat, as they are our natural enemy. Most of your gathering must be done after dark or before dawn, as that's when most humans are asleep. A human being is far more dangerous than a cat. They'll use all kinds of tricks to catch a mouse, and from the looks of this house I'd say there are quite a few humans around."

"Oh yes, there are, Mrs. Chubbly—Mother used to tell us stories about them. There's a mother, and a father, and a young girl with golden hair, and there's the housekeeper, Mrs. Hammond. Mother always said Mrs. Hammond was terrified of mice."

"There you have it Eency, she's the one most likely to be on the lookout for a mouse in her kitchen," I said.

"The kitchen! But Father said that's way across the other side of the house!"

I put my paws on his shoulders to reassure him. "I know it is, Eency, but the kitchen is where the food is, and although it's still light out, you must get to the kitchen and bring us back some civilized scraps to eat. Nothing fancy or heavy, mind you—just a little something so we won't go hungry tonight."

I felt him trembling beneath my paws. This was a large burden for such little shoulders.

"I'm frightened, Mrs. Chubbly," he said in a very small voice. I put my arms around him and hugged him close to me.

"A little fear can be a good thing, Eency. It will make you careful."

I found the sack hanging on the kitchen wall. It was well worn from Father Twingle's previous gatherings, and I showed Eency how to tie it around his waist so it wouldn't be in his way.

"Now, just a piece of muffin or some crumbs of cheese will do for tonight. You must stay close to the walls at all times and always keep your eyes open for a crack or crevice, or someplace to dash into should you be discovered." He nodded his head in understanding. "And something else you must remember: if you should be spotted by a female human, they usually let out a horrible war cry and bring everyone in the house running to see what the matter is. Then, they will either jump on the nearest chair, dancing wildly, continuing the scream, or if they are very brave, they will grab the nearest object and come after you."

"That all sounds so terrible and frightening," Eency said, his eyes wide with fear.

"Well, it's mostly a lot of harmless noise. The main danger you face is your inexperience. Most mice will naturally react to the scream by freezing in their tracks and staring at the unbelievable sight—that's the worst thing you can do. So, you must use all your self-control to keep moving—no matter what. Because if they catch you..."

I didn't want to continue, for fear of frightening the mousekin all the more, but Eency had to know the truth. It would keep him from acting foolishly. He looked at me with those big wide eyes.

"Go on Mrs. Chubbly, what will they do?"

"They do many awful things to mice, Eency. They might catch you in a drinking glass and toss you down a water-filled bowl to drown. Or they'll break your neck and throw you into the garden to be eaten by the birds," I replied.

"How horrible those humans are! But, why? Why do they behave that way, Mrs. Chubbly?"

"That, my dear, is a lesson for another day. Now you must hurry up and gather, and then hurry back. I'm sure lunch hasn't been cleared up yet and there should be some easy pickings on the dining room rug or the kitchen counter."

I walked Eency to the crackway and we both peered out cautiously, together. It was very still. Chesterfield was asleep on the rug near the fire. Not a single footstep could be heard in the entire downstairs. So, with a hug and a pat on the back, I sent Eency off on what was to be more of an adventure and learning experience than either of us expected. He checked the sack to make sure it was tied correctly and could be easily opened when he found a morsel. When he was certain it was right, he slipped off along the long entry wall, heading toward the dining room as if he had done it a thousand times before. I watched from the crack until he disappeared around the turn in the wall. Trusting the powers that be, I went inside to tend to the other mouselings.

4. Eency Meets Mrs. Hammond

When I arrived at the nursery I found both mousettes sound asleep. Mop must have woken up fussing, for Weency had taken her into the large bed and the mousekin safely snuggled up against her sister's warm fur. This little creature would be a wonderful mother someday. I cleaned up the rest of the playthings, tucked the covers around the sleeping pair, and continued on through the walls to explore my quarters and the rest of the nest.

Each room was decorated tastefully and the nest contained the most ingenious devices to make life easier for any mouse. I had just finished putting away my things in a charming dresser made from very ornate matchboxes that had been carefully stacked and glued together, when I heard an ear-shattering scream. I imagined it must be the housekeeper, Mrs. Hammond, and I could only pray that Eency remembered his lesson well. Mousekin Mop began to squeak and squeal, and I ran to the nursery to find a large lump in the bed. Weency had pulled the bedclothes over both of their heads.

"You're safe girls, I'm here now. Nothing is going to harm you." I sat on the bed and gathered them into my arms.

"Mrs. Chubbly! Where's Eency?" cried Weency, her voice high pitched and tense.

"He went to gather dinner, but I'm sure he'll return safely—he's a very smart mouse. From the sound of that scream, I think Mrs. Hammond is the one who's in trouble. He must have frightened that human out of her wits."

We sat quietly and waited to see if any other sounds from the big house would give us a clue to the whereabouts of Eency. After the initial scream, all we heard was the stomping about of heavy footsteps and some scuffling—some slamming of doors, and then all was quiet.

"Weency, play quietly with Mop while I go to the crack and see what I can see."

Weency took a large dried green pea down from the toy shelf, and singing a comforting song to her younger sister, she showed her how to play roll the ball, while I gathered my composure and hurried to the entryway crack. I peered out cautiously and saw Mrs. Hammond stomping about in her large black shoes, shouting and waving a broom in the air.

"Chesterfield! Where are you, you lazy cat! Where is that cat? The house is being overrun by filthy mice and that no good cat is nowhere to be found."

She is certainly a mean one! Imagine—filthy mice! I suppose she had no idea how neat and tidy mice really were, not knowing one personally. I ventured out a bit further and noticed Chesterfield slinking quietly out the French Glass doors to the garden, trying desperately to go unnoticed. I suppose he was going to hide out in the garden until Mrs. Hammond was over her rage about Eency. Meanwhile, I searched every crack and crevice I could see from the hall, and couldn't spot Eency anywhere. I assumed he was hiding somewhere safe; that was all I could do for the moment. Then I noticed that the crystal candy dish on the afternoon tea cart had just been filled with fresh chocolates—and not knowing when or if Eency would return, I knew I had to take it upon myself to get some nourishment for my hungry mouselings. Chocolate soup would be a fine dinner. I looked around once more to find the proper route, and then I slipped off carefully down the hallway toward the unguarded tea cart. The white lace cloth made an easy ladder, even for a mouse as old and unused to gathering as myself. In the twinkle of an eye, I was up on the cart top. I was a paw's reach from a sumptuous looking truffle when I heard the frightening sound of Mrs. Hammond's big feet stomping into the room—and I quickly slipped beneath one of the linen tea napkins that sat folded conveniently next to the crystal dish.

"Mr. Lovely, we've got to get another cat. Perhaps we can call the shelter and find a better mouser," she said harshly.

"Now, Mrs. Hammond, calm yourself. Chesterfield has always been a perfectly good mouser, after all everyone is entitled to a slip up now and then," he said, trying to soothe her.

"But Mr. Lovely," she whined, "you saw for yourself that brazen little mouse sitting right there in the middle of my nice clean kitchen floor, and Chesterfield nowhere in sight. Why, I myself had to chase the dirty thing out into the garden. I wasn't hired to keep the mice out of the kitchen. I think I have more important tasks to tend to, like the cleaning and the cooking."

Mr. Lovely slammed his newspaper down onto the couch. "All right! All right, Mrs. Hammond. I'll see about it first thing after tea."

Oh kitty whiskers! Not another cat in the house, and Eency out alone in the garden—why, the poor dear must be terrified! I peered out from the corner of the napkin. The garden doors were left ajar from Chesterfield's sneaky escape and the sun was shining brightly enough for any bird to easily find

Eency and snap him right up. I knew I had to work quickly and go searching for the lad myself. Just as I was about to move, the tea cart jolted across the floor and I found myself sitting ungracefully on my tail. My, oh my! Was I about to be discovered next? The cart glided some distance before it came, once again, to an abrupt stop in front of the couch.

"Will you be taking your tea now, Mr. Lovely?" Mrs. Hammond asked, in a tone I would never expect from a good English housekeeper. I held my breath and prayed, waiting for Mr. Lovely's reply.

"No, Mrs. Hammond, just leave the cart there. I'll help myself shortly."

Oh, thank The Great Creator; a reprieve. I had to think fast.

"Very good sir, I'll be in the kitchen if you need anything."

I listened to Mrs. Hammond's retreating footsteps, afraid to even peer out from my conspicuous hiding place.

"Hmmm, first things first. I've got to get a truffle back to the nest to feed the mouselings, and then quickly get out to the garden and find Eency, before another disaster takes place."

Suddenly there was a loud crackling sound and then the bump of falling logs. I looked out carefully.

"A bit nippy in here, now that the sun's going down—better get this fire going." Mr. Lovely mumbled to himself as he bent over, poking the logs with a long brass poker and puffing up his cheeks, blowing wildly at the first orange flames.

He was making such a terrible noise himself that I took my chance and grabbed a truffle, hurled it out of the dish and sent it flying off the tea cart and onto the rug. I scurried down the white lace cloth and ran for the truffle, grabbing it just as he turned around to get another log for the fire. Thank goodness the rug was a busy pattern, or he would have surely spotted me hovering silently over the truffle. But, as fate would have it, he turned back to his fire and I was free! I grabbed the truffle and hoisted it onto my shoulder, running the long distance to the crackway. The mousettes were waiting at the entryhole, just as I arrived breathless.

"Mrs. Chubbly! Are you alright? Where's Eency?"

"No time to talk now, Weency—feed the mousekin and yourself. I must go and help Eency. And don't spend any energy worrying, it's a waste of time for a smart mousette like yourself." Then I dashed off, leaving the truffle on the entryway rug. Well, life and death must always come before good table manners.

The way seemed clear as I ran straight across the open floor, once more, down the hall toward the garden doors. Then, just as I crossed the doorjamb, I was struck by the most horrible sight. Eency was nowhere to be seen and there sat Chesterfield Cat, his muzzle and paws covered with fresh blood. I was grief stricken and horrified.

"Chesterfield Cat! What horrible deed have you done to a poor innocent babe?"

"Mrs. Chubbly, whatever do you mean?" Chesterfield looked down at his paws, then back at me, and saw me staring at the dripping blood. "Why, you're not suggesting... I mean, you certainly don't believe that... I thought surely I would be commended. I certainly don't understand at all..." His voice trailed off sadly in his confusion.

"Nothing you can say, Chesterfield, will wipe the innocent blood of tiny Eency from your paws or from my memory!" I turned my face away, not wanting to see the brutal crime for a moment longer.

"Mrs. Chubbly! What a horrible accusation. You've got it all wrong." Chesterfield was interrupted by a tiny voice calling out from the tall grass behind him.

"Mrs. Chubbly? Mrs. Chubbly! Thank goodness you've come!" It was unmistakably the voice of Eency.

"Excuse me for a moment, Chesterfield."

I dashed to the grass behind him and there found Eency, crouching and hugging himself, terrified. His fine blue suit was torn and he was covered with mud from whiskers to tail. I picked him up in my arms as if he were still a tiny mousekin and cradled him to my bosom.

"It's all right now dear, it's over," I whispered softly and he began to cry like a babe as he realized with great relief that his terror was indeed over and he was safe in loving arms at last.

"Chesterfield, I believe I owe you an apology. And I do wish somecreature would explain," I said, pointing at the pool of blood.

"Oh Mrs. Chubbly, it was terrible!" Eency's eyes filled with fear as he explained. "It was a great huge ugly creature, covered with the strangest fur, and it had these two wide things that it kept beating in the air, and it had claws much larger than any cat's I've ever heard about, and between its eyes it had a sharp pointy nose as big as my whole head!"

"How frightening for you. Eency—you must never go outside the big house alone, never," I warned the young mouseling as gently as I could, considering the circumstances.

"Never, ever again, Mrs. Chubbly. But I really didn't mean to go out, it just sort of happened."

Chesterfield finished cleaning the last of the blood from his paws and lay down beside us, as Eency continued his tale.

"...you see, I had just reached the big kitchen and there wasn't a human in sight. I spotted a large hunk of cheese right on the floor, within easy reach—when all of a sudden across the room, another door opened. Then this huge human came stomping into the kitchen, the floor was shaking from her big feet—and that's not all." her said, trying to keep from crying. "She had a big long stick in her hand and there was a bunch of straw tied to one end of it. She began dragging it along the floor—"

"That was a broom, Eency." I explained.

"Oh? Well, she was heading right for the cheese when she spotted me, I looked at her and she looked at me, and then I barely had time to think before she let out the most horrible sound I have ever heard a creature make! I was frozen fast on the spot. I couldn't even turn my head to search for a crack in the wall." Eency searched my face for disappointment but found none, so he nestled closer to me and went on.

"She kept right on making that noise. Then the next thing I knew—she was yelling 'A mouse! A mouse in my nice clean kitchen! I'll get you, you filthy thing!' and she picked up that broom thing and just as she was about to squish me with it, I came to my senses and ran for the kitchen door." He was breathing hard, as if he were still running, and tears came to his frightened brown eyes.

"Thank The Great Creator you remembered. You're a very smart mouse, Eency."

"I thought I was safe, Mrs. Chubbly—but then she came after me! I felt that broom hitting the floor right behind my tail. I didn't have time to even look behind me, and everything was happening so fast. I couldn't find a hole or a place to hide—but I saw this wonderful light on the rug and I followed it out through an open door to this grassy place."

"You poor, innocent thing. Of course you did the only thing you could under the circumstances." I gave him a reassuring squeeze. "You did fine Eency, just fine."

"I did?" he said, brightening. "Well, I remembered what Mother had said about the big open place, the outside place with sunlight and the flowers..." At this I saw Eency's eyes grow watery again—remembering his dear sweet mother, and he had to gulp back the tears before he could continue. "It seemed that this was the beautiful place Mother had told me about, in bedtime stories. She called it 'The Garden', and said it was very fragrant and beautiful—but very dangerous for a mouse. I knew I had to find a place to hide, but before I could begin to search for a safe corner, a dark shadow surrounded me, blocking out the sunlight. Then I felt a terrible pain! This enormous ugly beast had me tightly in its claws, and then there was a terrible noise."

"It was a hawk, to be precise," added Chesterfield. "Quite delicious, really."

"Well, I was thrown to the ground near that thick grass, so I climbed inside and hid. The noise grew louder. There was screeching and growling—I was too afraid to even look out. I just sat there wondering how I would ever get home again," he whispered as he snuggled against me, and breathed a sigh of relief.

I looked at Chesterfield, and he was smiling shyly.

"Chesterfield, you clever creature! Not only do I owe you an apology for my accusation, but it seems that you've saved Eency's life. Very good, Chesterfield. All things accounted for, you are now a hero!" I said, returning his smile.

"Me! A hero? Why," Chesterfield turned his head modestly away, and began to preen his fur, "I was just having a bit of lunch."

Eency climbed out of my arms and walked over to Chesterfield. Then, stretching up onto his tippypaws, he placed a kiss on the embarrassed cat's nose.

"Thank you, Chesterfield," he said.

"Very nice, Eency," I whispered, walking over to Chesterfield and extending my paw. Chesterfield, remembering his manners, immediately took my paw warmly in his own.

"You're most welcome, Eency. We orphans have got to stick together you know." Chesterfield wrapped a paw affectionately around the mouseling.

"I suppose this makes us brothers of a sort, doesn't it, Chesterfield?" Then Eency added, thoughtfully, "If there's ever anything I can do for you, just ask."

The furry, black cat smiled broadly at the thought of little Eency helping him out of a fix.

"We must be going now. The mousettes have no idea what has happened, and we have some explaining to do back at the nest." I brushed off my apron, and took a serious look at Eency's suit. "My goodness, Eency, we've got to do something about your clothes!"

Eency looked down at himself for the first time since his adventure had begun, and even he was shocked at the condition of his fine clothes.

"What a mess," he said, brushing at the mud, uselessly.

"It does seem a hot bath and some mending is in order here."

The three of us started toward the house, only to find Mr. Lovely drinking his evening tea, and Mrs. Hammond, dusting in the dining room.

"Now what will we do?" I said, greatly annoyed at the way Mrs. Hammond had of always turning up in the wrong place, at the wrong time.

"I guess we'll have to stay out here in the dark," Eency said, looking into the warm lights of the drawing room. "I'm cold, Mrs. Chubbly," he shivered hopelessly. The sun was indeed setting, and the air was beginning to smell of snow.

"No, we won't Eency—I've got a marvelous idea that will help all of us out of this little fix. Chesterfield," I motioned him closer with my paw.

"Yes, Mrs. Chubbly?" The big cat leaned closer, to hear my secret plan.

"While I was trying to find Eency, I overheard Mrs. Hammond badgering Mr. Lovely about getting another cat. To be more precise, they are planning to call the shelter after tea to see if they can find a better mouser."

"A better mouser?" Chesterfield meowed, indignantly.

"It seems Mrs. Hammond's adventure with Eency was more than she could bear—and she's blaming you for the entire thing!" I said.

"Well, I believe these days a cat just can't win," he said, straightening up, now worrying about his own fate.

"Chesterfield, you have a problem. Eency and I have a problem as well, we can't get back to the nest without being in plain sight of Mr. Lovely and Mrs. Hammond unless..."

The door from the garden swung open wide and Mrs. Hammond nearly dropped her feather duster. In strutted Chesterfield Cat, proud and tall, and smiling in that way that cats have of smiling when they know something you don't know. In Chesterfield's mouth, there were two mice, a large one and a smaller one. He paraded them around the room in front of the gawking housekeeper. Mr. Lovely looked up from the evening newspaper and placed his teacup in the saucer.

"There you go Mrs. Hammond. It seems that Chesterfield has solved the problem nicely." He buried his face back in the newspaper, and Chesterfield, feeling rather roguish, took a last spin around Mrs. Hammond ankles, while she watched with her mouth agape. Then he trotted off down the hall toward the nest.

"Well, that'll make a stuffed bird laughI!" Mrs. Hammond said, closing her mouth at last. "How wrong can a person be?" She went off to the kitchen muttering to herself, "never seen a cat with two mice caught, before. What a sight. I guess I'll have to get ol' Chesterfield a bit of leftover cheese soufflé."

Chesterfield heard this from the hallway and rudely dropped Eency and I in front of the nest.

"Ouch!" cried Eency, rubbing the seat of his pants.

"Terribly sorry, Eency," whispered Chesterfield, "but there seems to be a sumptuous reward waiting for me in the kitchen."

"Oh, I understand, Chesterfield. I'm quite hungry myself," Eency answered.

"That's no excuse for rudeness, even from a hungry hero. Go on, run along Chesterfield, and claim your prize. We've managed to set everything right," I said. Then I attended to straightening my dress.

"Hopefully our next meeting will be far less eventful." We hurried inside the crackway, tired and dirty from our adventures. It had been a long busy day and Eency was so tired, he was dragging his tail behind him.

"Let's hurry to the nursery, the mousettes must be beside themselves with fear by now. I realize it's been a difficult day for you, Eency—but now, we must be the chief comforters for your sisters."

Eency's eyes were half closed as we made our way up the wallway to the nursery. What a brave mouseling he turned out to be! In one short day he lost his parents to a hungry cat, almost died twice—once at the hands of an angry housekeeper, then again in the talons of a hawk—and rode home in the mouth of a cat. Now the poor, sleepy creature was to be the head male of our nesthold and a comfort to his sisters. I put my arm around his muddy shoulder and helped him along. In spite of his young age and small size, I do believe that Eency will come up to the task and help me run our new family well. Thank The Great Creator that this day is almost at an end. Soon we will all be asleep in our beds. Chesterfield, fat and happy from his prize, will be curled up by the fire, and we will all be dreaming of better days to come.

5. Giving Thanks

Weency came running down the wallway, mousekin Mop wailing in her arms. When she saw our bedraggled condition, she gasped.

"Mrs. Chubbly! Eency! Look at the two of you! I just knew something awful must have happened."

"Never mind all of that, we're just fine, but Mop isn't." I took Mop into my arms but she went on crying and would not be comforted. "She's drenched," I said, patting her soggy bottom scrap. "We've got to get Mop changed and fed. Eency needs a hot bath and some fresh sleeping clothes."

"And food—I'm starving!" Eency added. "I haven't had a nibble all day."

We headed for the kitchen and Eency got his second wind as he began to tell Weency of his adventure.

"Weence, you should have seen the creature in the garden. It was huge and terrible—and it nearly carried me off to eat me. But Chesterfield saved me, and then..."

"Eency, save your tale for bedtime. We've got to get a fire lit and a dozen other things need to be done," I said, as I changed Mop's bottom scrap. It was soaked all the way through. She stopped crying as soon as I tied a dry one across her bottom.

"There now, you sweet little mousekin, sometimes all a mousekin needs is a dry bottom and she cheers right up," I cooed.

"Eency, I'd really like to know what you were doing out in the garden," Weency scolded him. "That was a stupid and dangerous thing to do—if Mother were here..." the twins both realized at that very moment their mother would not be coming back.

"Oh Weency," he cried out mournfully and fell into his sister's arms. They held tight to each other, sobbing hopelessly, then the three mouselings were crying their hearts out for their missing parents.

I tried to make things as homey as possible. First I took a shawl from the hook by the kitchen hole and I picked up mousekin Mop and tied her to my back. She seemed to like this and soon snuggled up to sleep, comfortable, with one paw stuck in her mouth. She sucked away at her paw and had the other paw wrapped in my headfur, holding tight as if to make sure I wasn't going anywhere.

Next, I put my arms around the crying twins and led them over to the table, sitting them down on two yellow stools.

"Now, everycreature try to be calm. I know how you both feel, but in spite of how we feel—we must go on. There are many things to do and you know your mother and father would have wanted you to carry on and take care of each other, isn't that right?"

"Yes, Mrs. Chubbly," they answered as they broke into fresh sobs.

"So what must we do, mouselings?"

"We must eat our supper and have our bath, hear our bedtime tale and say our prayers, and snuggle each other to sleep," Weency answered quickly.

"That's correct, Weency. And will you help me?" I asked.

"Yes, of course, Mrs. Chubbly," she nodded.

"I can help too," Eency said resolutely, "I'll light the fire."

I found the bathing tub. It was an old white china soap dish and it was quite deep. Inside the tub were two large cotton bath wraps. Jenny Twingle had taken the time to cross-stitch the mouselings' initials onto each one. There was even a smaller pink one, for Mousekin Mop. Near one end of the cupboards there was a pipe with a small cork plugging the hole. Under it was a caper tin that served as a basin, so I assumed it must be the sink. I carefully pried loose the cork and steaming hot water began to drip into the basin. How perfect! Mr. Twingle had thought of everything. I lifted the tin and poured the hot water into the tub. I had to fill the tin and pour it into the tub several times, but at last it was full.

"Now mouselings, we'll let the bath water cool a bit while I get supper started."

I pushed the heavy tub to one side and the hot water splish-splashed, sending up a cloud of steam. Then, I went to the pantry where Weency had stored a large piece of chocolate truffle, next to the stale cracker.

Eency was busy with a pile of wood chips and a stick match as long as his arm. He struck it carefully on a flint stone beside the hearth and set the huge flame to the chips, making a crackling fire.

I took the thimble that hung over the fireplace and filled it with hot water and a large hunk of chocolate. The fire was burning well now and the kitchen grew toasty warm. I placed the thimble pot on its hook and as the smell of the sweet chocolate filled the kitchen the mouselings sat dreamily at the table thinking about nicer times when they had chocolate soup with their mother and father.

When the soup began bubbling in the thimble pot, I went to the cupboard in search of some nutshell bowls. Instead of the customary nutshells, I found a delightful surprise! Inside the cupboard, stacked neatly, there was a matched set of bright red clay dollhouse dishes. There were dinner plates, a teapot with a matching sugar and creamer set and several serving dishes—all with hand painted yellow buttercups trimming the edges. I brought the soup bowls to the table and thought about the human girl in the big house. She must still be wondering where her dollhouse dishes had gotten off to.

Mousekin Mop was just beginning to stir when we all heard a scratching at the crack.

"Who could that be?" I asked aloud.

"May I go and see, Mrs. Chubbly?" Weency asked. She had been cooped up with the mousekin all day and though I wasn't looking forward to any more adventures, I nodded my approval.

"Be attentive Weency—we've had enough excitement for one day."

She dashed off toward the crackway and shouted back, "Oh, thank you, Mrs. Chubbly—I will."

A moment later, she was back carrying a large piece of cheese soufflé.

"Wherever did you get that?" I asked, amazed at the wonderful gift.

"It was right there in the crack—it seems as if somecreature had just stuck it there and left."

"Chesterfield Cat," Eency said, smiling.

"How peculiar," Weency said to her twin. "Why would a cat stick a piece of cheese soufflé in a mouse hole?"

Eency and I had to laugh.

"It's a very long story, Weence," answered her brother. "I'll tell you all about it at bedtime—meanwhile, I'm starving!"

I got a large serving platter and three dinner plates from the cupboard. The large hunk of soufflé just fit on the platter and I placed it on the table. Then I found a ladle next to the hearth and served each of us a double helping of chocolate soup.

There was a basket of dainty paw carved wooden forks, knives and spoons. Weency got the yellow cotton napkins from a matchbox drawer, then set a place for each of us at the table. Mop was awake and hungry so I took her off my back and sat her in my lap. After all we had been through in this difficult day,

I never imagined we would be sitting down together to such a lovely dinner.

The mouselings had not yet begun to eat and they eyed each other questioningly.

"What is it, mouselings?" I asked them.

"Father always gave thanks before we ate," Weency said in a whisper—afraid to offend.

"That's fine Weency, as it should be. Eency—you're the head male, will you give thanks please?"

"But Mrs. Chubbly, I don't know what to say, I've never..."

"Just say what's in your heart, Eency. After all—giving thanks isn't something one learns from a book. Being thankful is a feeling, it's a celebration of life and a way to let your fellow creatures and your Creator know how much you appreciate all the joy you have."

"Oh. I see—all right then."

Eency took my paw in his and reached over and took Weency's paw. Then he closed his eyes and was quiet for a moment.

"Thank you, dear Mother and Father, for giving us this lovely nest," he began in a faltering voice, but I heard the feeling mount in him and his words began to flow, "and for teaching us the important things—that we must stick together and love each other. And thank you, Chesterfield Cat, for being so uncommon and for giving us this yummy cheese soufflé. Thank you, Great Creator, for allowing us all to be here together to enjoy this wonderful meal—and for having Mrs. Chubbly come when we needed her the most. Please let her stay here to love us and care for us. Amen."

Then Weency added, "Amen for me as well."

And if it wasn't my imagination, I believe that Mop looked up at me with her toothless smile and said, "Me too!"

"That was just perfect, Eency." I said, cutting the Soufflé.

We ate and ate, and when we couldn't eat another nibble, Weency and Eency cleared the table.

I found some fresh peppermint leaves hanging inside a cupboard and made us a pot of hot tea. The mouselings were getting sleepy-eyed and the bath water was just right, so I helped them undress and I plopped them all into the tub together with a large flake of soap. Then I sat quietly beside them, sipping my tea as they all played and splashed and washed behind each other's ears.

I looked over at the mouseling and felt a strange feeling of familiarity, as if somehow, beyond this lifetime, we've always known and loved each other. Now, here is my new family. We were placed into each other's care by an unseen force. I gave thanks to The Great Creator—for where else could I have found so much love.

6. The Visitor

At last the twins were asleep in their bed. I was too tired to do another thing but Mop was looking around for her mother mournfully, so I brought her into my bed and we were both happy and comfortable with this arrangement. I snuggled her close to me under the warm bedclothes and she was soon sucking her paw and drifting off to sleep.

Eency's torn blue suit still lay on my dresser to be washed and mended in the morning. As I pulled the covers up under my chin, ready for sleep after a long day in my new home, I heard the wind howling beyond the outer wall—and I knew a heavy snow would be coming that night. I closed my eyes in meditation and thought about how long I had kept myself alone and in stillness. I had chosen to just be alone with myself, away in healing meditation, away from other creatures in need of love or care. It was a time of mourning the loss of my parents and my husband. It was a time to allow The Great Creator to hold me and remind me that I had more to do, more to give, and grand adventures that I couldn't yet begin to imagine. As much as I focused on being peaceful, I fell asleep thinking about the many, many things I would have to do to make my new family safe and sound in the coming winter months.

Just as I found the peace of my first dream, there was a loud scratching at the crackway. Then a whispering voice was calling my name.

"Mrs. Chubbly! Mrs. Chubbly, do come quickly!" Was it a dream? I heard somecreature calling my name, but I was still dozing. Again I heard it.

"Mrs. Chubbly, do come—I need your help!" The urgency in the voice brought me out of my deep sleep and I was up and dressed in a flash. I tucked Mop in tightly and followed the sound of the whispering voice through the darkness, to the crackway.

The fire was still lit in the big house and when I looked out, a dim orange glow filled the hall.

"Chesterfield Cat—it's the middle of the night!"

The big house was dark and my eyes were full of sleep but in the glow of the fire I noticed a lump of fabric sitting on the hall rug in front of the silhouette of a cat.

"I'm sorry to wake you, but this is urgent," he said, peeling open a flap of the fabric. Inside the fold was a young female mouse. She was crying softly and wincing. I watched as she alternately squeezed her eyes shut tight and then opened them wide with fear—unseeing.

"You see, it seems that she's ill, Mrs. Chubbly," he whispered, as he watched the young mouse. "I found her at the garden door, trying to scratch her way in. It was freezing out so I opened the door a bit. As soon as she saw me, she fainted. Can you imagine that?" He looked down at the mousette, his green eyes filled with concern.

I made my way closer to have a look at her. The poor thing was nothing but fur and bones.

"She's not ill, Chesterfield. She is starving though—and she's having a litter."

"Now? Here?" Chesterfield asked, amazed and embarrassed. "Well I suppose I brought them to the right place, after all—what could I have done?"

The mousette began to writhe on the floor and moan with pain.

"Chesterfield—there isn't any more time to talk. I've got to get her inside by the fire where she'll be warm. She's pretty far along."

"Oh? Oh my goodness! What should I do?" he asked nervously.

"There isn't anything else you can do, thank you Chesterfield." I began to pull her by the fabric, toward the crack and Chesterfield thoughtfully nudged her from behind.

Again she began to squeal and moan.

"Stop here," I commanded.

"What is it?"

"We must wait, she's having another contraction and it's too painful to move a birthing creature while they are contracting. It takes a lot of focus to bring forth life Chesterfield." I told him. I counted the seconds while I watched her. "A full minute- that's a long one. She's getting close. We'll have to hurry." As soon as she was calm, we both worked together to get her inside and I left Chesterfield pacing nervously in the hallway. She looked up at me for a moment and her eyes focused when they met mine.

"Everything is fine, dear. I'm going to help you. Put your arms around my neck and I'll bring you to a comfortable place where you'll be safe."

She was weak from hunger and pain and could barely lift her arms—but she managed to hang on as I lifted her, brought her into the kitchen, and laid her down in front of the fire. I looked up and found the twins in their nightshirts gawking sleepy-eyed from the wallway.

"Good to see you both ready—I'll need your help right away," I said as calmly as I could. The young lady mouse let out a horrible squeal and rolled onto her side to get closer to the tiny fire. Both of the mouselings looked down at our guest and then they turned to me—looking extremely frightened.

"What's going on? Is she sick?" they asked, together.

"No time to talk now. Weency—wash out the stew pot and fill it with hot water. Eency—put more chips on the fire, then fetch my black bag, it's next to my dresser."

The twins got moving at once, observing the urgency of the situation. In a moment the fire was blazing hot and a thimble pot of water was beginning to boil. My black bag sat on the floor next to me, where I knelt beside the labouring young visitor.

I assisted at the birth-time of many a young mousette in my calling as a nanny and a healer. Many were easy and some were hard, but every elder knows a difficult birth when she sees one.

Most litters come into this world calmly and quietly, without any help from anycreature but the mother mouse herself. One never has to interfere with a healthy birthing. The mother goes about her joyful pleasurable business, pushing her offspring into the world, cleaning them herself, tidying up her nest, and celebrating the new life—but something was definitely wrong here. This mousette was very young and too thin. She looked as if she hadn't eaten anything in days. She was shaking with exhaustion and her lips were cracked and dry. She was badly dehydrated. I didn't know if she would make it, and in her condition, I judged her mousekins didn't have much of a chance for survival either—but the work still had to be done, and of course there's always the chance of a small miracle. All we could do is roll up our sleeves and hope for the best. When I was young, I attended births as a helper with Mama Sandy as midwife. Sandy Fields was my husband Tailbit's mother. She taught me so much about birth and life. Birth always felt like a celebration with creatures cooking and playing music for the comfort of the birthing mother. The birthing mother was honored and adored and celebrated by every creature in the nest, after all, she was like The Great Creator, bringing forth life. It was a true rarity to have a stillborn, or a death. I witnessed very few. It was even more rare to lose a birthing mother. That's how Tailbot came to us. Sandy was attending his mother's birth. It was her first litter and she was very young. I heard it was a terrible night. Every mousekin in the litter was stillborn, all 7 of them, except little Tailbit. He was a miracle. And when at last the birthing mother heard him squeak, and knew she wouldn't make it, she handed little newborn Tailbit to Mama Sandy and whispered "He's yours now, please give him a good life." Sandy and her husband Woody saw this as a great gift. They had no mouslings of their own, so they adopted Tailbit and raised him lovingly as part of the Chubbly family. He grew up to become a fine strong mouse, and he won my heart with his sweetness and his charm. And then he was taken from me suddenly.

I looked over at the labouring mother struggling before me and whispered to the creator "Please help me save this precious creature".

She was breathing harder, deep in the throes of labour. I needed to focus.

"Weency, get me a teacup right away." As soon as I asked, it was placed in my hand. "Good, thank you. Now get a clean scrap and wet it."

There was no sound in the room except the laboured breathing of the young mousette and the scurrying of the twins as they quickly carried out my orders.

I opened my black bag and found several small sacks of herbs I kept on top, for emergencies such as this. I kept them all colour coded and easily found and untied the small red bag. I measured four large pinches of lobelia leaves mixed with red raspberry into the cup and held it toward Weency.

"Hot water, please."

She cleverly used the ladle and I sat the brew near the fire to steep, where it would stay warm. The next moment a cool scrap was in my paw.

"Listen carefully to me, young one," I spoke firmly, leaning close to the frail creature. "Everything is going to be fine now, but I need your help to be able to help you."

She was starting to have another strong contraction and she called out, "Mother!"

I placed the cool scrap on her fevered brow and held her paw tightly while she squealed.

"You must try to uncurl your body and relax. You're safe now—just breathe deeply and let nature do the work."

"Yes—yes!" she squeaked. "I understand—but I can't do it!" and then she was a tight ball again, crying out, "Ooohhhh!"

"I'm going to sit you up a bit and give you something to help make this easier—now you have to work with me, all right?"

She just nodded, her eyes glazed over from the pain and exhaustion. I turned to Eency. "Get me some cushions and as many clean scraps and bedclothes as you can—and hurry!"

Between the pains, she seemed fine but exhausted, so I tried to talk to her, to make her feel more at home.

"Can you tell me your name, little one?" I asked, as I searched through my bag for my litter cone. Her throat was so dry, I could barely hear her when she whispered, "Angel, my name is Angel. I don't like the way this feels."

"Of course not, dear, but we're going to make you more comfortable and then it will feel much better. Weency, get behind Angel and help her sit up a bit. We've got to get some of this medicinal tea into her."

Eency came back with his arms full. We piled cushions beneath Angel and placed a clean cloth on the scrap of fabric that was serving as her mattress. I sniffed the tea and knew it had steeped long enough and it was just right.

"Now Angel, you've got to drink this tea, all of it— slowly, one sip at a time. As you drink it, you'll begin to feel stronger, it will make this all much easier."

I put the cup to her dry lips and she drank thirstily. Her body relaxed and I saw the tension leave her pretty face.

Weency placed a fresh, cool, fabric scrap on her brow, and relieved some, she settled down into the pile of cushions.

"I'm going to try to feel your mousekins now. You tell me if I'm hurting you and I'll stop. Do you understand, Angel?"

Her eyes cleared and she smiled a wisp of a smile and nodded to me. I lifted her thin worn dress as high as I could and began to feel around for her mousekins. I felt three distinct lumps—but I felt no movement. I placed my litter cone on them and listened for their heartbeats. I heard nothing, but I didn't have much time. The contractions were coming faster now, one on top of the next. I knew I had to concentrate on just keeping the mother alive and helping her through the birth.

"Ooooohhh! Please! Help me!" she squealed in a frightened voice. She was getting close to the end.

"I'll help you, you're doing very well," I said, squeezing her paw. The herbs had begun to work, and she was handling her ordeal in a much calmer manner.

"Just breathe deeply and slowly. your mousekins are coming."

Again she cried out, "Ooohhhh!" her face contorted with the intensity of the contraction and she was squeezing my paw terribly hard. It seemed as if the contraction would never end, but she let her breath out in a deep sigh. It had passed.

"Here now," I said, tipping the cup to her lips. "Finish this tea and then we'll try to make you more comfortable."

She was breathing heavily but she managed to finish the tea, at my urging.

"Twins- we're going to turn Angel over onto the cushions. I'll need your help."

They both followed my directions and in another moment, Angel was leaning over the cushions with all of her paws on the cloth. Weency was above her head and the two mousettes held paws tightly.

"Eency—break off a tiny piece of chocolate and place it in Angel's mouth." He dashed to the cupboard and did as he was told. The sugar worked quickly and suddenly she was filled with a burst of energy. With the next grunt, Angel began to push her mousekins into the world.

The tea and chocolate had worked well, now nature seemed to be taking its course. The first of the litter arrived with a splash into my lap. He was black, wet and unmoving. I pulled the sack from him and began to rub vigorously, but still the babe had no life in him. I breathed soft puffs of air into his still mouth, and waited. There was no response. I sadly wrapped him in a cloth, and cleared my mind—ready for the next one.

I waited, hoping some creature would come through this alive. The next contraction came hard and Angel was up on her paws working with great fervor.

"Uuuuurgh!" She grunted and pushed. Another one, delivered wet and still into my lap. The sack was already off this one—not a good sign. Rub and pat as hard as I could, there was no sign of life. Once more, I wrapped a still mousekin in a cloth and prepared for the last. Angel was gasping for breath now. Exhaustion was getting the better of her. She moaned and fell to the cushions. In a moment she was up again, her eyes wide and blazing. She was grunting and squealing harder than before. The third was small and white, and was enclosed in a sack full of water. I tore the sack and the liquid spilled out into my lap.

"Please," I prayed in a whisper, "let this not be in vain."

I began to rub the mousekin's chest and I felt a faint heartbeat answer me. At first I thought it was my hopeful imagination—the movement was ever so slight. Then the tiny thing began to squeak and move more earnestly. She was alive!

"Eency, quick—get some chips on that fire."

Angel heard the tiny sound and quickly turned her head toward me, trying to see her new mousekin.

"Angel, you have a little mousette and she's beautiful!"

The new mother's eyes filled with tears of gratitude as she reached out for her little one. I placed the mousekin in her arms and they both sank comfortably into the cushions. The wet white mousekin nuzzled against her frail mother, searching for a nipple. She found a place to nurse right away.

I pulled the wet bedclothes away and replaced them with dry clean scraps, then I tucked a large sparrowdown quilt around the two exhausted creatures. Angel was smiling when she fell asleep. I took the two stillborns and wrapped them together in another cloth, then placed them aside so Angel could say goodbye to them properly, when she was rested.

The twins were wide eyed from all of the excitement, but I knew it was best to get them to sleep. Tomorrow was going to be another busy day.

"Weency, why don't you climb into my bed. Mop will be awake soon and she'll need comfort."

Weency just nodded, peeked under the quilt at Angel and her new mousekin, then ran off to bed.

"Eency, I'm certain Chesterfield Cat is still pacing in the entryway. Why don't you go and tell him we've had a mousette, then you can both get off to bed.

"Yes, Mrs. Chubbly."

Eency scampered off to the crackway, delighted to be able to share the news. He found Chesterfield Cat waiting nervously like an expectant father.

"Pssst. Chesterfield," he whispered to the pacing cat.

"Oh Eency, it's you. Is she well?" the large furry cat asked, as the mouseling ventured out into the hallway of the big house.

"I think so—quite well," Eency whispered, smiling. "She had a female—all white, very beautiful." Chesterfield considered this and then sat down for the first time that night.

"Quite amazing," he said. "Quite an amazing thing."

"Yes, Chesterfield, quite." The two male creatures sat there together in the light of the new dawn, each thinking his own quiet thoughts about the night's experience, thinking about the frail visitor and her brand new mousekin.

"Do you think we are the father now, Chesterfield?" Eency asked, in a whisper.

"I think we might be, Eency."

The cat sat up straight and pondered this. He realized that the family of mice would need his help now, more than ever. "We've got our work cut out for us, you know."

"I didn't think about it like that," Eency answered thoughtfully. "I suppose somecreature is going to have to take care of them."

Chesterfield nodded in agreement.

"Somecreature is going to have to feed them," Chesterfield said.

"And get wood for the fire—the mouseling is so tiny, I suppose she'll need to be kept warm," Eency added. Chesterfield rose suddenly.

"Stay here, I'll be right back," he said, padding silently off into the kitchen.

Safe in the darkness, Eency tip-pawed out into the hallway to have a look out the garden doors. As the sun began its slow rise into the grey morning sky, Eency was startled to see that everything was white.

It covered all of the strange green plants and rose in a mound against the glass doors, like powdered sugar. The wind sang to him through a crack in the door but before he could begin to figure out what had happened to the lush greenery he had seen yesterday, for the very first time, Chesterfield returned with his mouth full of goodies.

"Here," he said, dropping his packages, "you'll certainly be needing these."

There were two hunks of cheese, cheddar and Swiss, and a full box of stick matches.

"Wonderful! Oh, Chesterfield, I completely forgot to thank you for the delicious cheese soufflé!" Eency cried out, embarrassed by his lack of manners.

"Never mind, what's a little soufflé among family, right?" The big cat turned away shyly and began cleaning himself, licking at his front paws and then smoothing down his black fur.

"You are especially uncommon—thank you Chesterfield," Eency said warmly. Then the young mouse began to gather up the cheese and the box of matches.

"I wonder if they'll name her Chesterfield?" he said, very seriously grooming the white spot at the tip of his tail.

"Well it is a lovely name," Eency answered politely, "but you know—she is female."

"That's true, Eency. Maybe it's not feminine enough," Chesterfield said, sadly.

"I've got to get these things inside. Maybe I'll see you tomorrow and I'll let you know what they call the little thing."

"Good night Eency, see you then."

"Good night, Chesterfield."

Then the two parted ways, both of them deep in thought about the night's events and the odd occurrence that had caused their paths to cross and had brought two creatures so naturally opposed into such a deep kinship. Neither of them believed in accidents, and both of them knew they would be tied together forever for they had a bridge now that crossed their barriers. They were both males bonded in the mystery of birth.

7. The White Clay Cup

I had just finished making up a bed for myself next to Angel and her baby when Eency returned to the kitchen.

"Chesterfield gave me these," he said, placing the matches and the cheese on the table. "He was wondering if we'd name the new mousekin after him," Eency added, kneeling down beside the sleeping couple. He looked at Angel's sleeping face and pulled the quilt higher to cover her bare arm.

"Chesterfield certainly has done a great many things for us, but I think it's best to let Angel name her mousekin whatever she thinks most fitting," I answered, looking into Eency's half closed sleepy eyes.

What a long day this has been for all of us, what a day of new experiences for the mouselings and the young cat, all of these young creatures rising above their own needs to accommodate each other.

Now we are bound together in these experiences and a new family has been created—a strange new one. Where will

Angel and this tiny mousekin fit in? I'm sure there is a plan and we will each find our best place in it. But now it is time to rest for there will be much to do tomorrow and Eency's head was beginning to nod.

"Can I sleep here with you tonight, Mrs. Chubbly?"

I wondered if Eency was frightened to go off to the nursery all alone, now that his world had changed. His twin was in my bed with Mop and his mother was no longer a whimper away. I didn't want to ask him, though, knowing how hard he was trying to be grown up.

"I think you'll be more comfortable in your own warm bed, but if you'd prefer to make a bed beside the fire, I believe that would be fine—just for tonight, mind you."

He was delighted that I would allow him the choice and he stood up, quite excited.

"Oh, thank you, Mrs. Chubbly—I'll just get my things and be right back and then if you need any help with Angel during the night—why, I'll be right here!" He dashed off to get some fabric scraps, trailing his words behind him.

The weariness had come upon me and I knew that I would soon need to sleep. First I changed the fabric pad beneath Angel and the mousekin. The fire needed chips and I attended to it quickly, making a nice blaze to warm the visitors through the night. I noticed the thimble of water was still boiling and had just enough left for a cup of tea. I rummaged through my medicine bag and found the sack full of chamomile leaves.

Eency came down the wallway, sleepily dragging his bedfabric behind him, and quietly made himself a place next to mine. I watched soundlessly as he lay down and pulled the heaviest piece over himself as a cover. Just before his head dropped into the thick fluff of the fabric, he managed to whisper—"If you need me, I'll be right here." And then he fell asleep, breathing deep and heavy as only a young one can. Just watching the three of them made me feel all the more sleepy, but my paw found my special white clay cup and the hissing of the water in the thimble reminded me that I was about to make a cup of tea. So, I proceeded to place some leaves into my cup.

I carefully tied the pouch and tucked it back into my black bag, then closed the bag and placed it beside my bedding, within easy reach. I knew that Angel would need a strengthening brew should she awaken during the night.

The cloth thimble holder was hung next to the fireplace on a tack. It was made of the same yellow fabric that covered the kitchen stools and embroidered with pink thread to show trailing rosettes along each border—by the loving hand of Jenny Twingle. As I poured the steaming water into my white cup, I was filled with the memory of that delicate creature—how she loved those under her care! Though I had only met her for a brief moment, I knew her well from the beauty that now surrounded me. These lovely mouselings were indeed a part of her. They were gentle, helpful and kind—like their mother. I knew she was watching them this evening, from wherever the spirit goes when it joins The Great Creator—I'm sure she was proud of them, so smart and capable. I'm certain she was comforted to see their courage and strength. They were living proof of their mother's love and a job well done. She gave them everything they needed. Now they would be fine without her.

I sat at the table, my tired feet up on a stool, warming my paws on the shining white cup full of aromatic tea. The scented steam rose to greet me and the strong sweet smell of chamomile took me back to younger days, gathering herbs in the sprawling garden of my Uncle Makelroy, smelling the different herbs as he held each one beneath my nose. The sun was golden and almost too bright as it gleamed on the ripe yellow and white flowers.

"This one is chamomile—breathe deeply, Mousekin, and remember the scent. Look carefully at the flower, the shape of each feathery leaf—examine the pattern of the leaves as they turn along the stem."

I hung on every word as his gentle old voice instructed me. He spoke with the tired patience of one who has explained the same thing many times. With great care he taught me each property the plant owned, then he thanked the plant—and The Great Creator.

"The leaves are good, but the flowers are stronger. Each plant has many parts: the leaf, the flower, the root, the bark. Each part has its own special use. When the flowers blossom, you must gather them while they are fresh, then dry them slowly in the sun. That's the best way."

He reached over and touched my face with his big paw and looked into my eyes to make sure I was paying full attention. "If it is wet out, you can dry them slowly upside down by a small fire—slowly, mind you."

"Yes, Uncle," I said, trying hard to memorize each word and the smell of the chamomile surrounded me until I was dizzy with all of his words and the hot sun and the thick smell of the sweet flowers.

Each day we would walk together stopping here and there at different spots in the herb garden, in the orchard, in the woods. Each time he stopped, he would show me a plant and reveal something new. Then, at the end of that wonderful summer, he gave me a big black ratskin bag and watched with pride as I placed each colour-marked sack of herbs carefully, one by one, into my medicine bag. On my last day with him, he gave me a package tied with red and white gingham. It was quite heavy as he placed it in my paws.

"Oh, Uncle—what is it?" I asked, greatly surprised.

"It's just a little present I made for you, my darling mousekin. You have done so very well with your lessons and every great healer should have one of these—go on, open it."

I could barely pull loose the red ribbon that kept the package hidden. I was terribly excited! When it finally came undone, I found in my paws the most beautiful gleaming white teacup. Inside it, on the bottom, Uncle Makelroy had painted my name in curly red letters, "Lacey". Then I turned it over in my paws and saw his signature carved in the base, "Mak".

"Thank you, Uncle Mak—I will keep this forever and remember every single thing you taught me!"

He laughed at my deep seriousness and chided me. "Well, I certainly hope you remember. After all—I would hate to think I wasted an entire summer on a feather brain!"

Oh, how I missed that wrinkled old smile of his! I sipped at my tea and felt the soothing fluid calming me, sending me into a state of peace. The leaves were good but the flowers were better—when summer came I knew I would have to replenish my store of herbs. The garden out behind the big house was huge and would have most of the common herbs. I had saved many seeds from Uncle Mak's garden, just to be safe. Whatever could not be found could be cultivated.

I drank the last of my tea, rinsed my cup in the dish basin and placed it back in my bag, careful not to make a sound. Everycreature was breathing quietly, each in an exhausted sleep. The only sound that could be heard now in the cozy kitchen was the crackling of the wood chips and the whistling of the winter wind as it blew outside the kitchen wall, reminding me of how safe and warm we all were—protected by our Great Creator and our love for each other.

With that last thought I tucked myself deep into my bedfabric and said one last silent prayer of thanks for all the fine creatures that had been placed into my life; the wonderful mouselings, the visitor and her sweet mousekin, and marvelous Chesterfield Cat—my new friend and helper. I closed my weary eyes and sleep came fast.

8. Wendy With the Golden Hair

And then, it was suddenly Winter.

"Mother! Father! Look out the windows! It's been snowing!" Wendy Lovely came running down the steps from the upstairs nursery, bursting with excitement. Outside in the garden, everything was covered with the first sparkling white snow of December. The sun was strong and bright and danced on each snow-covered leaf in the garden. The first snow of winter always seems brighter and more magical than all the snow that will surely follow.

In the mind of a nine year old girl the first snow always brings with it snowball fights with father in the fluffy backyard, and the promising sound of sleigh bells as Father Christmas flies through the air with his team of reindeer. We know he'll be delivering wonderfully wrapped packages of longed-for presents and sweet goodies to be stuffed into overflowing Christmas stockings.

Mr. and Mrs. Lovely sat sipping their morning tea at the breakfast table. Mr. Lovely looked up from the morning paper and the vision of his beautiful young daughter, with her golden hair, dancing joyfully in her nightgown brought a smile to his lips.

"Yes dear, it is beautiful, isn't it?"

He looked over at his wife, Annabelle, sitting across from him, remembering how she once danced about gaily like his charming daughter. Over the last seven years Annabelle's expression had changed, and now she held all her beauty behind a small tight-lipped frown, her face pulled down into this sadness until he hardly recognized her at all. He needed to look back at Wendy just to remember how joyful his wife had been.

Wendy opened the door to the garden just a crack but the wind took full advantage and blew a cold hiss of snow across the drawing room floor.

"Wendy! Shut that door this instant!" Mrs. Lovely ordered in a high pitched voice, then she caught herself and more quietly she added, "You'll catch your death of a cold, now run upstairs and dress warmly." She pressed her linen napkin to her lips as if to keep any other harsh words from escaping and brushed at a wisp of stray hair that had fallen across her careworn brow. "Mrs. Hammond?"

"Yes, Mrs. Lovely." The housekeeper appeared immediately in the kitchen doorway as if she had been waiting there.

"Wendy will be down to breakfast in a moment, I should think a nice hot bowl of porridge would be in order for today, and perhaps a cup of hot chocolate."

"Yes, Mrs. Lovely, right away." Mrs. Hammond disappeared behind the closed door without another word.

"Edmund?"

Mr. Lovely looked up cautiously from his paper, still disturbed by his wife's harsh tone.

"Yes, Annabelle?" he said folding his paper shut, but keeping his thumb tucked in to mark his page.

"I wish you wouldn't encourage any wildness in the child. After all," she brushed at the stray hair and it stayed in its place from the dampness on her brow, "The world is such a dangerous place you know and little children are so... vulnerable, to so many things..." her voice trailed off sadly and her eyes filled with tears. Edmund took Annabelle's hand gently in his, to soothe her from her memories.

"I understand, sweetness, but you must remember that Wendy is almost ten and she is the picture of health. Why, she's never been ill a day in her life!" With that Annabelle's lip began to quiver and he realized that he had said the wrong thing.

"Oh dear, I'm sorry, Annie. I was only trying to say that what happens to one child won't necessarily happen to another—and children need a certain amount of freedom to be joyful."

She withdrew her hand and began to cry softly.

"Excuse me," she whispered as she dashed from the table and ran up the stairs to her bedroom.

"For peace sake, I can't seem to say anything right anymore." Edmund folded his paper on the table and placed his napkin beside it. Then he got up and walked to the garden trying to shake off the strange conversation. He thought for a moment of going up to his wife's room, but knew he would be of no comfort. They had had many similar conversations in the past. She always left him alone feeling helpless as she dashed away to have her private tears. He went after her many times but she would never allow him to comfort her and it always left both of them feeling much worse. So, after several years, he learned it was best to leave her alone with her pain and he continually hoped that someday she would come out of it.

Edmund pressed his forehead against the coolness of the glass garden door. His warm breath fogged the window and he remembered being a young boy in a much smaller, poorer house. Although he had grown up with four brothers in one crowded room, his family had been a warm and happy one, and when the snow came for the first time each winter he and his brothers would breathe on the drawing room windows and write their names on the icy cold panes. He brought his finger up to the glass now and drew an ornate letter "E".

"That's lovely, Father," Wendy stood at the bottom of the stairs smiling at him, her arms wrapped around an old Victorian dollhouse.

"Ah! I see you're ready to face the day, all brushed and dressed and shining. Here, let me help you with your package, Madame," he went to take the doll house out of her hands, "and to where shall I deliver this?"

"Oh, I thought the drawing room rug would be nice. In front of a cozy fire on such a frosty morning." She pranced into the drawing room and pointed to a spot as if she were the lady of the house and Edmund was just a delivery man.

"Dear me! I don't think your mother would approve of toys out of the nursery or you laying about in your good pink satin dress on the drawing room rug," he said.

Wendy pouted and clasped her hands together pleading in a fashion that always stole Edmund's heart.

"Father, please may I? After all, I'll keep everything very neat and won't crease my dress. And if Mother is upset with me, I'll just bring it all right upstairs in a flash."

He took Wendy's face in his hands and looked lovingly into her deep brown eyes.

"Well, you certainly presented an irresistible case for your defense. Perhaps when you grow up you will follow in my footsteps and become a barrister." He placed a gentle kiss on her forehead, releasing her. "Go play now, we'll ride out the storm together should your mother be upset at our infraction of the rules."

Wendy was on her knees before he could finish speaking. She talked incessantly as she swung open the enormous house and began setting all the tiny pieces of furniture in order.

"Oh thank you, Father, you won't regret it. I'll just be as quiet as a mouse and neat as a pin! Why, Mother won't even notice that I'm here. Now this piece goes here and the rug is all curled under the sofa. This place is a terrible mess! It could take me hours to set it all in order. What I need is a housekeeper."

She fretted and fussed joyfully as she rapidly moved her little hands from one room to another, taking out the rubber doll family and setting them aside one at a time on the drawing room rug: a mother and a father, two small children, a newborn baby in a handmade wicker cradle with real rockers carved of wood, a small rubber dog all spotted black and white with a red cloth collar, and an older sister that she used as a housekeeper and called Mrs. Nose-in-the-Air, because she never did as you asked her to do and as she played she was very fond of saying "One can never find good help these days," as she had heard Mother say to Father so many times about Mrs. Hammond.

Just then, Mrs. Hammond clomped into the breakfast room and plopped Wendy's bowl of porridge down at her place at the table.

"Breakfast, Miss Lovely. Please eat while it's hot or your mother will have me fix it again." Then she left the room muttering, "I wish this family would all eat at the same time, it would save me a lot of bother. But do they ever consider my tired feet?"

The kitchen door closed behind her, but Wendy could still hear Mrs. Hammond complaining to herself as she took her place at the table.

"Everyone is in such a horrid mood today," Edmund commented as he picked his newspaper up off the table and stuck it under his arm.

"Eat your breakfast, sweetheart, and keep out from under foot. I'll be in my study if you need anything."

Mr. Lovely disappeared behind the huge oak door to his study. When Wendy was sure that everyone was out of sight, she quickly gulped down her breakfast (in a very unladylike fashion), wiped porridge from her face on the back of her hand and dashed back to her house, anxious to get to work.

She held Mrs. Nose-in-the Air in one hand and made her voice as old and skratchy as she could manage. Then, she helped Mrs. Nose-in-the-Air carry furniture and tiny toys around the upstairs nursery, complaining the whole time.

"Why you'd think this family would have some consideration for my tired feet! I do nothing but work and work, day and night for them. Now, where did I put the new baby?"

Wendy spilled the baby out of his cradle and made a crying noise.

"Oh, there you are, you little rascal! It's time for your nap, and I have so much housework to do before Mr. and Mrs. Bendable bring the other children home from vacation."

She placed the baby into the little blue crib and covered him with a delicate, hand embroidered handkerchief that she pretended was his blanket.

"Now," she scolded, shaking Mrs. Nose-in-the-Air over the crib, *"you go directly to sleep. I won't have any fussing, is that clear?"* Then she moved Mrs. Nose-in-the-Air down the carpeted stairs into the drawing room and finished straightening the rug. Here and there she moved the housekeeper until all the furniture in the house was set in its proper place—all the while complaining in her old grouchy voice.

"I wish this family would be neater. I'm tired already and my day has just begun. Well then, the house is almost in order and I know the family will be home at any moment."

Wendy marched the whole Bendable family into the drawing room and had the mother say, "Dear Mrs. Nose-in-the-Air, the drawing room has never looked lovelier. You're doing such a wonderful job! Why don't you serve lunch in the dining room and take the rest of the day off." Then Wendy had the housekeeper curtsey politely and say, "Thank you, Mrs. Bendable, how kind of you." But when she moved her into the kitchen Wendy remembered that her little red clay dishes had been misplaced and Mrs. Nose-in-the-Air began complaining once more.

"You'd think this family could certainly afford a good set of china. Imagine having to set lunch out directly on the nice wooden table. Perhaps I should give notice and find a position with a better family."

The housekeeper set some pink wooden lamb chops on the dining room table, then placed a bowl of wooden fruit in the center. A large face with shining green eyes watched her carefully through the picture window in the rear of the house. She screamed dramatically *"Oh, a monster!"* and Wendy answered her.

"That's not a monster, Mrs. Nose-in-the-Air. It's just a cat! Come here, Chesterfield," Wendy called as she reached her arm around the house and picked Chesterfield up under his belly.

"There's someone I'd like you to meet."

She settled the fluffy cat comfortably in the lap of her pink satin dress. Chesterfield rubbed his head against the child as she scratched the thick hair at the back of his neck.

"This is the Bendable's housekeeper, Mrs. Nose-in-the-Air." Then she brought the rubber doll up to his nose and said, "Mrs. Nose-in-the-Air, this is Chesterfield."

He meowed loudly and Wendy had Mrs. Nose-in-the-air scold poor Chesterfield.

"How do you do. I would appreciate you not spying through the windows of my doll house, as you scared me half to death!"

Chesterfield thought this was all very amusing and he was enjoying the attention. Then he saw the handmade cradle on its side lying on the rug and all he could think about was how he might slip it into his mouth unnoticed and bring it as a gift to his newborn baby mouseling.

Wendy ruffled his fur with both her hands and gave him an exceptionally nice scratching that set him purring and thinking about how nice it is to have a little girl of one's own. Then he remembered the cradle and decided to create a little distraction. He stretched in Wendy's lap as if he were bored with her attention, then he poked his head into the dollhouse drawing room and proceeded to turn over the furniture and make an awful mess of things.

"No, no, Chesterfield! You mustn't do that!"

She shooed him away with her hand, "Bad kitty! Stay out of the doll house! You'll ruin everything!"

"Well, that's the point," thought Chesterfield, meowing sweetly. Then he lay down quietly on the rug with his belly covering the beautiful cradle.

"Now, that's a good kitty. If you promise to be good and still, I'll let you be in the game too." Then Wendy proceeded to straighten the drawing room once more.

"Miss Lovely," Mrs. Hammond called from the kitchen door, "Your chocolate is ready. I'm sure you mother wouldn't approve of your drinking it in the drawing room."

The housekeeper placed it on the table and cleared breakfast, quickly disappearing into the kitchen once more.

"Oh, how nice," Wendy exclaimed as she dashed over to drink her chocolate.

"Really," thought Chesterfield."Very nice!"

He meowed as he watched his little girl sipping the sweet drink.

"And thank you, Mrs. Hammond." He meowed once again before he slipped the cradle gently into his mouth and dashed off unnoticed, down the front hall.

9. The Namesake

The first one to awaken on that crisp winter morning was baby Mop—but of course, she was the only one who had escaped last night's ordeal. And little mouselings are always the roosters of any household, waking everyone else with hungry cries.

Weency rolled over and put her arms around her fussing sister, patting her furry belly and cooing sweet words of comfort. The little one wanted her mother and would only be content when her belly was full of warm mother's milk.

The wallway was freezing cold. Weency had Mop wrapped snugly in a soft scrap of pink velveteen, but the cold air was biting at them both, and the little one squeaked and squealed all the way to the frosty kitchen. Weency's warm breath steamed in the cold air and she worried about the new mother and the newborn mouseling. She hurried to see if the fire had indeed gone out, thinking it might endanger them in their frail condition.

The inhabitants of the kitchen had slept through Mop's crescendoing cries, exhausted beyond waking. Even the newborn lay quietly in half sleep, suckling at her mother's breast, kept safely warm by the heat of her mother's body and the thick fabric surrounding them both. Eency was snuggled up against Mrs. Chubbly and the elder mouse had him wrapped in her arms and her quilt, both of them smiling, lost in a comforting dream.

As was the custom when any nursing mouseling loses its mother, Weency tucked Mop in next to Angel and young Mop happily began to nurse herself back to sleep. Angel stirred for a moment and then snuggled down deeper under the bedclothes, nursing the two little mousettes as if this is what she had always done.

Weency blew repeatedly on the wood chips she had stacked on the coals. The last dying embers came suddenly back to life and she tossed in some larger pieces, then set the thimble of water over the fire to boil for tea.

The kitchen was warming up nicely. There was a quiet symphony of the crackling fire, the deep breathing of the sleeping mice, the high whistling sound of winter wind as it blew outside the walls of the protected nest, and the rising and falling hum of the cooing nursing song from the hungry mousekins. Then, as Weency turned to the cupboard ready to start breakfast, she was startled by a scritch-scratching at the crackway. SCRITCH SCRATCH SCRITCH! There it was again!

She considered waking Mrs. Chubbly. She looked at the sleeping elder's peaceful smile and then turned slowly and cautiously headed for the crack. SCRITCH SCRATCH SCRITCH!

"Who is it?" she asked, trying to sound like her mother. She did not look out, but waited a paw's length from the hole.

"Chesterfield," a muffled voice whispered back to her.

"What did you say?" she asked and her curiosity was more than her fear—she peeked out in time to see a wicker cradle fall to the hall rug.

"It is I, Chesterfield Cat."

He was very proud of his gift to the newborn and crouched, smiling, an inch behind the beautiful handmade cradle. Weency had never seen a cat before, at least not outside of a picture book. She drew her breath in sharply, smelling his cat smell, as her eyes measured the length of his long white fangs exposed by his smile.

"Goodness!" she squeaked, frozen in place, "You're a cat!"

"Of course I'm a cat." He stuck out his paw. "Chesterfield Cat, friend and accomplice to your nanny, Mrs. Chubbly." She gathered her wits, hearing Mrs. Chubbly's name, and extended her paw, awkwardly introducing herself.

"Weency Twingle, nice to meet you Mr. Cat," she said faintly.

"Oh, no formalities, please call me Chesterfield. I feel as if we are almost family." He chattered warmly at the tiny young mouse, "And I've brought our new mouseling a little gift. I do hope it's appropriate." He nudged the fine wicker cradle closer to Weency and waited while she looked at the handiwork. He was so warm and charming that she had almost forgotten she was standing outside of her nest for the very first time, conversing with a large cat who claimed to be "almost family."

"This is a lovely cradle, Mr.—ummm Chesterfield, it's the mouseling's very first gift."

She looked up at him self-consciously, like a city mouse standing in front of her class unprepared to recite for the first time. Her paws clasped tightly behind her back, she rocked back and forth nervously, not knowing what else to say.

"I... uh... I've never talked to a cat before, I... um... have never even seen a cat before, I'm sorry, I'm a bit nervous." She flushed under the peering green eyes of the cat and turned her face away.

"Well, that's understandable considering predators and prey and such. In most cases you should really stay away from cats," his voice took on a fatherly tone, feeling such a guilt-ridden love for the little mousekin, "but of course, I am the exception to that rule as I have vowed to protect your family as long as you all shall live here. So how is the new addition doing this morning?" he asked, politely changing the subject.

"They were all sound asleep when I left and the new one seems fine, I don't mean to be rude, but I really must hurry back to check on everyone."

Even after his reassuring words, she was still naturally ill at ease and wanted to get back safely behind the wall.

"I understand completely. Can you manage the cradle?" he asked as he nudged it closer to the crackway. She hefted its weight against her hip.

"Oh yes, I'll manage. It's not very far." she began to work the clumsy package through the opening to the nest and then feeling his large green eyes still upon her, she realized she was not being very courteous. "Thank you so much, Chesterfield. It's a very lovely gift."

He felt so relieved at her words that he couldn't help purring loudly, proud of himself.

"Yes, you're quite welcome. I thought it was just purrrrfect."

She hurried into the nest, feeling breathless, and was happy to be in familiar surroundings.

By the time she carried the huge cradle into the kitchen, I had made the morning tea and was busy stirring a steaming bowl of cracker porridge, happily humming to myself. Weency clunked the cradle down next to the table and took in the sweet smell of the porridge.

"Good morning, Mrs. Chubbly, that smells delicious!"

"Good morning to you Weency, and what a lovely cradle." Mrs. Chubbly smiled a playful smile at Weency "Have you been out gathering?" The mousette laughed at my silliness.

"Oh Mrs. Chubbly, you know very well that I've never gathered. Isn't it fine though?" Weency asked, as she rubbed her paw over the delicate wickerwork.

"Yes, it is truly a lovely gift, and I can only imagine that Chesterfield Cat is feeling like a new father this morning." Then I added quietly, "I must have a talk with him about stealing."

I placed the large red bowl on the table and examined the cradle with a more practiced eye, looking for sharp edges, testing the rockers to see if it could be easily overturned.

"It seems to be fine, nice and deep, very well made. I'll have to sew some cushions for the mattress." I began measuring the inside with myr paws, "Six paws long by three wide."

"We've got just the thing!" Weency interrupted excitedly, "Wait just a moment while I check Mother's sewing room."

Weency scurried down the hall and was back in a flash with an exquisite pink satin cushion trimmed in the palest pink lace, paw embroidered with delicate red tea roses and tiny mint green leaves trailing along the bottom border. It was so dainty and charming and it fit perfectly into the waiting cradle.

"Your sweet mother was a very talented seamstress," I said, as we both stood looking into the cradle.

"Yes, yes she was." Weency added softly. "Next year when I turned ten, she was going to fix a corner of her sewing room just for me. " Weency bowed her head sadly. "We were going to have special time together, everyday. She was going to teach me how to embroider."

She began to cry quietly, thinking about the special time. Now that hope was gone. She would never have that time with her mother. I took her face into my paws and looked deeply into her bright eyes.

"I understand how you feel, Little One. Waiting patiently for Mop to be old enough so that you could spend some special time with your mother, some "just females" time with her and now she's been taken away from you." She fell into my arms and I hugged her and held her tightly.

"You know Weency, my Aunt Bibi was a very good seamstress. When my mother died, my Aunt Bibi and my Uncle Mak took me in and she taught me quite a few lovely stitches, not as fine as Mother Twingle's but as soon as things quiet down here, we'll set up that special spot in your mother's sewing room and I'll show you every single thing I remember. All right, Dear?"

"Mrs. Chubbly, you are so wonderful." Then she added in a small uncertain voice, "But do you really mean it? Do you promise?"

I looked into the young creature's eyes and saw mirrored there, all the dashed hopes I felt in my own bosom when my own beloved mother had been eaten by a cat. I remembered how suddenly uncertain all of life felt, how ready I was for disappointment.

"Yes, Weency, of course I mean it. I never break a promise. As long as The Great Creator allows."

I turned back to the business of ladling porridge into the red clay bowls I had set upon the table, as Eency yawned loudly and shook himself out of his covers.

"Good morning, that porridge smells yummy. I'm starving!" Eency said cheerfully, as he pulled one of the spools over and straddled it. He poked his twitching nose too close to the hot bowl of mush and licked his lips hungrily.

"Eency! You get up from the table this instant! Put your night clothes away and get dressed and don't forget to rub your teeth."

I only had to turn my glance to Weency and they both answered in unison (as twins tend to, often) "Yes, Mrs. Chubbly."

Then they were gone to the nursery to become properly ready to start the day. I covered the mush with saucers, (no youngster will eat it cold, I know) and sat down to drink a fragrant cup of rose hip tea. I sipped the tart warm liquid, enjoying the momentary quiet, centering myself in my morning tea meditation and silently giving thanks for my many blessings.

"What is your given name, please?" the soft high pitched voice asked from beneath the bedclothes.

"Good morning Angel. It's Lacey, Lacey Chubbly. And how are you feeling this morning?" I asked, kneeling beside the young mother.

"I'm feeling weak but very happy and it seems that little Lacey is doing very well," she smiled at me warmly, "Thanks to you Mrs. Chubbly."

I felt my bosom swell with pride, I never thought I would have a namesake and such a lovely namesake! Little Lacey clung to her mother's breast, nursing like a healthy mouseling. Her fur was smooth white, like velvet and her headfur was silver-blue. She looked exactly like her mother. Little Mop sat up next to Angel looking a very deep grey next to the white mice. Her black mop flopped back and forth. She stared at Angel, then at me and said questioningly, "Mama?"

"Angel, this is little Mop Twingle, she was orphaned yesterday, and I do believe she has just spoken her first word." Angel drew Mop closer to her and patted her tenderly.

"Nice to meet you, little Mousekin. I've been wet nurse since she woke up around dawn. It would be my pleasure to continue, if it wouldn't be any trouble for Lacey and me to stay on for a bit."

I was delighted that she asked to stay on knowing what a help it would be for Mousekin Mop to have a wet nurse.

"Well Angel, I was hoping that you could stay with us for a while, but of course I must discuss it with the little ones. This is their nest, you understand." I worked as we spoke, changing the wet scraps on the two mouselings and removing Angel's soiled fabric bedding, sliding a clean scrap beneath her.

When everything was clean and neat, I examined Angel and little Lacey. To my amazement, they both came through the birth in excellent condition, and considering the difficulty of the event, they were fit and well.

"You must be very hungry."

"I feel as if I haven't had a nibble in days!" She looked around the kitchen for the first time and spotted the bowls on the table. "Do you think I might sit at the table and eat?"

"Certainly, as long as you are up to it! Let's put Lacey in her new cradle."

I held the tiny creature in my arms and looked at her newborn-sleeping smile. Then I tucked her into her new cradle and covered her with a scrap of pink velvet.

"There you go, Sweetheart, a cradle fit for a royal mousekin," I whispered in her soft pink ear as I swaddled the scrap tightly around her. I gave the cradle a gentle rock and the motion sent her right back to sleep.

"What a pretty cradle, is it Mop's?" Angel asked, sitting up to look more closely.

"No, it's a newborn gift to Lacey from Chesterfield Cat. And that is a long story." I answered as I helped Angel to the table. "Don't you remember how you came to be here at the nest?"

"Cats and kittens!! I thought I was dreaming! I remember scratching at the door and then I fainted. I dreamt I was riding in the mouth of a cat. I thought for certain I had died in birthing." She uncovered the porridge and was eating hungrily as she spoke.

"That was no dream, Chesterfield carried you to the crackway. He thought you were ill and wanted me to heal you. When I explained your delicate condition, he paced the hallway till dawn waiting for news of the outcome. Then he brought this present for the mouseling. He's a very young Tom and in a way he feels as if he's a new father." I ladled a second helping into her dish as I explained.

"Then I wouldn't be alive right now if it weren't for Chesterfield," she murmured thoughtfully, "and neither would Lacey. We would have frozen to death in the garden." she added.

"Yes, that's true. He's a very noble cat."

Mop had her arms in the air and was struggling to get up, so I reached over and took her into my lap. She reached her paw into my bowl and tried her first taste of porridge. Then she began wildly sucking it from her paw so I spoon-fed her some and she sucked it down greedily.

"A very uncommon cat. I'll call her Lacey Chesterfield Smoothstone, in honour of the two important creatures that helped bring her into this world."

Angel scraped the last of the mush from her bowl and I gave her a medicinal brew of red raspberry and rose hips. She drank the tea all up and I helped her back to her place by the fire.

"That's a very unusual family name, Smoothstone. I had an Aunt Myra on my mother's side who married a mason named Chipper Smoothstone." I tucked the bedclothes around her and put some wood on the fire.

"That's my Great Grandfather, Grandpa Chip! I guess that makes us cousins." Angel and I were both delighted to discover that we were family. We had quite a bit of catching up to do, since I hadn't seen that part of the family in many years.

But before the tired dear could say another word, the warmth of the fire had gotten the best of her and in mid-sentence—something about Great-Grandma's oatmeal cakes—she was fast asleep. I tucked Mop in beside her for a nursing and a nap, then I looked in on my newborn cousin Lacey and set the cradle rocking gently. My foot kept time on the wooden rocker as I hummed her a mousey lullaby, one Aunt Myra used to sing to me when I was a little one. And as I waited for the twins to come to breakfast, I thought about how pleased Chesterfield will be when we tell him that Angel did indeed name her new mousekin after her brave rescuer.

10. The Grand Tour

The vote was unanimous. The twins wanted Angel and her new mouseling to stay on as much as I did. As they washed the breakfast dishes and tidied up the kitchen, they chattered excitedly in hushed tones about their new "sister" and their new mousekin. Each in turn reminded the other to be quiet, lest they should wake the new addition. When everything was hung up and tucked in its proper place, Eency stoked the fire against the chill December wind.

"I think this should keep it for awhile," Eency announced shoving a large chunk of wood scrap on top of the pile of burning chips. The fire roared in agreement. I knelt down and checked Angel's bedclothes to make sure that they were tucked snugly around her, safe from the sparks and embers.

"Do you think we could leave them alone to sleep for awhile?" Weency whispered as she looked down adoringly at Little Lacey tucked tight in her new cradle. From years of caring for little ones my hearing has grown quite acute and I've developed a fine set of "Mother's Ears."

"We can if we don't go too far out of my range. What are you thinking, Weency?" I asked the smiling young one.

"You haven't even seen the nest, and I thought Eency and I could give you a guided tour." Eency was beside her, nodding vigorously.

"Please do say yes, Mrs. Chubbly! I can show you father's workshop," Then, so as not to be left out of the adventure planning, Weency interrupted excitedly,

"And I can show you mother's sewing room!"

"And I'll show you the library, and the storeroom, and..." Lacey began to stir in her cradle.

"Quiet, you two, or we're not going anywhere," I said rocking the mouseling back to sleep.

"All right, as long as we're not out of ear shot, I would be delighted to see the nest."

Before I could say another word each had me by a paw and we were down the hall beyond the kitchen and nursery off on our grand tour of the wonder-filled nest.

We slipped silently past my quarters and I noticed they did not stop to show me what I supposed was Mr. and Mrs.

Twingle's bedroom. We followed the wallway and turned to the right. I began to smell a deliciously familiar scent, ancient and musty. A rush of fond memories rose in me as I recalled standing in my Aunt Bibi's workroom, surrounded by her paw copied manuscripts. Leaning at her wooden desk, watching as her fine grey paw moved across a white page, stopping only to dip her quill pen into the glass vial filled with blackberry ink, then continuing its scrolling journey across the clean page. I remember being filled with awe. "What are you doing that for?" I asked her.

"I'm writing down the elder tales, making copies of them," she explained patiently.

"Why?' I asked again.

"So they won't be lost. So you and your mouselings, and your great mouselings, will have the tales forever, you curious little dear!"

She bent herself back to her task, "Now, hush, and you may stay and watch."

The long shelves of old manuscripts had enfolded me then, with their warm darkness. A safe place to be, a solid place, surrounded by the ancient history of my foremothers.

"This is the library," Eency said proudly, guiding my gaze around the dark room with a sweep of his paw.

"Mmmm... I know."

I nodded, breathing in the sweet smell of the old books. We were respectfully quiet as we slowly toured the beautiful room. It was a room that commanded respect. The shelves reached from the floor to a towering height of four EM's and considering that one Elder Mouse was five inches, they must have been at least twenty inches high. Each shelf was paw carved of hardwood with an eagle feather pattern I have seen in other good libraries. The feathers trailed along the edges of the shelves and met at a carved walnut in each corner. The ladders reached up to the highest shelf, also of the same hardwood, with a matching pattern of quills and walnuts, and Herbert Twingle had cleverly attached two cat's eye marbles at the base of each leg. With the touch of a paw, the ladders moved easily across the library floor, and I climbed up to peruse the more obscure volumes on the top shelves.

The books were each a work of art, paw written, paw made. Each volume was bound carefully, stitched by an artist in fine fabrics. The volume I chose had a sculptured rat-hide cover—the leather embossed with scrolls and curlicues.

The title painted in gold leaf was "Florapedia", and neatly pressed into the leather in humble letters, "By Makelroy Chubbly."

"Oh, I just knew it!" I said, quickly descending the ladder.

"What is it, Mrs. Chubbly?" The twins scurried over to see what was causing my excitement.

"A volume on plants by my Uncle Mak!" I sat in a thick cushioned, brown velvet reading chair and placed the heavy volume in my lap. Mr. Twingle had cleverly gnawed a hole through the exterior wall and covered it with an ornate silver encased monocle. The sunlight poured in brightly through the round window and fell perfectly on to the book. The twins leaned on either side of me, looking on expectantly as the sunlight glittered on the golden letters.

"Oh, it's so beautifully done!" Weency touched the cover very gently with her pawtip. I opened the cover carefully, as it was quite old, and began to turn page after page. Aunt Bibi's fine lettering and her intricate copies of Uncle Mak's drawings reminded me of my first summer as an apprentice. Weency "oohed and aahed," enthralled by the lovely book. Eency got bored by the whole thing and drifted away, muttering to himself, "I don't see what all the fuss is about, just a lot of leaves."

I thought then, that perhaps when spring came, Weency might be interested in learning about the ancient healing arts. I was very pleased. I never thought I would find a young apprentice and believed the family healing arts would die with me.

11. Father Twingle's Secret

Eency was getting impatient.

"Mrs. Chubbly, can't we please go now? You can visit this old library any time," he whined.

"Father's workshop is much more interesting," he said, shuffling around impatiently, directly in my light.

I rose from the chair, tucking the volume under my arm, and took the energetic young mouse by the paw.

"All right, Eency, but you never have to whine to get my attention. It's very rude and no mouse will ever respond well to you if you cannot express yourself without whining. Besides, you're far too old for that sort of tactic," I replied, leading him toward the opening to the wallway.

"Some mice think libraries are much nicer than stuffy rooms filled with dirty old machines, little twin," Weency added with a flourish as she followed us out. Weency was a full twenty minutes older and sometimes she liked rubbing it in as a reminder that being first born does give one certain privileges.

We turned to the right once more and pushed aside a heavy black velvet drapery, entering a room that was crowded and dusty. Strange machines and contraptions haunted the dark room. Their looming shapes hung about us like hungry tomcats in a pitch black cellar. We stood perfectly still, allowing our eyes to grow accustomed to the dim light.

"Cats and kittens!" Eency swore, "I've forgotten to bring any matches!"

I reached down into my front apron pocket.

"I've got two," I replied, pulling out a broken piece of stick match, the firing end still intact. "Is there a lamp?" I asked, knowing that Mr. Twingle was the clever sort.

"No, father always preferred the smell of wax to oil. There should be a bit of candle somewhere on the workbench," Eency replied, reaching for the match bit in the darkness. "Here, let me..."

"No Eency, it's far too short, I'm afraid you'll singe yourself," I replied.

I held the broken stick as far from the end as I could, then struck it quickly against the bench. The room suddenly came to life, shadows dancing eerily back and forth as I walked with the torch toward the candle and set the flame to its wick. The candle took over and the room brightened into a steadier light, giving us all a view of the oddities that surrounded us. I blew hard on the match and sent a cloud of dust from the floor into the air. All of us began to cough.

"Ahhhhchoooo!" Weency sneezed loudly. "Father never cared much about what the workshop looked like. He was so eccentric about his inventions, he wouldn't even let Mother in to clean."

I placed the Florapedia on the workbench and tentatively began to look around, then I felt Eency take my paw.

"Let me show you," Eency said, tugging at my arm.

"Have you been in here before? I thought your father..."

"Yes, well. Father didn't know," Eency replied sheepishly. "Sometimes, early in the morning, before Father woke up, I'd sneak out of the nursery to come and see what he was building. Father spent a lot of his time working here alone."

I looked at him reproachfully, though I didn't need to. He already knew he was wrong.

"I couldn't help myself, Mrs. Chubbly. He was so incredible and I just had to know. Sometimes he would bring something out—a gift for Mother, like her sewing machine... but mostly he would work and work and never show what he was working on."

"Curiosity killed the cat, Eency." I said.

"Thank Goodness!" Weency answered, chuckling.

Eency pulled and we followed behind him. We treaded carefully through piles of metal and wooden parts and a collection of gathered objects that had been categorized in a way I didn't understand. We threaded our way beyond the small workbench, then on past the main workbench. There were several large shapes covered in sheets of filmy fabric. I stopped at the first and tried to read the paw printed card that hung on the face of the machine. My spectacles were covered with a fine layer of dust and the dim light made the job impossible. I removed my glasses and polished them with the underside of my apron—the only part of me that wasn't covered in dust.

When I sat them back on my nose, the room seemed considerably brighter. I read the card aloud.

"Mother's helper—Clothes washer"

"And it really works!" Eency exclaimed, pulling the sheet off of the Mother's helper. "You see this base? The tin can? This is where you put the clothes, and you fill it with hot water through this funnel at the end of the water tube."

The thing was brilliantly devised. Mr. Twingle had created a sort of eggbeater in a tin can. On the left side were two large rubber erasers attached to some kind of lever that seemed to open and close them.

"Then you turn this handle here," Eency said, demonstrating. "And this beater turns the clothes and beats the dirt right out of them."

He picked up a scrap of fabric from the floor to assist us in imagining the job, and placed it on the bottom eraser, ' Next, you place your washing on this rubber pad and pull this lever, and TA DA!!!" He pulled the lever and the erasers came together and squeezed the scrap tight.

"Your washing is wrung out and ready to be hung by the fire."

Weency and I were both delighted.

"Wonderful! Just this contraption alone could make nestkeeping so much easier, especially for a young mother with twins," I commented.

"But why didn't he give it to Mother?" Weency asked him.

"He never brought anything out unless it was perfect. It probably wasn't finished."

Eency's voice trailed off sadly, then he brightened. "Maybe I could finish it?"

"I'm sure you could, Eency—you've got your father's paws and his curiosity."

He was smiling and I was glad to see his heart lighten with his new interest.

"We haven't much time," Weency said, considering the mousekins sleeping in the kitchen.

"True, perhaps we should be getting back," I answered reluctantly.

"Not yet. There's something else you've got to see."

Eency had my paw again and was off with us in tow. We passed another machine, larger than the first. This one also had a card, but it was marked "Food Keeper".

"Hmmmm," I thought to myself as we hurried by, "I'll have to see that one later."

Eency brought us to a halt in front of a large shape about three EM's long by two EM's high. It was covered by a large sheet of black cotton. The wall behind it was covered by the same fabric. The whole thing had a mysterious, theatrical effect, with its long flowing drapes and vaguely familiar covered shape.

Eency climbed upon the workbench, a corner of the black fabric held tightly in his paw—then he announced in a booming ceremonial voice,

"Elders and mousettes! Permit me to unveil Father Twingle's Flying Machine!" With a sweep of his arm, Eency tugged at the fabric and in one smooth motion it slid into a large black pile on to the dusty floor.

The flying machine stood before us like a final monument, marking the genius of Herbert Twingle.

"Great litters of kittens!" I gasped, moving close enough to touch the strange creature with my paw.

The flickering light of the candle shone on the gleaming metal machine. Mr. Twingle had fashioned it out of thin sheets of aluminium in the shape of the most familiar flying thing he knew—a woodpecker. It was majestic, even as it stood flightless, its metal feathered wings folded gracefully against its body. Its headcrest was hammered from copper halfpence, as was the long pointed beak. Not only was it designed aerodynamically for flight, but it was designed for beauty as well. The copper beak and crest were polished to a red brilliance, the body gleamed silver, and the eyes were fashioned from two oval watch crystals set into rims of copper that gave the machine an almost frighteningly life-like quality.

It stood perched upon two steel legs that ended in sharp talons, and each talon held a hard black rubber ball.

"How very clever indeed!" I thought to myself. If it could fly, it even looked as though it could make a safe landing.

Weency had disappeared behind the great bird, then I saw her as she came around from behind the tail. She looked mesmerized by the sparkling creature. Her eyes held a far away look, as if she was seeing something none of us could see. She touched the wings then ran her paws along the sides until she came to the underbelly. Eency watched her in amazement, as if this wasn't his familiar twin at all, but some new mouse he had never seen before. Her concentration was intense. Her paw came to rest on the breast, where she felt along the seam in the aluminum, searching, then stopping. She seemed perplexed, then she turned to look at her twin, as if to question him.

"Push it hard," he said, waiting for her reaction.

She pressed the breast of the great bird and something clicked. Then the hatch released and a door with a built in ladder slowly lowered to the floor before her.

Weency gasped. In the semi-darkness of Mr. Twingle's workshop, the mysterious hatchway looked like the passage to another world, at that moment none of us realized how close to the truth that was. But we would, and that is another tale.

Before I could utter a word of warning, Weency had bounded up the steps and disappeared into the darkness. I was right behind her, almost stepping on her tail, and I felt Eency follow me closely. I stood up in a space that seemed impossibly large. The hatch stairs ended in the main cabin. When my eyes adjusted to the darkness, I found I was in a large barrel-shaped room. There were six panels in the interior walls, three on each side, held up by loops of ropes hanging on small metal knobs. I unhooked the one nearest me and a comfortable seat folded down from the wall. On the seat was a roughly sewn cushion and a blanket—Mr. Twingle's paw work no doubt. Then I heard a sound and turned to the doorway to my left. There were two permanent seats in the front of the great bird and the candlelight shone through the watch crystal windshield on Weency and Eency sitting in the cockpit, looking all too ready to take off. I scurried up front and stood between the twins, amazed at the complicated switches and knobs on the dashboard before me. Eency had his paw on a steering lever, happily pretending to be flying. Weency was staring straight through the windshield, deep in thought. She was mesmerized and breathing very slowly and deeply as if in a trance.

"I do believe I could fly this thing," she stated quietly.

"And what makes you believe that, Weency?" I asked her.

"Call it mousette's intuition. I know this may sound silly, Mrs. Chubbly, but I just feel it deep inside of me somewhere, somehow when I sat down here, and looked around, it all seemed oddly familiar, like I have dreamt this moment many times before and... I just understand it, that's all," she answered, sounding happy and frightened at the same time.

"It doesn't sound at all silly to me, Weency. We are all capable of things far beyond our wildest imaginings, and we are all one. We have access to the knowledge of everything, now and throughout all of creation, without the boundaries of time or our imagined physical limitations, through The Great Creator. I'm sure if your father created something that could fly, somewhere in you is the knowledge of how to fly it. You are your father's daughter, you know."

"Oh go on, you two, with all your mysterious talk of wild imaginings! Weency, you're just a female! A writer of tales and someday a mother of many litters, and maybe a seamstress, like Mother. Look at how complicated this great bird is! If anymouse could have figured out how to fly this thing it would have been Father." Eency folded his arms across his chest angrily as if to close the subject, but Weency was furious.

"Oh really, little brother? A few days ago you were a mouseling in a pretty nursery and now, beyond your wildest imaginings, you are head male of a household, and have been gathering in the big house kitchen, and out playing in the garden with a hawk! Open your mind and imagine that."

"Enough, you two," I silenced them sternly. "We're not going to settle this debate today. I have a new mother and two mouselings waiting for me in the kitchen, and it really is time for us to get back. When we decide to go for a trial flight, Weency, I designate you as the pilot. I trust intuition more than most of the foolish thinking I've heard in my long life. Now, we must go."

I turned and walked down the hatch steps and the twins followed behind me, Eency pouting angrily and Weency already off in a flight of fancy. I wondered how Mr. Twingle planned on getting the huge bird out of the nest as I pressed the hatch door shut and picked up Uncle Mak's book. Eency brightened a bit when I allowed him to snuff the candle, but we were all silent with our own private thoughts of the past and now of the strange possibilities for the future during the long walk down the wallway and back to the kitchen.

Once again, it was proven to me that every time I believe that life is about to settle down to a nice calm routine, the good powers that be present me with the opportunity for another incredible adventure, another learning experience with higher peaks to climb. And though I like the idea of settling down, I always keep my traveling bag packed.

12. The Story of Angelvoice

It was a beautiful sound, high, clear and sweet. It came lilting down the wallway and stopped us in our tracks. I put my pawtip to my lips and motioned for the mouselings to be quiet and still. We stood entranced, listening to the violin-like tones of Angel singing to the little ones.

"Fuzzy little ones, close your sleepy eyes.

Fuzzy little ones, close your sleepy eyes.

Fall into your mousey dreams,

Mountains of cheese and bowls of sweet cream.

In your sparrow down bed, rest your little sleepy head.

On pillows and sheets of fine velveteen

You'll fall into your mousey dream.

Father's a gatherer and every night,

He'll bring you a trinket for mousely delight,

Mother's a baker and maker of song,

She'll sing you a lullaby, sweet, soft and warm,

then fill the cupboard with sweet oatmeal cake,

and you'll fill your belly a-when you awake-o."

She continued the melody, humming the bright tune. Her voice was familiar, kind, like Aunt Myra, but there was a haunting bell-like quality that rang over and over in my mind and brought back a lost memory of a night many years ago. I had gone to hear a young singer at the "Mouse Trap Cafe," a boisterous music hall down on the riverfront. My cousin Sprout's son, Silver, had married a beautiful, talented mousette, and they invited us down for the night to hear her perform. When she took the stage, she appeared so delicate and very beautiful. And when she sang she glowed with an inner light, much brighter than the many candles that surrounded the stage. While she sang, the large rowdy crowd became suddenly silent. They sat mesmerized, friends and strangers alike, savoring her song. Though it happened years ago, when I was much younger, the memory was crystal clear, and the voice I heard now seemed the very same.

"That was lovely!" I broke in as we entered the kitchen. She smiled shyly, as if unused to compliments.

"Thank you, I didn't know anyone was listening." Then she was silent, and with Lacey asleep in her cradle and Moo tied in a sling on her back she moved gracefully around the kitchen tidying up. I almost felt useless, then I realized, with Angel so willing and able to help, I would be free to spend more time with the older mouselings, something they sorely needed right now while adjusting to orphanhood—and I was greatly thankful.

The twins were looking around the cupboards now, hungry after our long tour, and surprised to find all the cheese gone but too polite to say anything. Angel saw this and brought a large platter to the table.

"Lunch is served," she chimed, as she uncovered the dish.

The cheese was cut neatly into bite-sized pieces and surrounded by bits of leftover cracker. Next to the platter she set out a trivet made from a beautiful paw painted bottle cap and on this she placed the red clay teapot full of hot water. Weency got teacups for all of us, while Eency greedily sat down to eat without a thought of helping.

"Eency, where are your manners?" I asked quietly. He put his head down, embarrassed at being caught again.

"Sorry, Mrs. Chubbly. What can I do to help?"

"Why don't you bring us some dried peppermint and get my bag so I can make some medicinal tea for Angel?"

He nodded and brought the herbs to the table, placing my bag at my feet. I fixed Angel a mixture of raspberry and fennel for her milk, then after a prayer of gratitude, we all sat together merrily eating from the beautiful cheese platter and sipping our tea.

"Angel, we must take you on a tour of the nest. We had such a wonderful time this morning," Weency said, excited to be sharing with an older sister.

"Well, Weency, I would really love it, but I don't know how much walking I'm up to. After all, this was my first litter," she said, glancing over at Lacey so beautiful and peaceful in her cradle. We could all see in Angel's eyes the tender love she felt for her new daughter.

"That's wise, Angel, I believe in three days of bed rest after a birth. You may sit at the table to eat and to move around the kitchen a bit, but you need at least two more days to heal, and this is an important time for you to spend quietly nursing Lacey." Then I remembered the stillborns, wrapped and left in the corner of the kitchen and though none of us wanted to talk about it, it was a matter that just couldn't wait any longer.

"Angel, after lunch, I'd like to do a ceremony for the stillborns and give you a chance to properly say goodbye to them," I said, watching her for a response

She nodded her head and began playing with her cheese like a distracted young mousekin, no longer hungry, trying not to think about it. She looked suddenly very young and vulnerable, as if she needed her mother.

"I don't want to pry, dear, but is there someone we can get a message to, for you? You must have some family somewhere that would want to know."

She shook her head sadly and wrung her paws in her lap, repeating over and over again, "I don't know, I don't know, I just don't know Mrs. Chubbly."

"What do you mean? Where is your mother, little one?" I asked.

Then Eency, without thinking asked, "Was your mother eaten by a cat too?"

"Oh no, it wasn't like that at all. When I left, I was in such a terrible state, I'm not even sure I remember it correctly."

Then we all listened quietly as Angel recounted her tale for us.

"I was born in a nest in the back storeroom of a music hall down on the River Thames. It was a wild place, a sailor's bar. My father, an instrument maker, had turned the place into a lovely cafe, and after he married my mother, Lily Angelvoice, they set up a stage so she could sing."

"That must be my cousin Silver, one of the triplets. Uncle Chip had one of his pianos in their parlor. It was the first I had ever seen, a real work of art," I interrupted.

"That's right, that was my father, Silver Smoothstone. He built pianos for everyone in the family and then started doing it as his trade. He never loved building them as much as he loved playing for my mother. Anyway, I'll make a very long story short," she said drumming her paw tips on the table, not wanting to go on.

"When I was a babe, I would lay in my cradle in a darkened corner away from the bright stage and the crowd of strange mice, listening to my mother's nightly performance." She adjusted the sling on her back and Mop found her little paw and began sucking on it.

"My mother had the most beautiful voice I had ever heard. Sometimes friends or distant cousins would stop by and sing a few songs, but it wasn't like listening to Lily. Her voice didn't lull me to sleep. It hypnotized me. I could lay there awake for hours, listening to her in a half dream."

She looked away wistfully, as if she would never hear her mother's voice again.

"I know, she was really magical." I said.

"How could you know? You've heard her?" she asked surprised.

"Yes, my dear, I heard her years ago and I remember it like it was yesterday. I went to the Mouse Trap Cafe with cousin Ebony. It must have been just after you turned two, about fifteen years ago, I'd say. It was the first time in years I had gotten together with the cousins, your father's brothers, and some other relatives. I can't even recall the occasion but they brought us to Lily and Silver's place to hear your mother sing. I've never forgotten the sound of her voice, to this day—and you sound just like her when you sing, just lovely."

She smiled shyly when I said this and turned away embarrassed.

"Thank you so much, Mrs. Chubbly, that's the kindest thing you could have said, but I find it hard to believe I could ever sound as lovely as Mother."

"Not kind, dear, honest. You sound very much like her. The Great Creator has given you a very special gift, and of course you must share it with us."

"Oh yes, Angel!" the twins added together, "You have a wonderful voice, we'd love to hear you sing again."

"Sometime I will, Mouselings. Though my mother could sing as soon as they lit the stage candles, I can only do it when my heart moves me. But I was trying to tell you about the fire."

"Fire?" Eency asked, terrified. All mice are frightened of fire, we have all heard tales of a fire whipping through a nest and killing entire families instantly, or turning them into homeless wanderers, and none of us imagined that fire might be the reason Angel was with us this morning.

"Yes, fire! It was a terrible nightmare! I was sound asleep when a drunken human man came wandering into the storeroom very close to the nest. He smelled horrible as humans do when they've been drinking, but you little ones wouldn't know anything about that horror, growing up in this beautiful mansion, in such a safely placed nest."

The mouselings' eyes were wide, imagining living in a nest in the back room of a music hall, picturing the drunken men wandering into their home—and Angel continued.

"He fell down, quite near to my bed, then picked himself up muttering angrily about the barkeep who wouldn't serve him another shot of rum, then stumbled again, this time to an old pile of newspapers that made up the outside wall of the nest. I held my breath from the terrible stench and sat still watching him. We had company over that night, Midnight was there, sound asleep on a mat near the piano."

"Who is Midnight? Your brother?" Eency asked.

"No, no. I have no brothers. They were stillborns too. Midnight is Lacey's father, but I'll save that story for another time. Midnight was sleeping and so was Lily, but my father heard the sound of the human falling and was up on his bed, watching, waiting to see if he would have to move us to safety. Then the man got a cigarette out of a package in his shirt pocket and also a stick match. I couldn't move, though I sensed what was happening, somehow the fear froze me. The man was moving sloppily, several times dropping the matchstick and then picking it up again, cursing it. Then he struck it on the bottom of his shoe and lit the stick in his mouth. He dropped the match onto the papers and I saw him and the whole stack of papers burst into flame."

She shuddered and began to shake her head again, as if she were just hearing the tale for the first time and couldn't believe it at all.

"I could feel the heat of the first flames and smell the terrible acrid smell of the man burning and the horrible screaming, but I couldn't move. My father must have carried me out. The next thing I knew, I was sitting in the snow in the back alley. My father said 'Wait here, Angel, I'm going in for Lily.' I wanted to stop him. I could see the black smoke pouring out of the door and I was afraid that I would never see my papa again, but Lily was inside and he loved her more than life. So he went."

Angel droned on in a flat, dull voice, devoid of feeling, not at all like the gay lilting creature who had just sang a lullaby to the newborn mouseling. It was painful to listen to her go on this way, but she had to tell it all, to spill it all out of her, or she couldn't begin to heal.

"Then something happened that I still don't understand. Father scurried in through the smoking doorway to save Lily. I sat there watching the door, waiting for my mother and father to be beside me, safe in the wet snow. I'm ashamed to say I wasn't even thinking about Midnight, just my parents.

She shifted her thin body uncomfortably on the stool, so I rose and took Mop from her back and lay her to sleep on the bedding near the fire. Angel waited, watching me until I was once more seated across from her.

"Mrs. Chubbly, it was a nightmare. I see it every time I shut my eyes."

"What was, dear?" I asked, touching my paw gently to hers.

"I don't know, I really don't know." She sat silently again, pressing her lips together tightly, holding back her words until the emotions that were welling up inside her had subsided.

"I felt the air around me being sucked away, it was cold and the building seemed to be sucking in air, drawing it in like it was taking a huge breath. I held tight, digging into the earth beneath the snow to keep from being sucked away too, then there was a noise. A huge booming sound. The building rocked, the earth shook beneath my paws. Glass shattered around me like a thousand crystal arrows and living balls of flame burst forth from the window holes and the doorway. The whole building went up in a flash of flames, it all happened in an instant. My mother and father and Midnight, I don't... I just don't know." she pressed her paws on the table, hard and tight as if she was holding on. Silent again, squinting her eyes, looking back, she was trying to recall exactly what had happened, and I felt the power in her words directed at me, as if, if she told it well enough, clearly enough, I would be able to give her the answer to the unanswerable.

"I woke up in the bushes a good distance from the place. I must have been blown away by the force. My head was aching. Maybe I struck it on the ground, I don't know. I couldn't remember where I was, what happened, and then it all flooded back to me and I turned to look at the back door and it was gone!"

She pressed her paws to her eyes to make the image disappear and then, drained from the telling, she went on almost in a whisper.

"The sun was up now and I was sorry that it was. I was sorry that I had escaped the fire, that I was alive and alone, but then I felt Lacey move, she rolled inside of me as if she could read my thoughts, and I knew that I wasn't alone and it gave me courage. It gave me the will to go on."

She looked at me, searching my face for understanding and though I had never had a litter of my own, I knew what it was like to go on for others, to take strength from caring for those who needed me when I felt I had no strength left for myself.

"The sun was shining on the mound of burnt-out remains of the building. It was ugly and beautiful at the same time, covered with ice, dripping with long sparkling icicles that hung in rows on the debris like giant cat fangs. It was frightening and I began to run. I ran and ran for a long time. I was tired and cold but so numb inside, all I could do was keep moving and when I could no longer run, I walked. I walked and talked to my growing little ones, telling them it was going to be alright, not knowing myself how it ever could be, but I told them over and over that it would be."

She looked over into the cradle again and it seemed to give her strength, just seeing the newborn sucking at the air in her sleep, nursing in her dream, knowing she had someone left.

"I walked till my paw-pads were sore and then I was in labour. I knew I had to find a safe place to litter and I guess my instincts kept me moving. It must have been days, maybe three or four, I don't know, but the sun kept coming up again and again, and then it was night and I knew my time was near. Somehow I found myself at the garden door, dazed and exhausted, scratching to get in. I have no idea how I got here, I just felt I had to go on and on like I was being guided by something I didn't understand, so I went on and on until a small voice inside of me said "Here, you are here now, and you will be safe" You know the rest." She rubbed her face with her paws and I took her by the arm, led her over to the bedding and laid her down beside Mop to rest.

"You need to sleep now, Angel. You've been through too much."

She was about to protest, to try to get up again, but I pressed her gently down and tucked the bedclothes around her. She was asleep quickly.

I sent the frightened mouselings off to play in the nursery until dinner, sure that they'd had too much elder business for one day. But life goes on, and I never believed one should hide reality from mousekins, after all, birth and death are part of our experience. If you hide experiences from them, it turns them into frightened unprepared elders. But of course, everything in moderation. And though I've seen and heard worse, Angel's tale had shaken me to my core and I knew the mouselings would need some play time to sort through their thoughts and understand it all.

Kindly, Chesterfield dropped by after tea and left us a fine half sandwich of nut butter and strawberry jam and a whole chocolate truffle. I knew we'd have a fine meal that night and no one would have to gather until tomorrow.

I spent the rest of the afternoon changing wet bottom scraps and keeping the mouselings quiet and happy so Angel could rest. When everycreature was settled, I prepared a dinner of chocolate nut soup and strawberry jam on bread.

As I worked, I thought about the drunken man with the match and the consequences of his actions. I thought about Mrs. Hammond and the humans in the big house and all the other humans that I had known or been told of and I wondered about them. Were their lives filled with the same loss and pain we mice suffered? Were they given so much tragedy to overcome? Do they have the joy and closeness we mice share with all of our brothers and sisters and our fellow creatures? It's hard to tell about humans, they behave so strangely so much of the time. I believe they are the cause of their own misery. From the stories I've heard, it seems they are predator and prey to each other, but at the very least, they never have to worry about being eaten by a hungry cat.

13. Annabelle Lovely

Annabelle sat by the French windows overlooking the garden. She pulled the worn, brown woolen shawl closer around her shoulders and rocked methodically back and forth in her old wooden rocker. She had one knee drawn up on the chair and just the tip of her slippered foot touched the floor, pressing over and over while she rocked. The moon was full and the bright light it shone on the garden was sharp as day, casting huge shadows everywhere. The air was cold and crystal clear as it always is after a large snowfall, and Annabelle sat sleepless, rocking and staring at the large white shape in the winter sky.

The only thing that looked out of place in the beautiful room was Annabelle. She looked grey and pinched and tired from thinking constantly about the past, thinking the same thoughts over and over in a spiral that returned to itself, always unresolved. Always full of guilt and self-blame and rage at the whole universe. She was deeply angry and she didn't know what to do to make it stop. She sat rocking and thinking in the beautiful room. It wasn't the brightness of the moon that kept her awake at such a late hour but her constant rethinking. Once, she was a lively passionate woman, but she had turned the passion into a constant beratement of herself and those she loved.

Sometimes she was aware of how miserable she made herself. But she was helpless to stop it and rather than push Edmund and Wendy further away, she simply withdrew and chose to spend her time thinking and crying alone in her room. She wanted them to be free from her anger and self loathing. She loved them both fiercely so she protected them. Annabelle protected her family, by disappearing. In the beginning she had come to the little spare room to sew. It was an attic room with a large dormer and leaded French glass windows that let in plenty of light. When Edmund first bought the house and she saw the little room, she knew right away that it would be the perfect place to sew. All that sunlight and fresh air and the magnificent view of the formal garden, perfect for her. When Doctor Hartley told the Lovelys they were going to have a baby, she ran right up to that room and began sewing in her every spare moment. She handmade sheets for the baby cot, and beautiful dresses with matching booties.

After she lost Michael, she would come up to the room and sit looking at the bolts of fabric and the racks of brightly coloured thread with no desire to touch anything, and soon it was all just gathering dust. She liked it there alone, finally away from Edmund's pleading eyes and Wendy's round, cherubic face. When she looked at Wendy, she saw Michael.

And when she looked at Edmund and saw how openly he loved her, she loathed herself all the more for what she was so helplessly doing to her family.

After a while she gave up the pretense and had the room done over as her own bedroom. The decorator chose bright blues with dramatic peacocks for the curtains and the bedspread. The bedframe was brass but very feminine and ornate, and the walls were covered with a watered silk fabric, also in a bright blue. The room was lovely, except for Annabelle. In the beautiful blueness of it all, she was a dark grey stain. Her hair that had once been a bright rich auburn was now peppered with grey, though she was only thirtyfive, and her complexion, once a smooth alabaster with a girlish blush high on her cheeks, though still perfectly smooth, was now ashen.

She heard the familiar scratch at her door and without turning she answered, "Come in Chesterfield. Here, kitty," She patted the lap of her flannel nightdress, hoping the large cat would accept her invitation. Chesterfield liked to play a little game with Annabelle before he settled in for their nightly chat. Instead of taking his place in her lap, he spent a few moments rubbing the back of his furry black head against Annabelle's leg. Then he circled her outstretched foot once or twice, always stopping briefly to rub his head against her leg.

"Here, Chesterfield, be a sweet kitty," she pleaded again, patting her lap and reaching out with her arm. After a few more good solid rubs and some purring, sure that he was in charge, he jumped into her lap and settled himself for the nice scratching he would receive while she talked.

She sat silent, rubbing the soft white fur on his belly while he purred loudly and tossed his paws carelessly in the air. He always knew where to find her, and each night he would arrive and they had their quiet time. She caressed him and scratched behind his ears, then he would curl up in her lap and snooze while she would talk in a warm, droning tone that never failed to lull him to sleep.

"What a pretty kitty you are," She crooned to him, "and you've grown so large this year."

She watched him stretch to his full length as she ran her hands through his thick fur. Then he settled again, purring, as she absently played with his long tail.

"Sometimes when I'm sitting here alone it feels like my life has been one long endless night, rocking here." She paused, her weight coming to rest on her toe, then they were rocking again, back and forth, back and forth.

"I can't bear the thought of leaving this room! I used to care what Edmund would think, and Wendy, and Mrs. Hammond. They probably all think I'm crazy. But I just can't stand the thought of having to go downstairs and sit at the table, looking at them looking at me the way they do. Sometimes I feel like an infection of rage and grief. And I don't want them to catch it"

She began again rubbing his back fur, sometimes going up against the grain of his fur, then smoothing it down from his head to his tail. He purred loudly to let her know she was doing a fine job.

`"I just don't care anymore, about anything. Sad isn't it?" she asked, looking down at him.

"There was a time when I cared so much about everything that I felt I would almost burst. You know, I used to be quite a gardener. Most of the flower beds, I planted them myself." She held her hands up in the moonlight and looked at them hard. They were long and strong, with slender fingers and a delicate wrist. Then she folded them into tight fists and dug her fingernails into her palms till she could squeeze no longer. She dissolved into tears and hung her head till Chesterfield could feel her moist breath on his face.

"I just can't feel anything anymore, Chesterfield. Nothing at all, and I wonder why I am still alive. Walking around this huge house like a ghost, while everyone else seems to be going about their lives."

He was drifting off, almost in a dream, listening to the pain in the sad human's voice.

"When we first came, I wouldn't let Edmund engage a gardener, and did everything myself. Planned the beds, designed the paths. I even planted some of the younger apple trees. That one there," she said pointing out the window. "The one near the fountain, I planted that tree ten years ago. It was August and I had just found out that Edmund and I were going to have a baby. I went right out and planted that apple tree. And as my belly grew, I watched it grow. Now it stands there and mocks me. All my careful planning. 'My children will play in that tree,' I thought, the day I planted it. I saw them gaily climbing in its broad branches, sitting cradled in its arms, picking apples, running to show me their bounty, delighted."

Her mood turned suddenly sour.

"What right has that tree got to live? People are dying all the time! What right has it got to go on growing and maturing that way, when innocent babies can't breathe and suffocate, innocent victims, their own bodies betraying them? Do you ever think about that? At any time your body can betray you and drag you down into the grave. When Wendy was a toddler, I would take her to the Kensington Gardens. She would run and play, chasing the other babies. All of them with their cheeks so fat and rosy."

She spat the words out as if in disgust.

"And now all those children are grown and strong, having their lives, having their joy. What about mine?"

She rocked faster, violently pushing her foot against the floor.

"I should call the gardener right now and have him come out tonight and chop down that tree! Just kill it! Dig out its roots and fill the hole! Cover it with sod! In a few years no one will even remember it existed. Like Michael."

—A LETTER HOME TO THE APPLE TREE NEST—

To: Mak and Bibi Chubbly from: Mrs. Lacey Chubbly

#1 Old Apple Tree Nest c/o The Twingle Family
Babble Creek, England 22 North Chelsea Lane
Chelsea, England

Spring 1904

Dear uncle Mak and aunt Bibi,

I love and miss you both down to the tip of my tail. I hope this letter finds you both well and serene in your apple tree nest and that The Great Creator has filled your time with joy and peace.

I certainly don't mean to be abrupt after not writing since last spring but I'll bring you up to date quickly, due to lack of spare time (I've got mousekins to care for).

I began working for the Twingle family at the very end of last November. The nest is marvelous beyond my expectations and is scfely located in the entry walls of a fine old formal mansion in Chelsea, quite near the Kensington gardens and not very far from the River Thames.

My charges are Eency and Weency (twins now eleven years of age), and a yearling, Mop (going on sixteen months, to be precise).

Unfortunately (and by providence) the parents were devoured by a reckless young tom named Chesterfield shortly after my arrival. In fact, the very same day I began employment.

However, Chesterfield was young enough (an orphan from the shelter) that I was able to straighten him out and bring him over to a more correct way of behaving and now we have formed a strange alliance with our new guardian (more on this when I see you).

Because of these events, I am the only elder in the nesthold and it seems The Great Creator has given me a permanent family to raise and nurture (a strange turn of fate, considering how you two had come to raise me).

To complicate matters even further, and to my great delight, Angelvoice Smoothstone (Cousin Silver's offspring) arrived a few days later in the final stages of labour with her first litter. After a very difficult night, she birthed two solid black stillborn males and a very healthy all white female with a charming silver lock. She looks just like Cousin Silver's wife Lily. It was a brutal delivery but mother and mousekin are well now.

The new mouseling (my namesake) is called Lacey Chesterfield Smoothstone. I'll explain the Chesterfield part of her name when next I see you.

Angel told me of a terrible fire at "The Mouse Trap Cafe". I wonder if you've heard anything? Are there any survivors? Angel believes she's lost Lily and Silver, and Midnight (Laczy's father) in the fire. Any forthcoming news—for better or worse—would aid in the healing of her wounds.

I have been nanny to the Twingle family for over six months now. Little Mop is walking well and talking a bit. She calls me "Ma Chubby" and s nce Angel is wetnurse, she calls her Mama Angie.

Young Eency (full of false bravado when first we met) has turned out to be quite the gatherer and all around repairmouse, like his father, Herbert. Of course, he gets a great deal of assistance from Chesterfield Cat and Clatter the Mailman.

His sister Weency is showing tremencous interest in studying The Great Healing Arts (she has excellent intuition). I found a copy of your Florapedia in the Twingle family library. It was quite a pleasant surprise as I know Aunt 3ibi made very few copies of the manuscript. I wonder how they came to own it? Do you know anything about this? Please let me know, as it has made me quite curious.

How are Uncle Chip and Aunt Myra doing? Please send them and all the cousins my regards and my regrets about Silver and Lily.

Have you heard from Uncle Woody and Aunt Sandy? I still have the beautiful apple wood spoon woody made for my medicine bag, it's like having a piece of your nest with me always. I hope that Cousin Weaver and her husband Swifty have straightened things out, please send them and their boys Nip and Tuck all my love. Would you ask Weaver to send me some of her tales? I know the mouselings would love her stories, she's got such a fantastic imagination!

I think of the apple tree nest often and miss the farm and all of you much more than words can express. My fondest memories were born there and the great loves of my life. I would love to share some of that magic with my new family. Lacey is crawling now and I know she would love to learn stair climbing on your endless staircase. And I'm sure Aunt Bibi would enjoy watching her attempt it! All of my city mice would love the farm, they've hardly been out of this luxury nest and it would give them a chance to get in touch with their true nature.

Weency would certainly be encouraged in her studies of The Great Healing Arts, if she were able to spend more time with you, my dear Uncle Mak. I believe she is just about the right age, though she is older by a few years than Tailbit and I were when we began our studies of The Great Arts.

I can't imagine how we would find our way up to your nest, but were you to invite us, I believe The Great Creator would prepare our way. It has been ages since I've been home. I'd give up an inch of my tail this very minute just to see your two smiling faces again.

Is Curly Goldentop still living in the upstairs nest? How are her two little ones and her handsome son, Lancelot? Please send then my best wishes.

Well, I've got dozens of exciting stories to share with you both, but I'll save them. I bel eve they would be much better told in front of a crackling fire, all of us sipping our tea and watching the young ones play.

Again, I love you and miss you both and hope with all my heart to see you very soon.

My deepest love and affection,

Lacey

14. The Apple Tree Nest

Upstairs at #2 Old Apple Tree Nest, Curly Goldentop had had just about enough. "I told you mouselings, stop your endless bickering and eat your breakfast."

Arthur and Guinevere looked up at their mother and then turned back to each other, pouting as only two seven year olds can. As soon as her back was turned they renewed their argument with great fervor.

"I tell you, Gwen, it's not possible to drop an acorn from the top of a tree and then run down and catch it on the ground!" he pounded his little paw hard on the table, as if to prove he was right.

"Oh Arthur! You're so narrow minded. Anything is possible, you know, it just shows how much you know about the universe!" she yelled back at him loudly.

"I'll settle this," Lancelot said as he walked into the kitchen. Lancelot was very tall for an eighteen year old, taller than all the other mice his age. He was very handsome with his sleek golden pelt and curly gold headfur, but his alarming good looks didn't seem to affect him, he was the kindest mouse on the farm.

If you could say anything at all wrong about Lancelot, it was that he was too terribly shy. He wasn't always shy, but in the last few years after his father died and he came of age to be wed, with all the young mousettes of marriageable age paying such extravagant attention to Lance, he changed. He was still kind and respectful to everycreature but he kept to the nest more and more, helping his mother with the twins, and basically keeping to himself. This only fascinated the young mousettes all the more and he had to constantly give them tea and ask them politely to leave after they had come to visit to try and pique his interest, asking him all sorts of foolish questions to try to "bring him out," as they called it. His mother, Curly, mostly kept quiet about it, although she worried that he would never have a family of his own. She was also wise enough to know that someday the right mousette would come along and open his eyes.

"The truth is, Arthur, if a creature was fast enough, they could catch the acorn before it hit the ground," he said, ruffling his little brother's headfur with his paw. "But, Gwen, I've never seen any creature fast enough to do it. So, you're both right."

"Thank you, Lance. I hope the little ones turn out to be as reasonable as you, dear," his mother said, kissing him good morning on his cheek. Just as they settled down to finish their walnut mash there was a loud rapping at the entryhole.

"Who could that be at this hour?" Curly asked herself, thinking it was an early calling suitor for her handsome son.

"Mail call!" came the voice from the entrance branch. Then the rap, rap, rapping sound came again, louder this time, to be sure some creature knew he was there, waiting.

Clatter Woodpecker had been the mail bird for as long as anycreature could remember and it never satisfied him just to knock once. After all, he was a woodpecker, so Mrs. Goldentop knew he would keep right on hammering away till he saw her face at the hole.

"All right, all right, Clatter! Hold your feathers! I'm coming." she called as she poked her curly gold head out of the entryhole. Clatter was perched at the entrance, two letters in his beak, his bright red head crest ruffling back and forth impatiently. His mailbag was full to the brim, but Curly wasn't surprised. Spring was always a busy time for Clatter. All those long winter days indoors inspired everycreature to write to near and distant relations with news of the daily goings on.

"Two letters! Well, that's a first!" she said, reaching her paw out to receive her mail.

"Nope," Clatter answered, handing her a small yellow envelope. "Just the one for Mrs. Curly Goldentop. Letter from your sister Nelly, though she lives just over the other side of Babble Creek, you'd think she'd run over here herself for a visit and a little chatter. The other's for the Chubbly's," he said waving the thick pink package, sealed with a hard lump of magenta sealing wax, stamped with a fancy curlicue "L".

"Letter all the way from their niece Lacey, in London." he said, hefting the weight of the letter in his wingtip.

"Must be a doozy, she hasn't written since last spring," he whispered conspiratorially. Then, as an afterthought, he tossed a rolled-up newspaper into the nest. "Here," he said as it landed, "for you and the little guys."

Curly picked up the paper and unrolled it. "Clatter, I believe you've made a mistake here. This is the Rodent Herald Record, and my subscription ran out last winter."

"Well, I had an extra copy. Warren Weasel says his eyes are going and he just isn't interested in the outside world since the Mrs. passed. Take the paper, you should keep those little guys informed. It's a big wide world out there," He said, spreading his wings wide to dramatically make his point.

"Thank you, Clatter, that's very thoughtful of you."

"You might want to pay old Warren a visit. Gets real lonely for a fella when he can't see much anymore," he said, turning to leave.

"I think I'll do just that, and maybe send Lancelot over with some soup. I don't believe this world would keep spinning if it weren't for you helping it along, Clatter. Now, you have a good day."

Clatter flapped down to the ground floor but before he could knock, he heard Bibi Chubbly's voice calling out to him.

"That you, Clatter?" Bibi called from the entryway.

"Yes, ma'am, got a nice little surprise for you and Mak today," he said, shoving the pink package at her. "Letter all the way from your niece in the big city."

Bibi took the package and turned it over in her paw, tracing Lacey's familiar seal with her pawtip. Clatter perched there a moment thinking she would open it and share the news, but she knew this was special and she was saving it for Mak.

After an awkward moment Clatter said, "Well, I best be going." And he patted his full mail bag. "Got a full day's flying ahead of me, all the winter news, ya know. Oh, here's your paper." Again he tossed a copy of the Rodent Herald Record.

"Clatter, I just don't know how you can keep track of so many creatures' business," she said, her eyes sparkling as she teased him about his gossipy nature, but her chiding went right past him.

"It's a difficult job but somecreature has got to do it. You have a fine day now, and say hello to Mak from me." And then he was a black and white blur as he flew off, singing to himself.

Bibi rubbed the seal again and was tempted to break it open and read the thick letter but then she thought better of it and decided to wait until after tea. She and Mak would read it together. Besides, her eyes were getting tired and she loved listening to the warm sound of her husband's voice when he read aloud to her. So, she'd wait, as she always did.

Mak and Bibi had lived on the farm for almost fifty years. And all of those wonderful years were spent here together in their only home, the apple tree nest. Most mice choose their own nests and make them home a bit at a time, gathering here and there the things they need and the things they most want to have around them for pleasure. But this nest was different. It was a wedding present from Mak's youngest brother Woody. Woody knew Mak well and he knew what would make his big brother happy, so when he heard they had decided to get married, he packed his carving tools and some supplies and set out across the long field of corn to the apple tree. He camped there for months, working steadily day by day, carving out the beautiful entry hole, sculpting a circle of apple blossoms around it, then, room by room, he carved out the interior of the tree, careful to leave the heartwood intact and coating the center core of the tree with a thick wax, so that it would live a good long life. He cut and smoothed each floor, until at the end of six months he had finished his finest masterpiece. The nest was four stories high, each apple wood floor smoothed to a fine shiny finish and paw rubbed with bees-wax. Inside the exterior wall was a circular wooden staircase that wound round the inside of the trunk like a bedspring, starting at the first floor and ending at a carved porch on the fourth floor. On the third floor he created a library, for he knew how the young couple loved books. He painstakingly carved floor to ceiling bookshelves into the tree trunk on every wall. Every detail was considered carefully, and he edged the shelves with quills and walnuts and finished the top of the doorway with a bas relief of the sun coming up over two mountains and a shimmering stream.

He managed to get his paws on a nice large piece of red cedar, and carved Bibi a beautiful desk in the shape of a cat. He always had an odd sense of humor. So there, in the middle of this fine library, stood a large red cat on four long wooden legs, its tail curved around its square body, an inkwell hole in the top of its head and a nice flat polished back. A fine place, he thought, for Bibi to copy her books. Later, he told them that the cedar would make the room smell sweet and keep the bugs away from the paw copied manuscripts. He was an unusual mouse, but very practical.

The whole nest was a work of art. He cut out windows in almost every room to make the place light and airy, then carved tight fitting shutters to keep them warm from the winter wind. He gave special attention to Bibi's sewing room and carved the doorway with long scrolling ribbons and bows dangling from the mouths of sparrows and wrens, then carved a border of spools and needles half way up the wall encircling the whole room. The kitchen was the grand finale. He carved rows and rows of pantry shelves, each edged in a pattern of strawberries and curling tendrils, and when he was finished, it appeared that a whole strawberry field had taken over the room and made itself at home along the walls. Then, because he loved family so and he knew that Mak did as well, he carved them a long sturdy table of apple wood. It was a simple table, just a great long oval with a set of matching oval stools but it was big enough to have fifty mice over for dinner. Later, Bibi commented that she believed he did it because he loved her cooking and wanted to assure himself room at her table.

The family whispered about the nest for months before the huge wedding. No one had actually seen it, but whenever there's a family secret the rumors start building up and going around in circles until everything is blown right out of proportion. The only difference was, this time no one could blow out of proportion or exaggerate what Woody had done. It was beyond even their wildest imaginings.

After the wedding party was over, Woody walked the couple across the field to their new nest in the apple tree. Room by room he showed them their home. Mak gasped openly at each new proof of Woody's brilliance, but Bibi was breathless and quiet until they arrived at the library. When she saw the one-of-a-kind cat desk she started to cry and she tried to throw her arms around her rotund new brother to hug him and thank him, but he was far too round and she was too slight.

Instead, he picked her up and hugged her, then whirled her around and placed her into Mak's waiting arms, saying, "I'd best be going. You two can go see the love birds I carved in the bedroom all by yourselves."

They only did get to spend one night alone together. Clatter Woodpecker had told everybody in the neighborhood about the nest (he was the only one who flew in and actually saw it) and by the next day, everycreature that could make it over to the apple tree was there for a tour. No creature who saw it left less than amazed, especially Sandy Fields, a little brown field mouse midwife, who fell in love with Woody's work, and shortly after fell in love with Woody, but that's another story.

Though the nest was big enough for a large litter of mousekins, unfortunately, it was never to be. So they lived in their lovely nest, alone but happy, for fifteen years. Then in a moment of tragedy, when Onyx, Mak's older brother, was eaten by a cat, Mak and Bibi Chubbly took in Onyx's daughter Lacey and at long last they had a mousekin to love and teach and raise and they did this with the gusto of two elders who had waited many years to have a mousette of their own. When Lacey was older and left the nest, they gave the top floor of their home to Mr. and Mrs. Goldentop and their little ones, so they always had the opportunity to enjoy the pitter-patter of little feet. After Mr. Goldentop was swept away in the flood, Bibi and Mak had Curly and the mousekins to care for and it helped to keep them busy when they were missing Lacey the most.

Bibi carried the letter into the strawberry kitchen and found Mak, already back from his morning stroll, sitting at the end of the long table with two cups of peppermint tea—hot and steaming. She pulled up a stool and sat close beside him, placing the pink letter on the table next to his white clay cup.

"I see," he said looking down at the curly "L" on the stamp. "Well, it's about time. Let's see what's happening in the big city, shall we?"

Bibi sat sipping her tea, watching him as he broke the seal and carefully unfolded the many pages of the letter. then glanced through it without saying a word.

"Do you want the whole thing, or should I sum it up and give you the important parts?" he asked her, already anticipating the answer.

"The good parts first, then you can read it all again after breakfast," she answered.

"Now, how did I know you were going to say that?" he asked smiling, and they both laughed together at themselves and their old, ingrained way of doing things.

"She says here that she loves and misses us," he said, reading through the first page. "She's got a new family, orphaned by a cat the day she came, but she straightened out the cat."

"That sounds like my Lacey!" Bibi said smiling, "How many mouselings?"

"Twins and a yearling. But Cousin Chip's great-grandmousette Angel arrived there last winter quite by serendipity and had a newborn mousette. Named her Lacey Chesterfield Smoothstone, got a nice ring to it. Lost two males, both stillborn; I think it runs in that side of the family. Anyway, little Lacey is doing well, starting to crawl and saying 'mama'. Says she's very beautiful and looks just like Angel and her mother Lily. She says Angel lost her family in a fire down on the river and wants to know if we know anything about it. That explains why we haven't heard from my nephew Silver. We'll have to get a letter off to cousin Chip and see if he's heard anything. Says here the yearling's name is Mop, toddling around now, and the little darlings call her Ma Chuby. She writes that one of the twins wants to be a healer and she'll be eleven this year. We'll have to invite them up and talk more about it."

"Makelroy, we haven't seen Lacey in years. I'd love to have her and her new family up. It'd be so nice to have some young ones around here for awhile.

He looked at her hard with a tight frown. "Are you accusing me of being old and boring?"

"Just old, Mak. Go on and read the letter."

"All right, I just want to make sure you're not going to put me out after all these years," he said in mock seriousness.

"I will if you don't read the letter."

"She asks about Cousin Weaver, wants to know if she's written any new tales, asks about her husband Swifty and the mousekins, Nipper and Tucker. Also asks if we hear from Woody and Sandy and how they're doing. Says she found a copy of my old book "Florapedia" in the library at her new nest. That's a surprise! We didn't make too many copies of that one, wonder how they got their paws on it?"

"What else? Go on Makelroy!" she said, impatient to get through it and to make sure there wasn't any more bad news or tragedies to deal with.

"Well, it seems that she's very happy and so is her new brood. Everycreature is doing well there. The mousekins sound lovely and bright, they have a house cat who caused a great ruckus at first but now that Lacey has the matter in paw, he's been helping with the gathering. Imagine that! He must be a very unusual cat. Myself, after losing my brother Onyx to that Siamese, couldn't imagine befriending a cat! But of course, there's good and bad in every species. She also sends regards to Chip and Myra and all the cousins on that side of the family. There's a bit in here about Tailbit. Mostly it sounds like she's homesick and needs a visit."

"You know, Mak, I think it's about time for a family reunion. What do you think about that, my love?" she asked, taking his paw in hers.

"Yes, Bibi, I do believe you're right."

"I'm going to go right up to the library after breakfast and start writing some letters."

"Bibi, it's been so long since we've all been together, let's plan it for the summer and give everycreature in the family plenty of time to figure out how to get here. I'd like to see the whole family present this time, not just the Chubbly's."

"Are you really up for it, Mak? Do you realize how many creatures there are on both sides of the family?"

"Yes, I do, dear. Probably enough to fill this whole table and spill out onto the porch." He answered, smiling happily at the thought of finally having their huge table full of family.

"And that's without counting the mousekins. I think it'll be wonderful!"

"Your right, it would be wonderful to have the whole group together, but before you start sending out letters of invitation, get a quick one off to Lacey just to let her know how much we love and miss her too."

15. The Family Secret

The sky was a clear, cloudless blue for the first time in many days. It appeared to Wendy Lovely that spring had fallen quite suddenly into her garden. Why, just the other day she had noticed the first bright yellow head of a crocus peeking out from the snow. It seemed impossible, but now, as she meandered around the formal garden, she was surrounded by lush green lawns and flowering bushes and trees that had burst into bloom overnight.

All around her the nightingales were searching for worms to feed their nests of hungrily chirping babies. The long unheard sounds and smells, and the kaleidoscope of spring colours, made her feel lighthearted and gaily adventurous. She strolled down the cobblestone path, swinging Amanda, her favorite doll, by the hand. Then, she gathered the doll up into the crook of her arm and chatted with her.

"Oh, Amanda, it's such a beautiful day now that the rain has stopped. Doesn't everything smell perfectly wonderful?"

Wendy hoisted Amanda up into the air, pressing her white porcelain nose into the pink blossom of a flowering cherry tree. "This is a cherry tree, and after the blossoms fall we'll have sweet red cherries to eat and cherry pies."

Then, she held the doll by her delicate hands, and humming loudly to herself, she waltzed down the garden path and plopped on to a bench under the rose trellis. She propped the black haired doll next to her and wiped at a spot of mud on the miniature white lace dress.

"Mother certainly wouldn't approve of you being out in the garden, and look at what you've done!" she scolded, "You've gotten mud all over you best dress, now we'll certainly be in for it."

She rubbed harder at the spot but this only served to spread the brown mark into a larger mess, "Never mind. She'll probably never even notice if I don't tell her, so let's not think about that right now. All right, Amanda?"

Wendy looked around, then whispering to Amanda she said, "Now, don't you tell!" She slipped off her white patent leather shoes and her pink stockings and carefully placed them on the bench next to Amanda.

"You sit right there," She implored, shaking a warning finger at the doll, "and don't get into any more trouble while I'm gone. Now, be a good girl." And she walked off barefoot into the thick green grass, giggling at the delightful sensation of the cool mud seeping up between her toes.

"Sweetheart, are you out there?" Her father's deep voice called from the garden door. Wendy quickly wiped her feet against the new grass and scrambled back up to the bench, her heart racing furiously. Before she had begun to get her stockings on, he called again anxiously, "Wendy, are you there?"

"Yes, Father. By the rose arbor," she said, struggling to get her stocking on her muddy, wet foot.

Edmund Lovely hurried up the garden path, crisp in his black pinstripe suit, not noticing the beauty of the garden.

"Wendy, sweetheart, I need to speak to you right away."

Wendy had her shoes behind her and her muddy feet tucked demurely under the bench, but Edmund was so distracted that he didn't seem to notice.

"Why don't we go back to the study and we'll have some tea?" She was about to get Amanda, but she couldn't think of how she would manage to get to the house without her father seeing her bare feet.

"But, Father, it's such a perfect day. Can't we stay out here in the garden for awhile?" Edmund looked at his beautiful daughter and smiled for the first time that day.

"Certainly, sweetheart. We'll just sit here," he said, sitting down beside her on the bench. Then he was frowning again and silent.

"Father?" she asked, concerned. "Is it Amanda? I know I'm not supposed to bring my dolls out of the nursery," then she looked down at her dirty feet, "and I know I'm not supposed to take my shoes off in the garden." She was frightened now, and crying, "but I didn't think anyone would know, and it was such a beautiful day."

Edmund looked at her quizzically, not understanding her tears. Then he noticed her muddy feet and placed his arm around her to comfort her.

He touched her face and wiped her tears, then he brushed her long blonde hair back from her forehead and tucked it neatly behind her back. Wendy couldn't remember the last time anyone paid her this much attention, and it only frightened her more.

"Wendy, never mind those little things. I don't care that your doll is in the garden, or that your feet are bare and muddy. The problem is just that. Children need to run barefoot in the garden. I can't remember a single spring when my brothers and

I didn't get into the mud up to our ankles and we had our favorite toys with us everywhere." Edmund went on sadly, "things have been wrong around here for too long, and I've been too much of a coward to take matters in hand."

"Oh Father, don't say that! You're the bravest man I know."

"No, darling, let me finish. Maybe I've been too busy with my work, or maybe I have been a coward, but that's not important. The important thing is, now I've decided to do something about this mess."

"Father, I don't understand anything; what are you talking about?" she said, shifting about uncomfortably on the cold bench.

"You know, dear heart, when I first married your mother she was just like you. gay and sweet, imaginative and very pretty. For the last ten years, your mother hasn't been herself. She's been nervous and melancholy, turned in to her own sad thoughts most of the time. I always believed that the problem would solve itself. So, we kept our dark secret from you, and I looked the other way most of the time, watching and waiting for the day when she would come back to herself, when she would be the same gentle, loving woman I first knew. And I thought eventually she would be able to love you the way every mother should love such a delightful child."

Wendy was surprised to hear her father speak to her this way. He never said a thing against her mother. Besides, she had always known her mother to be dark and withdrawn. Then at other times she would be nervous and fussing, always fussing over so many things, and making too many rules for the young girl. And so strict! Heaven forbid Wendy should forget herself and not keep to her mother's hundreds of rules!

Of course, there were happier times, and she remembered them well and kept them silently in her heart. There were the summers in their country home on the South Downs of Sussex. They would drive down from London at the end of May and spend the long summer out in the country. Her mother seemed happier there and free from her usual cares. There they would take long walks on the rolling green hillsides, picking apples and berries, picnicking out in the sun. At the end of August, her mother's spirits would darken and the ride home was always silent and full of regret.

Edmund turned to face his daughter, he took both her hands in his and held them tightly.

"What I have to say to you, darling, isn't easy. Last night I called Doctor Hartley and asked him to come see your mother."

"But why Father? Mummy isn't sick, is she?" Wendy asked, concerned.

"Well, it's not like she has influenza, honey, but she is sick. Very sick. But it's an illness of the mind, not the body."

Wendy sat confused, not understanding what this illness could be that was in her mother's mind. How could a person be sick but not in their body?

"Haven't you noticed?" Edmund continued gently, " Mother has been keeping to her room? She's hardly been out in weeks. She rarely has her meals with us anymore. Hasn't this concerned you, sweetheart?"

Wendy thought about this for a moment, embarrassed by her sense of relief at not having her mother's brooding and fretting figure across from her at the dining room table. What could she possibly say to her father? She was silent.

"But, of course, you're just a child, filled with childish thoughts. Now I feel I must impose the adult world on you, much to my sorrow."

Wendy's hands were sweating uncomfortably and she pulled them away and wiped them on her yellow satin dress.

"Doctor Hartley thinks your mother needs a rest. I'm going to send her away to our country house in Sussex for a little while. The doctor believes that if Annabelle has a few quiet months in the country, she'll return to her old self. Of course she'll also be receiving some treatment. There's a very old doctor who has a farm near our home and he'll be seeing your mother regularly just to talk to her and report back on her progress to Doctor Hartley. But you don't really need to know any more about it."

"But, Father, won't Mummy be lonely out in the country all by herself?"

"No, sweetheart, I'm sending Mrs. Hammond to cook and care for her. She'll be fine, and we'll go up and see her some time later this summer," he said, patting her hand. Wendy's face brightened suddenly.

"Then, it will be just you and me here, Father? But, who will cook and clean and do the washing?" The excited child went on without waiting for an answer. "We can do it ourselves, you know. It could be a real adventure, just you and me and Chesterfield Cat. When my studies are over, we can picnic in Kensington Gardens and go to the theater the way we used to."

"Yes, my dear, it will be a real adventure. But I am going to hire someone to come in temporarily and help in the kitchen and to keep an eye on you while Mrs. Hammond is away. Now, put on your shoes and stockings and let's walk for a while," he said, brushing off her dirty feet, helping Wendy with her stockings, and then placing Amanda in her arms.

"Father, please don't let's get anyone else in while Mother is gone. It would be so nice, just the two of us. I'm certain I could care for myself while you're working, and I promise not to do anything naughty. Please, Father, please say yes," she begged Edmund, showing her most charming pout.

"I'll think about it, dear heart, but no more asking. Let's just see how it goes, all right?"

"Yes Father, no more asking."

She stood up brightly and Edmund offered her his arm. Together they began a slow stroll down the cobblestone path, winding into the rose bushes and over to the fountain. The wrens were bathing and splashing about in the large stone pool and they seemed to take no offense in being watched. The father and daughter stood quietly, the sun shining brightly on the pool, the breeze playing softly in the many trees surrounding the silent pair.

"Tell me, Father, do you know what makes someone sick in their mind, sick like Mother?" she asked, breaking the silence.

"No one knows exactly, sweetheart, but there's a famous doctor, Doctor Sigmund Freud. He has written quite a lot about the illness of the mind. He believes that when someone experiences a trauma—a frightening experience, that sometimes it changes them, and makes them sick the way your mother is sick. But he also believes they can be made well again, through a kind of talking cure." He looked at her hard, to see how much the girl was understanding.

"What was it, Father?" Wendy asked plainly.

"What was what, darling?"

"What was the trauma that made my Mummy so sick?" She asked, crossing her arms firmly across her chest, as if to protect herself from his answer.

"Dear me, I didn't expect to be discussing this with you today." Edmund took out his monogrammed handkerchief and wiped the sweat off his brow. Then, he removed his favorite cherrywood pipe from his other pocket and spent a few moments re-lighting it. Wendy watched his careful movements as he drew in the smoke and blew it out again very slowly, deep in thought.

"You know, Father, I'm not a little girl anymore. I'm already ten and eleven twelfths," she stated flatly.

He looked down at her and saw how grown up she really was. Somehow in his mind she was still his baby, still a young innocent. Then he studied the sharp lines of her face and the seriousness in her eyes and realized that lately he hadn't really been looking at her and seeing her truly at all, but only seeing a chubby toddler that had grown much taller in the last few years.

"Yes, sweetheart, you're quite right. You are very grown up and I've been treating you like a child. Now I have something very grown up to tell you, but before I begin I want you to know that we always intended to tell you when the time was right, but somehow that time hasn't been quite right until today." Edmund sat on the edge of the fountain and motioned for Wendy to sit down beside him. Then he drew on his pipe again, sending a curl of familiar, comforting smoke up into the air.

"How shall I start? When you were born, you were not alone. You were one of a set of twins. It was quite unexpected. The doctor was surprised, to say the least, but your mother and I were delighted.

"You came first, a strapping, pink, squealing baby girl. You were healthy and hungry, but your brother, Michael, was not as fortunate. He was half your weight and sickly from the start. The doctors didn't know if he would survive. But he did, for a while." Edmund hung his head sadly, reliving the terrible time from the telling of it. He tapped his pipe against the stone fountain and let the ash fall to the grass. Then cupping the warm bowl in his palm, he continued quietly.

"There were some problems with his lungs, a congestion of some kind, but they managed to clear it, and though he had to remain in the hospital for a few weeks, soon we had him home and we believed all was well. There were other things after that. In his weakened state he had several infections and colds—but he always fought them off bravely, one after the other. You were always ahead of him, walked first, talked first, but your mother fretted so badly over Michael that it impaired her ability to notice how wonderfully you were blossoming." He looked at her then and saw the silent tears rolling down her pink cheeks, but he looked away knowing he had to go on.

"When you both turned a year old, Lottie, your nanny, had you out in the garden for an airing. You were sitting in the sun, you in your pretty blue perambulator and Michael in his matching red one. She left you both there napping for a moment while she came inside to warm some milk for your mid-day feeding. The weather grew strange, a cool breeze came up and brought with it an April shower. By the time Lottie got out to the garden, Michael was soaked and shivering, and the two of you were crying mournfully." Wendy was crying openly now and hugging Amanda tightly in her arms.

"I remember, Father. I remember Michael." she sobbed.

Edmund pulled her onto his lap and gathered her in his arms.

"Dear Lord, do you really?"

"Yes, of course. We were twins, always together, but I didn't remember until now. It's as if a black curtain were drawn across part of my head, keeping something hidden," she said, laying her head against the large man's shoulder.

"Michael woke with a barking croup that night. We called Doctor Hartley immediately, but it didn't matter. He went from bad to worse. Annabelle stayed with him every moment. No one could tear her away to rest. The cold settled in his lungs and became pneumonia. He was a fighter, that boy. He struggled against the illness for months. By then your mother was worn to a frazzle, and when we finally lost him she was so beside herself that the doctor had to give her sedatives to help her sleep—to keep her from being hysterical. She never recovered." Edmund held Wendy tighter, not so much to comfort her as to comfort himself. His throat tightened terribly and tears threatened, but he held them back.

They sat locked like that for some time, until Edmund collected himself and turned his attention back to Wendy.

"Are you all right, sweetheart?" he asked, wiping her cheeks with his handkerchief.

"You know, Father, I've always felt something was missing, something was a little off. It was like knowing something and not knowing it at the very same time. Now I see. I wish Michael was here now and we could both turn eleven together, and I would have a playmate and a classmate and a brother. It makes me feel very lonely knowing that I had a twin and he's gone." Then she broke into fresh tears and Edmund felt ill-equipped to handle it. He patted her arm mechanically and thought about Annabelle, away in her room, sulking and distant, while he carried on and kept their lives pulled together, fathering Wendy and Annabelle both. He realized his daughter was a motherless child, and was glad then that he had decided to bring the matter out in the open and do something to change things.

They stood up together and began walking back to the garden door, hand in hand. Edmund felt very courageous for the first time in a long time and this gave him great comfort and the conviction in his heart that somehow, it was all going to be all right in the end.

16. Weency's Chance

E ency sneezed loudly "Ahhhh Chooooo!" then he was tugging at my bedclothes. I woke suddenly and reached to feel his forehead.

"Mrs. Chubbly," Eency wheezed miserably, "I feel terrible."

He was burning up with a bad spring cold and what sounded like a croup.

"You've got quite a fever," I said reaching for my black bag. My paw found it easily, right beside the bed, and I opened it up and began rummaging around. I removed a red fabric bag of willow bark and took off the ribbon, then measured a small piece of the bark with my pawtip and broke it off.

"Here, chew on this while I get dressed Eency. Lay down on my bed and rest yourself."

Then I was up and dressed in my cotton spring frock and apron, and had Eency in my arms, trudging down the wallway to the nursery.

"Ohhhhh, Mrs. Chubbly, my head hurts awfully, ahhhhh chooooo!" I rubbed his head gently as we walked, then I deposited him on his bed and woke Weency.

"Get up, my dear, we have a very sick mousekin on our paws and I'll need your help to get him settled."

Weency woke groggily from a dead sleep and rubbed at her eyes.

"Mrs. Chubbly, is it morning?" she asked, sitting up and pulling down the covers.

"No, not nearly. It's still the middle of the night, but Eency has the croup and a bad fever. I need you to make a fire and boil some tea water."

Weency didn't answer but jumped up and dressed. Then she was off to the kitchen and back in a flash with a steaming teapot full.

"Get me a scrap soaked in cold water—no, bring the scrap and a bowl of cold water, so we can keep it refreshed. He's burning up."

"Can't we do anything for him to bring it down?" Weency asked, obviously worried about her little brother.

"Well, dear, I've already given him a bit of willow bark, that should take it down slowly, but actually the fever isn't the culprit here." I continued as I filled a teacup with some peppermint and eucalyptus leaves. "The fever is actually a very good thing, it's the body's way of burning off the infection."

I placed the scrap in the bowl and then wrung it out thoroughly. "The problem with the fever itself is not the highness or lowness of the temperature, it's how quickly the fever rises or falls. If the body doesn't have time to acclimate, it goes into shock. It's best to let the fever run its natural course. The only reason we are working to bring it down now is for the comfort of Eency. He needs to sleep so his body can begin to heal." I placed the cold scrap on Eency's fevered brow.

"I'll do that," Weency said, taking over the job.

"Let's sit him up a bit and get this tea into him. That croup sounds frightful." I placed the hot cup beneath his nose. "Drink this, in slow sips and breathe in the hot steam. That should clear you."

Eency did as he was told and gasped as the sharp-smelling medicine began to work.

"Oh no, Mrs. Chubbly!" Eency groaned. "Today is the day I was supposed to do the gathering!" He looked pained, not from his illness, but from the fact that he would not be able to provide his family with their food, and it was his responsibility.

"I can do it!" Weency stated boldly. I looked at her and believed she could. She was such an intuitive determined mousette, though six months earlier she had never been out of the nest before. Neither had Eency, and he had done well even though he was grief stricken from losing his parents.

"Yes, Weency, you may do the gathering. As soon as we get Eency settled and sleeping again, I'll take you into the kitchen and show you how to begin."

Eency was soon breathing deeply in a relaxed sleep, so I quietly took Weency by the hand and led her down the wallway to the kitchen.

"This is the gathering sack," I said, taking the well-worn bag down off its hook and demonstrating on myself the proper way to wear it.

"Now, you try it," I said, handing it over. She had no problem copying my motions and soon the sack was in place and we were walking toward the entryhole.

"Are you nervous?" I asked, checking the bag one last time.

"No, it's still quite dark out, I imagine the humans are sleeping. But what about the cat?" Weency asked.

"Chesterfield? I believe he's fine, but, of course, be cautious. Even the most intelligent creature is capable at any time of reverting back to its base instincts," I said, and she nodded in understanding. "I'm sure Eency has told you all I've taught him, it's the nature of twins. However, for safekeeping, we'll have a quick review." She nodded once again and gave me her focused attention. Her eyes, clear and bright, drank in every warning about screaming housekeepers and brooms, and she knew enough to stay away from the garden after Eency's day out with the hawk. "Just keep close to the walls and look for cracks or objects to cover you should you be spotted, though I doubt you'll encounter any human at this hour of the morning."

I sent her off with a hug, knowing if anycreature could get back safely to the nest, Weency could.

17. The Strange Occurrence

Wendy Lovely couldn't sleep. She tossed and turned, then finally decided to go down to the kitchen and get herself a warm cup of milk.

If it had been a week earlier, she would simply have called to Mrs. Hammond, and the housekeeper (grumbling all the way) would have warmed the milk, sprinkled it with cinnamon-sugar, and brought it up to Wendy's room. But as providence would have it, Mrs. Hammond had taken Annabelle Lovely up to the country house in Sussex the week before.

Wendy was determined not to wake Edmund, but to take care of herself, in the hope that he would not see fit to employ a temporary housekeeper. She liked being alone with her father. She missed her mother's dark presence, but only as one misses the familiar and comfortable. After the two women left, waving at her from the back seat of a long, black, hired automobile, a dark cloud seemed to lift from the Lovely household.

As the old saying goes, "Rules were meant to be broken." And so they were. Wendy gaily set up a large tea party for her best porcelain dolls, right in front of the drawing room fireplace on Mother's best sofa. And they all had real tea and real biscuits to eat! Father gladly participated in the game and had his tea at the party along with the others.

Wendy had watched Mrs. Hammond cook for ten years. She remembered everything, and made the tea perfectly. She blushed bright red when Edmund commented on how well she had done.

In just a few days, Edmund and Wendy had cemented their new relationship with a carefree joy and playfulness that Edmund had long since forgotten. Wendy managed to make hot porridge and do the dishes, Edmund did the washing and remembered all the charming bedtime stories his mother had told him as a child. The father-daughter pair were blossoming, and putting back together all the broken pieces of their love.

Wendy put on her slippers and her satin robe, and took Amanda along, for she knew Amanda was afraid of the dark and wouldn't like to be left alone. Then she shuffled quietly down the carpeted hall and took the steps one at a time, carefully skipping over the seventh step, as it always squeaked so loudly.

The house was quiet except for the far away breathing of sleeping Edmund, and the loud ticking of the grandfather clock in the drawing room. But it was silence to Wendy, for she had heard those two familiar sounds all her life.

She reached the kitchen and turned on the light, forgetting the warm milk completely. There on the wooden counter sat the cutest mouse Wendy had ever seen, dressed in a miniature pink flowered frock, complete with tiny lace ruffles. The creature was bending over a piece of cheese left behind from Father's bedtime snack. Try as she might, she just couldn't get it to fit into the small sack tied to her waist. Wendy could hardly believe her eyes! Time stood still, the way it does when something unbelievable is happening, and it seemed a very long time indeed that the two stood still, staring at each other. But it was just a flash really, and almost immediately after the room was lit and

Weency saw the human girl looming over her, she gasped and said,

"Gracious me!" Then dropped the cheese completely.

"Did you just say 'Gracious me'?" Wendy asked the mouse, perplexed.

"Certainly, I did! What would you say if you were trying to gather your dinner and a giant appeared suddenly when everycreature knows humans are supposed to be sleeping!"

Not knowing what else to do, Weency grabbed the cheese and began again trying to get it into the gathering sack.

"I suppose I would have said 'Gracious me!', or maybe I'd have screamed and ran away—but of course that all depends on the size and ugliness of the giant," she answered thoughtfully, watching the pretty mouse struggling with the awkward piece of cheese.

She was just about to offer to break it in half for her when the kitchen door flew open and in ran Chesterfield Cat at full speed, leaping for the counter.

Now, you and I know it was his intention to get Weency into his mouth and dash safely back to deliver her at the entryhole of her nest, but all Wendy saw was a big hungry tomcat leaping at her new friend.

Before you could say "kitty whiskers," Wendy scooped the mouse into her hand—cheese and all, mind you, and deposited her into the rather comfortable pocket of her pink satin robe.

"Chesterfield Cat!" she shouted. "How could you? You were just about to eat my new friend!" Wendy moved to get the broom to chase Chesterfield out of the kitchen, and she nearly fainted when he turned to her and said, "I had no intention of eating Weency, actually we're very good friends as well."

Then, more to himself than anything, he sighed, "Never before in the history of felines has one cat's intentions been so often misunderstood."

"Chesterfield, you can talk!" Wendy said shocked and perplexed. She looked down at his gleaming green eyes and wasn't a bit surprised when he smiled at her. It was a patronizing smile, but a full one from ear to ear.

"Why, of course I can talk. I'm not an idiot, you know." Then Weency stood up and looked over the top of the lace trim on Wendy's pocket, first at the cat, then at the beautiful human girl, and as Wendy had already claimed her as a friend, she thought it best that they be formally introduced. She saw that Chesterfield and the human girl were already friends, so rather than introduce herself she thought it better form for Chesterfield to perform the introductions.

"Pssst, Chesterfield," she whispered to get his attention, "We haven't been properly introduced."

"Why, of course! How rude of me. Mrs. Chubbly would have my head for such bad manners," he said, still smiling.

Clearing his throat, he gracefully stood up on his hind legs and performed a formal bow.

"Wendy Lovely, allow me to introduce my dear friend," he pointed to her pocket, "Miss Weency Twingle." Weency reached out her paw over the lace trim of the pocket.

"Weency Twingle, allow me to introduce my very sweet human, Wendy Lovely." Then to a chorus of 'How Do You Do's', the two creatures proceeded to shake paw and hand.

"Gracious me!" Wendy said, shaking her head hard, "I do believe I'm dreaming—there's no other reasonable explanation."

"There! You see, Wendy," Weency said from the pocket, "you just said it! 'Gracious me!'"

Weency smiled and got both her paws over the edge so she could more easily see the girl, although the view was mostly the underside of Wendy's chin.

"You're quite right, but it was the perfect thing to say."

Just then, Wendy realized she was talking to a mouse who was standing in her pocket. She pinched herself hard on the arm to see if she could wake herself from the dream before it became too bizarre, as dreams have a way of doing just when you think they are safe and fun. She had to pinch herself again, but nothing happened except a smarting pain, and she thought that she might be awake but still couldn't think of any reasonable explanation. She was having a very good time conversing with her house cat and the cute little girl mouse, so she decided not to mind the whole business of figuring it out.

"Well, you two seem to be getting along famously, and I was in the middle of a very important nap," Chesterfield went on dryly as he fell back to all four paws, "so, I'll just be running along now. I was having the most marvelous dream. Oh. Weency, if you need anything, just squeak!"

Then Chesterfield was off to find a warm place on the drawing room hearth, and the kitchen door swung closed behind him.

"Can I help you with that cheese?" Wendy asked, carefully removing Weency from her pocket and sitting down on the kitchen floor. She gently placed the mouse down in front of her and laid her doll beside her.

"Would you? That would be very kind."

Weency offered the huge hunk of cheese to Wendy and the girl broke it into four even pieces and gingerly stuffed them into Weency's gathering sack.

"Do all mice speak English or are you an enchanted princess, or something like that?" Wendy asked seriously.

Weency giggled.

"Don't be silly, that's stuff out of fairy tales. From what Mrs. Chubbly has told me, all creatures in England speak English. Perhaps in other lands they speak other languages," Weency said, enjoying her talk with another young female.

"And who is Mrs. Chubbly? How does she know these things?" Wendy asked, growing more fascinated by the moment.

"Mrs. Chubbly is my nanny. She's the smartest mouse I have ever met. She knows just about everything," Weency claimed, proudly.

"You have a nanny?" Wendy asked, surprised. "How old are you?"

"I've just turned eleven and so has my brother, Eency."

"I'm almost eleven! I'm having a birthday next week, so I'll be eleven years old in six more days. Perhaps you and your family can come to my party?" Wendy asked, delighted to have found some guests.

"I'll have to ask Mrs. Chubbly, but I don't have any family except for my twin and my little sister Mop." Weency said, sadly.

"You know, Weency, I was a twin, but my brother Michael died when he was a baby," Wendy told her, glad to be able to share her secret at last. "Where are your mother and father?" she asked the little creature.

"My parents were eaten by Chesterfield Cat. That is why he's made a vow to Mrs. Chubbly to take care of us and protect us. He was the creature who turned us into orphans."

"Oh, how terrible for you." Wendy commiserated. "My mother went mad when my twin died and now my father has sent her away to the country house in Sussex, where some doctor is supposed to help her get better again," Wendy finished.

"Oh, how terrible for you! But at least she wasn't eaten by a cat. I'm sure she'll get better, and then you can have your mother back. I can't have that, but we have Mrs. Chubbly to love us, and she is truly wonderful. Who is your nanny?" Weency asked.

"I don't have one. We have a housekeeper, Mrs. Hammond. She is away with Mother, taking care of her. My father and I, we're taking care of ourselves right now," Wendy told her friend, proudly.

"That sounds like a very grown-up adventure—to be taking care of yourself without a mama or a nanny," Weency said, thoughtfully.

"Well, we've just been doing it for a week and it is exciting. I feel very grown up. My father wants to hire some help but I hope he doesn't. I like doing it this way, on my own, no one to answer to, no one to scold me. But it does get lonely— do you have many friends?" Wendy asked.

"Just my twin, and Angel. She's a cousin of Mrs. Chubbly. She came to live with us this winter when she was having her baby. And I have my little sister, Mop, and Angel's little baby, Lacey, but they're not eleven like you and me, and they're not twins like you and me."

Weency smiled at Wendy, feeling like she knew the human girl very well, indeed.

"As far as I can see, the only difference between you and me is that you are a mouse and I am a human. Aside from that, we're very much alike. Do you like to play with dolls?" Wendy asked, excited at having found a real, true friend.

"Yes, it's one of my favorite things to do! Mother sewed me a whole set of cloth dolls, a family of mice, of course, and she also made a set of other creatures, but I don't have any human dolls. Do you like to sew?" Weency was racing now, trying to fit in as many words as she could, and as many questions, for she knew it was getting light, and soon she would have to leave her new friend and get back to the nest, before they became worried.

"I don't know how, but I think I would like it very much," Wendy answered.

"I can teach you. Mrs. Chubbly has taught me so many stitches, and embroidery too," Weency went on, "You'll have to have a needle and thread and a scrap of fabric, a large scrap— and then I can show you how."

"Well how can we meet, I mean—where do you live?" Wendy asked.

"I live in a beautiful nest in the walls of the front entry hall."

"Really? Imagine that. And we've never met before." Wendy said.

"Wendy, I've never been out of the nest before today," Weency said, embarrassed that Wendy would think she was overprotected.

"Oh, that's all right, I haven't been too many places either. My mother is always worried something terrible is going to happen to me if I'm out of her sight for more than five minutes," Wendy said, sadly.

"My mother was the same way. She was sure that the moment I left the nest I would be gobbled up by a cat or drowned by a human—oh! I'm sorry Wendy—I didn't mean it like that," Weency said, sheepishly.

"That's all right, most humans don't like mice and I know that they can be very cruel and thoughtless. But I like mice, I like all types of animals. Most of the time I like animals better than people."

"You're a very special human, and I'm very glad we're friends. Do you have many friends?" Weency asked.

"No, Mother always thought that if I played with other children I would catch some terrible disease and die. Isn't that silly? So she hired a private tutor and I learn my lessons at home. I do get to play with other children when someone comes visiting and brings them along, but it's been so long, and they never bring girls the same exact age as me."

The sun began to rise, and the sky filled with a pale violet light. Both girls heard the birds in the garden and knew their time together had grown short and would soon be over.

"When can we meet again?" Wendy asked, sadly knowing that her friend must leave now.

"My brother has a cold—so I'll be doing the gathering, but only until he gets well again, then it's his job," Weency answered sadly.

"Can I come and knock on your little door, and will your nanny let you come out and play with me?" Wendy asked her hopefully.

"I don't know, I suppose so. I can ask, but mice aren't supposed to play with humans," the little mouse answered mournfully.

"I've got an idea! Will you show me where your nest is?"

"Yes, certainly, but why?" Weency questioned her friend.

"Wait here a minute." Then Wendy jumped up and began going through the pantry. In a moment she was back, her robe tucked up in front of her filled with all kinds of sumptuous delights. "Come on," the girl said, extending her hand onto the kitchen floor. "I'll take you back to your nest."

Weency climbed into Wendy's hand and rode joyfully all the way down the hall to the front door of the big house.

"Here," she said pointing downward with her paw, "Put me down, and I'll show you."

Wendy gently placed her friend on the hall rug and the little mouse motioned for the girl to follow as she walked over to the small entryway crack. "This is it, my front door, but it's really just a crack," Weency said smiling.

Wendy unloaded her robe onto the rug and began rummaging through the goodies.

"I don't know if these will fit, but we can try and get them through the crack," she said, opening a package of biscuits.

"Wendy, this is wonderful! There's enough food here to last two lifetimes!" Weency giggled, delighted, and started passing the biscuits in through the crackway. "We'll never have to go gathering again."

"And I can bring you more any time, I would love to," Wendy said, gladly. She was poking some blueberries through the opening with her little finger, and getting ready to break up a very large piece of Swiss cheese.

"Wendy, because we are now friends, there's something I must confess to you," Weency said, seriously.

"Yes, what is it, Weency?" Wendy asked as she opened a tin of chocolate truffles.

"A few years ago, my father was out gathering. He was an excellent gatherer, you know. He could fit more into a gathering sack than any mouse I've ever read about. He came home one morning with a beautiful set of red clay dishes." Weency hung her head, embarrassed by the confession.

"I see. So that's where they got off too. Well, never mind, Weency, I'm sure you've put them to better use than I ever could. But, it's nice to know that I didn't just carelessly lose them, I appreciate your telling me," Wendy said kindly.

"Do you? Oh, I was so frightened you'd be angry and not want to be my friend anymore," Weency said, helping Wendy push the truffles through the crackway.

"Never would I let a set of dollhouse dishes come between me and my best friend!" Wendy stuck out her hand and Weency stuck out her paw and they shook on it.

"Best friends, all right?" Weency asked.

"Best friends!" Wendy said, "I've got to get back to my room. Father will be waking up soon and I don't want him to suspect a thing."

"Come and knock. I'm sure when I show Mrs. Chubbly how kind and generous you are, she'll allow me to come out and visit."

"Wonderful! Then I'll see you very soon," Wendy said, gathering up everything that was too large to fit through the tiny entrycrack.

"But it can only be when there are no other humans around," Weency cautioned.

"All right, you have my word."

Then Wendy started down the hall, and stopped to look back at the mouse working hard to push all the food through the hole. Just to make sure it really had happened after all, she called out, "Goodnight, Weency," in a loud whisper.

"Goodnight, Wendy."

When Wendy got back to her room, Chesterfield Cat was waiting there at the foot of her bed. He rarely came upstairs to visit her there and she was surprised to see him. He looked at her seriously for a moment, and she fully expected him to meow and lay down to sleep.

Instead, he sat back on his tail, crossing his hind legs, and put one paw down on his knee. Then, leaning low against the white eyelet bed cover, he cocked his head to one side like an old gentleman about to give a lecture and very plainly said, "You know, you must never tell anyone."

"Tell what, Chesterfield?" Wendy asked, still half believing she was having the most marvelous dream. Chesterfield looked impatient.

"Children!" he growled loudly. "You must never tell anyone that you spoke to me, or Weency, for that matter. It is not allowed."

"I would never think of telling anyone," she said, reassuring him. "But who doesn't allow it, and why? Why don't animals go around talking like people do?" She asked, stifling a yawn against the back of her hand.

"The Creature Council doesn't allow it. Years ago, creatures did speak to humans, from time to time. But they only made a fuss about it, and it inevitably got the creature into terrible trouble. Humans can be very cruel and dangerous, so the Council decided it would be best for us to create secret languages, to communicate among ourselves, and to allow humans to believe that we were just stupid beasts. It's safer that way." He finished and rose to leave.

"Wait! But why did Weency talk to me? And why did you?" She asked him quickly, before he leapt off her bed and onto the floor.

"She's innocent, never been out of the nest before. It's quite likely that no creature ever told her, because no creature ever expected her to meet a human and have a chance to talk to one."

"And you, Chesterfield?" Wendy asked again.

"It seemed like the right thing to do at the time," he answered, cleaning his front paws, extending his claws to stretch and then pulling them back in again.

"Are you still my kitty?" Wendy asked, reaching out to scratch behind his furry black ears.

"No, but you're still my human, and you may scratch all you like. But for heaven's sake, don't call me 'kitty', it's quite demeaning." Chesterfield moved closer and curled up in Wendy's lap, to assure the child that their relationship had not changed. She attended to his ears and then gave his belly a nice long scratching.

"Chesterfield, did you really eat Weency's mother and father?" He rose suddenly then and puffed into full attack stance.

"Mind your manners, young lady! There are some things one does not talk about! Besides, I was young and foolish then."

18. A Friend is a Friend

Weency had to climb over a mountain of food to get back into the nest. She listened carefully for a moment, and realized no creature was stirring in the nest. So she attacked the monumental task of stocking the kitchen cabinets. She moved quickly and quietly from the entrycrack to the kitchen, over and over, until each cupboard was filled and could hold no more. Then, because there was still so much left, she began stockpiling the food into a storage closet that had once been used as the surplus pantry, but hadn't been touched since Father Twingle had died.

"Mrs. Chubbly will be delighted." Weency said aloud to herself as she packed the last biscuit into the closet and pulled the curtain shut.

Angel came quietly into the kitchen, Mop toddling along behind her, still walking with her knees locked, the way mouselings do when they're first learning to get around on their hind legs. Her pajamas had sewn in feet and they made a pat,

pat, pat sound as she tentatively put each foot in front of the other. Weency turned to the sound.

"Good morning, little sister. Good morning, Angel. Where's Lacey?" Mop couldn't manage 'good morning' yet, so she waved her tiny paw at Weency.

"Hiiiiy Weence," she squeaked in a long drawn out squeal, delighted to have her big sister's attention. Weency picked her up, placed her on her hip, and rubbed noses with her affectionately.

"Lacey's still fast asleep, thank The Great Creator. Sometimes I just don't know how to manage the two of them now that Lacey is crawling and into everything. You're up early."

"Eency has a fever and a bad cold, so," She continued proudly, "I've been doing a little gathering. " She swept a cupboard curtain aside, and Angel gasped when she saw the incredible array of food stuffed on to the shelves.

"Great mother mouse! How did you manage this?" Angel asked, trying to imagine Weency single handedly bringing all of this food back to the nest. "Was it Chesterfield?" she asked, even though that too seemed impossible.

"No, not Chesterfield," She said, laughing aloud about her secret. "I don't know if you will even believe it!" And she unveiled the other cupboards and the enormous storage closet. "I did have help, but I'd like to tell you about it when Mrs. Chubbly is up."

I was just coming down the wallway and overheard the last bit of conversation.

"I am up," I said wondering what all the commotion was about in the kitchen. I placed the empty teapot on the table and set it beside the red clay bowl full of water and the scrap. I turned slowly and eyed the open cupboards, mentally recording as I turned; Cheese, Swiss and cheddar, enough for at least a week; Strawberries, blueberries, lady apples, six tins of orange marmalade, three tins of gingerbread, a heel of whole wheat (uncut), dozens of truffles, a paper sack of cashews spilling out onto the shelf (I must remember to tie it shut), sugar snap peas, enough to last a month, two small tins of nut butter, a sack of popping corn, also pouring out on the shelf, a tin of candied fruit, and more tins of biscuits than I cared to count so early in the morning. I was beside myself, but tried to keep my composure.

"Weency, I believed when you left to gather that you would do well and come back to the nest safely, but it appears that you have performed a large miracle. Would you please explain, dear?" I said sitting at the table, knowing the explanation would have to be extensive. A real cat tale, I thought to myself.

Before Weency could utter a word, there was a scratching at the crackway.

"Sounds like Chesterfield. I'll go, you mousettes keep your ears perked for Eency. He was sleeping peacefully, nice and cool when I left him, but keep your ears open anyway. If he's still barking from the croup, brew him some of the herbs I left at his bedside—one half paw mint, a pinch of eucalyptus to one tea cup of water, steep it for five minutes—I'll be back," I said as I left the kitchen.

I was correct. It was Chesterfield. I had come to know the sound of his scratching well in the last six months. He was almost a nightly visitor at the nest—usually late in the evening when the mouselings were sound asleep. I would come to answer his scratching and we'd sit quietly chatting at the entryway crack, often late into the night. But Chesterfield always slept in the morning, usually in front of the fire. If I chanced to have a peek out into the big house I'd often see him there, stretched out on the hearth, his paws running in some sweet dream as he chased his invisible prey. So, I was disturbed to find him calling at this unusual hour, and felt that something must surely be amiss.

"Mrs. Chubbly, I must speak with you right away," he whispered, pacing the hall nervously.

I couldn't recall seeing Chesterfield behave this way since the night he brought Angel to us in labour. Something is greatly wrong, I thought as I left the crackway. Staying cautiously close to the wall, I looked down the long hallway. No human was near as it was still quite early in the morning, so I ventured closer to the waiting cat.

"Yes, Chesterfield, what is it? You sound urgent."

He moved closer and lay down on the hall rug, also checking the hallway for movement. Then, he leaned his face close to mine, keeping his voice to a whisper as if he expected some creature to overhear us.

"Something unheard of occurred last night in the kitchen." He shook his head as if he was having trouble going on.

"I think Weency was about to tell me the same thing," I said, interrupting his thoughts. "When I looked in the cupboards they were stuffed to overflowing with more food than I've seen since winter preparation at Aunt Bibi's nest," I finished.

"Food?" He asked, surprised, "I don't know anything about that, I had nothing to do with it, if that's what you're asking. Though I would love to take credit for such a marvelous deed." He smiled his most charming smile. "That's not what I've come about," he said, licking nervously at his paw pad, a habit I've seen him use many times while gathering his thoughts.

"Chesterfield, " I said, trying to comfort him, "It is me—Mrs. Chubbly, that you are speaking to. Is there anything so terrible that you can not possibly tell me? Haven't we been through the worst of it together, already?"

He cocked his head, considering this.

"Unless you've eaten the mouselings—and I know you haven't, for I've just left them safe in the nest—what could possibly be so tragic that we can't find a way to fix it together?" I sat next to him and waited patiently for his reply.

"All right, Mrs. Chubbly. I'm sorry for stalling, I'll get on with it." Then he heaved a deep sigh and blurted out, "Weency has spoken to Wendy."

"What do you mean?" I asked, quite shocked, "In English!? Spoken to her?"

He just nodded at me. We sat there for a moment pondering the magnitude of the situation in silence.

"Great Creator! I never thought to explain the rules, I told her everything else she would need to know about gathering, even about cats, but never for a moment did I consider the possibility that this might happen." I held my tongue, considering what was to be done.

"She is just a human child, and a very kind and loyal one. I spoke to her myself and she seemed to take it fairly well," he said sheepishly.

"You spoke to her as well? Great mother mouse! It seems as if the whole thing has gotten quite out of paw." I began pacing the crackway. I was now as nervous as Chesterfield and with good reason, this could bring disaster down upon our heads.

"Mrs. Chubbly, I'm not that worried about Wendy, but I am concerned about the situation in the big house. Her mother was sent away with Mrs. Hammond for a rest cure. Now, she's alone with her father and they've gotten quite close—Do you think she'll tell him?"

"Chesterfield, if I were a human child and you were my father, and I told you that my house cat and a cute little mouse had spoken to me in the kitchen—would you believe me?" I asked him, pointedly.

"If I were Edmund Lovely, I'd probably say, 'That's nice, dear heart, say hello to your kitty and send my regards to your mouse' then I'd go back to my office and chuckle about my daughter's vivid imagination," he said smiling.

"Exactly. So, I don't believe we really have anything to worry about, but I do think Weency should be here. Let us just get this out in the open, and perhaps solve the mystery of the full pantry." I dashed back into the nest and bought Weency back with me.

"Sit here, dear." I motioned to a spot close to the crackway, to ensure her safety should the humans awaken suddenly, and I stood nearby.

"Chesterfield was just explaining to me that you spoke to a human last night. Is that correct, Weency?" She looked at me as if she was going to get quite upset and then checked herself.

"Wendy is my friend—she's not just a human!" she said indignantly. Then her face became very animated and she went on, brightly, "She's my best friend, we shook on it. You have no idea how much we two are alike—I'm eleven years old and she'll be eleven this week, I'm a twin and she's a twin—though her brother died when he was a baby— we both love to play with dolls, neither of us have any other friends—and both of us have lost our mothers. So you see, it doesn't matter that she's a human and I'm a mouse. We're perfect for each other! We were meant to be friends!" She said this with such a great deal of passion that I was dumbstruck for a moment. I gathered my words thoughtfully, trying hard not to patronize the intelligent young mousette.

"Weency, all that you've said is very true. The two of you are very much alike, but we must remember our history or we are doomed to repeat it. Whenever in the past an animal has spoken to a human, terrible tragic things have happened. I know you really like this human child-"

"Wendy—call her Wendy, please, Mrs. Chubbly," she said angrily.

"Fine, Weency, I know you really like Wendy—but she's a person and you're a mouse, and nothing in creation can change that simple fact. Humans and mice simply cannot be friends, my dear, it's too dangerous an affair—not just for you, but for all creatures."

She looked at me hard and then turned to look at Chesterfield, then she smiled broadly as the thought struck her.

"Mrs. Chubbly, here we sit, you and I, and your very good friend Chesterfield CAT. Since when have cats and mice ever before been friends?"

I couldn't think of a single instance.

"Touché! You've made your point well," I said smiling back at Weency. Chesterfield rolled on the rug, laughing at the clever mousekin, and I was forced to eat a bit of crow. "Weency, I'd like to apologize to you for being so narrow minded. In all species there is good and there is evil. The problem is that the Council has not been able to find many good homo sapiens."

"Well, I guess they never met Wendy Lovely—and she's the one who brought all the food to our nest," she said smugly.

"Did you ask her to help you? Did you suggest it?" I inquired.

"Oh no, not at all. It was not only her idea completely, but she made me wait while she went in to her pantry and brought it all out as a great surprise. Then she carried me back to the nest and helped me get all the food inside."

Chesterfield came to attention, "Did Wendy do all that? I knew MY human was different. She's always been very affectionate and loyal—and kind to animals. Last spring she saved a baby robin that had fallen from its nest. She nursed it and hand fed it until it was ready to fly, then she set it free in the garden." We all nodded our approval at once.

"You see, Mrs. Chubbly, she is different," Weency said.

Apparently the two of them had joined forces and were teaming up, but I had already come over to their side, partially.

"She sounds like a very special human. I'd like to meet her," I said cheerily, and hoped my ulterior motives weren't showing. I didn't want Weency to ever know that I was going to meet her 'friend' for the sole purpose of making sure she wasn't a danger to us.

"Wonderful! I'll tell her when she comes to visit me," Weency said, delighted that I was interested in her new friend.

"Mrs. Chubbly, I believe it would be much more practical if I arrange the meeting. I can speak with Wendy as soon as she arises, and set an appointment for this evening, after bedtime," said Chesterfield, sounding like an official ambassador of mice. "If you don't mind riding in my mouth, I can bring you up to her room and wait for you."

"Chesterfield, I've ridden in your mouth before—not that I would choose it as my most favored mode of transportation, but I would be grateful if you would take care of things and arrange it for tonight." Then I remembered Eency. "Oh, Eency is still feeling poorly. He woke up ill in the middle of the night. Perhaps we should set the meeting for tomorrow evening at bedtime? I'm sure Eency will be over the hump by then."

Chesterfield bowed and extended his paw to me, and then to Weency, and we shook paws ceremoniously. He loved the formality of all the niceties I had taught him and practiced his manners whenever he could find an appropriate moment, and he had grown quite charming.

"I'll take care of everything. Till tonight then," he said, and he was off down the hall. Weency fell silent. I believe she felt slighted that I hadn't allowed her to set up a meeting between Wendy and me, but sometimes one must place practicality before emotions.

19. The Invitation

Angel was inspired by the full cupboards and set about making a lovely breakfast of stewed cashews and fresh strawberries, and a large pot of hot chocolate. The air in the kitchen was filled with delicious smells of fresh food cooking and there was a feeling of festivity and celebration.

I entered to find Eency up and about, looking like his healthy old self. Mop was sitting on her high stool, and Lacey was crawling about trying hard to keep up with Angel's feet as she moved here and there, stirring the chocolate, setting the table, and slicing the succulent strawberries.

"Ma Chubby! Ma Chubby!" Mop chanted as I sat down. Then she began banging her spoon on her dish with the hungry fervor only a yearling can muster. "Num num num," she said, smiling at me.

"Are you hungry again, you chubby little mousekin? Why, I'm sure we remembered to feed you yesterday," I teased, putting a slice of strawberry on her red plate. "You look well, Eency."

"I feel terrific, Mrs. Chubbly. Whatever that thing was that I was sick with last night, it seems to be gone now," he said, licking his lips hungrily as he watched Mop chewing on a hunk of strawberry and succeeding to paint her face red with the juicy pulp.

"Good, good. But don't be misled. You still shall rest today in bed. Now have some strawberries, they have lots of vitamin C and that will help your immune system to chase away your infection. Don't be surprised tonight if your fever returns, that's when the body does its best healing."

We were all seated now and the table was full. What an unexpected feast!

"I'd like to give thanks, can I, Mrs. Chubbly?" Weency pleaded. "It's 'may I', dear, not 'can I', and of course you may."

Just then there was a loud knocking, it sounded like it was coming from the library. Eency and Weency both jumped up and yelled "Mail!" Then together they said, "May we get it? Mother always let us."

Everyone was so excited by the event that we all went together, the whole tribe, carrying mouselings and scurrying down the wallway to the library window.

We reached the library in time to see Clatter Woodpecker push open the monocle window and stick his large head into the room.

"Mail call!" he cried out, smiling. The mouseling Mop made a mad dash for it, but Weency won the race and had her paw out ready.

"Now take it easy, mousette, this letter is addressed to Mrs. Lacey Chubbly, and I'd get my wings clipped for certain if I handed it to the wrong customer—infraction of rule number 491 A," he said officiously. Then he winked at me and handed the letter over to Weency anyway.

"It's from Babble Creek. Now, who do you suppose it might be from?" he teased.

"I can't imagine," I said, having a bit of fun with a dear old friend, "but you better have brought me good news," I said, gratefully accepting the letter from Weency.

"Let me see too!" Eency was trying to get past the little ones, in hopes of getting a better look at the intricate paw drawn pictures Aunt Bibi had used to decorate the envelope. The seal was Aunt Bibi's special occasion seal—an apple with two leaves on the stem—pressed into the white wax. Just looking at it gave me a nice, familiar feeling.

"They asked me to wait for your reply," he stated, ruffling his red head crest impatiently.

"Oh, dear me—we were just about to sit down to breakfast. When do you make your next run to London?" I asked him.

"Day after tomorrow. Soon enough for you?" Clatter asked.

"That would be plenty of time, thank you Clatter. You've made this a wonderful day," I said placing the unopened letter in my apron pocket.

"That's the way it goes. Good news and they love me, bad news and they want to wring my neck—tough life being a messenger. See you in two days." He withdrew his head, popped in a copy of the newspaper, and was off. Angel closed the window behind him, and together we walked back to the kitchen and the feast that awaited.

As we took our places around the tale, I withdrew the letter from my pocket and broke the seal.

"In my family, when we would receive a letter, my Uncle Mak would always read it aloud to all of us at the breakfast table."

The twins looked delighted when they heard this, knowing now that their curiosity would indeed be satisfied and that I didn't intend to keep the letter to myself.

"Yes, Mrs. Chubbly, let's do it just like that! Will you read it for us?" they asked, excited. Angel looked fearful, knowing there very well might be news of the fire—wanting to know and not wanting to at the same time. She held Lacey and remained silent.

"Of course I intend to. Weency, would you pour the tea, please?" As she filled our cups with the aromatic peppermint, I removed the letter ceremoniously from its envelope, the way I had seen Uncle Mak do dozens of times. Everyone was silent and I felt all their eyes upon me, waiting for me to begin. I read the letter word for word, slowly and clearly.

—A LETTER FROM THE APPLE TREE NEST—

To: Mrs. Lacey Chubbly from: The Chubblys

C/o The Twingle Family

#1 Old Apple Tree Nest

22 North Chelsea Lane Babble Creek, Chelsea, England

Spring 1904, reply to your letter

My dear, sweet Niece Lacey,

Your letter was sheer delight! We are so happy that The Great Creator has given you a fine family, but this family misses you endlessly.

After your Uncle Mak read me the letter, we realized how long a time it has been since we were all together at the big table. We've set a reunion for the last two weeks of summer. I do not know how you will come, but I implore you to find a way and bring your lovely new family. I'm sure you must need a rest from the little ones and I know several Aunts (myself included) who would be happy to have one on the hip again. Many letters have gone out to both sides of the family, and we await reply—but I'm sure it will be a wondrous turn out as it has been too long since the last gathering.

Great grandfather Sage sent notice right away that he and Crystal will certainly attend.

He'll be 125 years old this winter! With the old family patriarch present, I'm sure all will want to be there.

Mak sent a letter off to Myra and Chip regarding the fire. I'm sorry to say we haven't heard back from them yet. When we do, I'll get a letter off immediately to let you know about silver and lily.

If it does any good, please let Angel know that the family loves her and her new addition, Lacey, and we will always be there for her at any cost, should she ever need us. In my heart I believe that they have survived. Silver was far too clever and loved Lily far too much to go out that way. Have faith and go on believing the best.

Mak was delighted to hear about Weency's growing interest in The Great Healing Arts. This is the first time in years that he's brightened this much, out early in the morning, checking on the herb garden. He's even begun setting up some practice sacks. It's really given him something to look forward to.

About the Florapedia: do you remember your mother's wild sister, Aunt Matilda? We gave her a copy of the manuscript in 1840, right before she ran off with that crazy inventor. That's the only copy we haven't been able to trace. Could be that he was a Twingle. I'll ask your Aunt Myra this summer. We lost track of Aunt Tillie after that. Never heard from her again, as a matter of fact. It seems that your adopted family just might truly be family after all. Check the page on wild rose hips, if it's Tillie's copy, you'll find an inscription there (I used to call her Rambling Rose).

The Goldentop family is doing well, those mouselings are so intelligent, it gives Uncle Mak a great deal of pleasure to be able to spend time with them. Lancelot is still a bachelor mouse. Curly worries constantly that he'll never find a mousette that interests him enough to get him out of the nest, and she fears that she'll grow old without grandmousekins to keep her busy. It's a sad thought.

Thank The Great Creator that Mak and I had you to raise, or I too might have had a broken heart. You'll never know how much you give us still. I love you more than I can ever say, and will meditate daily on a way to bring you home to me and Mak.

Well, I await your reply, and I will watch for Clatter every morning with great anticipation.

Love and devotion,

Bibi and Mak

As much as I tried to keep my composure in front of the mousekins, I was teary eyed from the letter, but their excitement broke me out of it quickly.

"Can we go? Oh please, can we?" the twins practically shouted at me.

"Mouselings! That's no tone to take at the table, lower your voices this instant." I waited until they seemed settled, and I had my own emotions in check. "Of course, I would love for us to go to the family reunion, and I'm sure that two weeks down in the country would do us all a lot of good. I cannot think of how we could get there. It is much too long and difficult a journey for tender paws as yourselves. It would take us many weeks to get there." I said sadly.

"We can take Father Twingle's flying machine!" Eency piped up.

"And I can pilot it!" Weency added.

"I would love to go, I've hardly met any of the family and neither has Lacey. Aunt Bibi sounds so kind," Angel said, thinking of Lily and Silver.

"I'll need some time to think about this, to work out the details, but, yes, we'll go! Yes, indeed, we will! If The Great Creator wants to bring us there by flying machine or flying carpet, it's fine with me—and we will be there for the Chubbly family reunion." I raised my teacup high and the others followed, even Mop—though she needed two paws. "Here's to the love of family—a love that knows no bounds, no limits and no judgments. To the open arms that are always there to draw a loved one home—where the heart is. May our Great Creator provide us safe passage—and watch over us as we make the long journey back to my apple tree nest. Amen and Aho"

And to a chorus of "Amen's" we began our celebration feast.

20. Mrs. Chubbly Meets Wendy

T he next evening, after all the little ones were sound asleep, and Angel lay reading quietly in her bed, Chesterfield came to the crackway at the appointed hour to fetch me.

I had carefully dressed in my best and prettiest apron, the same one I wore to my interview with the Twingles, and I had my walking stick at my side. I had never conversed with a human before and was feeling particularly nervous—after all, I was brought up with the idea that other creatures should never, under any circumstances, speak to a human being. I had to constantly remind myself that Wendy Lovely might be different, and so I hoped—for Weency's sake.

"Are you ready?" Chesterfield asked, lowering his face to the rug.

"Quite," I replied, climbing into his open mouth. He began the walk down the hallway and gracefully climbed the long stairs to the second floor. If it weren't for the dreadfully strong smell of cat that set all of my instinctual nerves on edge, the ride would have been quite comfortable. Chesterfield was careful to keep his mouth open and his lips pulled tightly against his teeth. He moved in such a way that I shouldn't be jarred around, and proceeded to push Wendy's bedroom open with his forepaw.

She slept in the nursery, like most English children, and the room was very beautiful indeed. The canopy bed was covered with a lavender floral print, and the bed was done in white ruffles with a matching white eyelet cover. There were more toys and dolls than a mouseling could even imagine, and an enormous formal dollhouse furnished lavishly with real wooden furniture and turquoise velour upholstery. Everything in it seemed to be a copy of an original, down to the handmade wool rugs.

I looked up and saw her smiling, sitting cross-legged on her bed in a long, white cotton nightshirt, her long blonde hair loose about her shoulders. It was a strange jarring feeling, to be willingly present and at the mercy of a human being. They are such volatile creatures. I took a deep breath and I trusted in The Great Creator, and the oneness of all beings, "Aho-Maste we are one" I whispered to myself as a reminder. It was no accident that I was here meeting this human child, against all of the rules and dogma of the Council of Creatures. In fact, it was a stunning moment that felt universally important beyond what I understood while gazing at her innocent face. This was not two creatures meeting, but a bridge being built across a long held belief in the illusion of separateness, for "safety". Then Chesterfield leapt upon the bed and deposited me gently on the cover. I was fine from the ride, but slightly damp. I straightened my apron while Chesterfield made the introductions.

"Wendy Lovely, I'd like you to meet my very dear friend, Mrs. Chubbly."

She reached out her hand and took my paw gently between her fingers.

"I'm so pleased to meet you, Mrs. Chubbly. Weency has told me so many wonderful things about you," the young girl said in a most charming manner.

"Delighted, my dear. Weency has also spoken quite highly of you, and you certainly are as beautiful as she said you are," I told her.

"Well, I think it only appropriate that I wait at the door," Chesterfield said politely as he leapt onto the rug. Before he turned to walk away, he added, "Do call if you need me."

"Thank you, Chesterfield, that will be fine," I answered. And he was gone, leaving the two of us alone to sort things out.

"I hope you and your family are enjoying the things I brought out of the pantry. I wasn't at all sure of what mice like to eat, " she said shyly. I watched her carefully as she spoke. She was so innocent, such a gentle soul, trying hard to be inoffensive. It was easy to like her and I understood immediately how Weency could choose her as a friend.

"It was all wonderful. I thank you on behalf of the whole family. A great deal of our time is spent on gathering food for survival, and this generous gift of yours will leave us more time for the important things," I answered honestly, smiling back at her.

"I'd like to do it regularly. If you'll just let me know what it is you need, I would be happy to get it for you. We have so much, I'm sure Father would never notice—and Mother is away," she said, sadly.

"You sound like you miss her very much."

"Oh, yes, I do. Although it wasn't very nice having her here, she wasn't very nice to me. I suppose people get used to things being a certain way—oh, I don't know, I just miss her and wish she was home and well again."

Her eyes filled with tears, but I could see that she was desperately swallowing and trying to hold them back. One doesn't cry in front of company, if one can help it. She wiped her tears, ashamed of her feelings, and my heart went out to her.

"Wendy, would you pick me up in your hand and bring me closer?" I asked, feeling an instinctive trust for the vulnerable child. She reached her hand down and gently lifted me up, close to her face. I looked into her deep brown eyes and saw her broken heart.

"I may be much smaller than you, but I am much, much older. I have taken care of many little ones in my time, some of them motherless, some of them fatherless—and some of them orphans altogether. I, myself, became an orphan when my parents died. I was only thirteen then, and I was frightened and lonely. All creatures, whether human or cat or mouse—all creatures feel the same things, the same love, the same fear, and the same loneliness." Then I gently touched my paw to her soft, pink, furless cheek, and like a baby mousekin longing for its mother's touch, Wendy turned her face to me for more. So I petted her and spoke to her in soothing tones—no matter that she was a human—she was a motherless child and I was a nanny.

"You know, dear, your father loves you very much. It seems he has worked hard to provide you with everything you need—and from what Weency tells me, you love him too."

"Oh yes, very much Mrs. Chubbly. My father is a wonderful man. And it has been so nice to have this time with him. I hardly ever got to see him before Mummy went away. Now he spends lots of time with me," she said happily.

"There, you see—that is how something good comes out of something bad. Life is always like that. If you know how to look at things, you will always find that The Great Creator provides us with something wonderful, while small minded creatures are busy believing that things are just terrible," I said firmly.

"Yes, I see. That is very true. But I wish that Mummy was well and home from Sussex so we could be a family again." She continued mournfully, "I'm going to have to wait till the end of summer before I'll be allowed to go down to the country and see my mother again."

"Ah, Sussex is a beautiful place! I'm sure that she will get well there—even the air is healthy in Sussex, and then you'll go visit her and things will be more wonderful than ever before," I said, trying to encourage her to be positive in her thoughts, knowing her feelings would then follow.

"How do you know about Sussex?" She asked, surprised.

"I grew up there on my Uncle Mak's herb farm," I said, smiling.

"Did you really? I never knew mice could get around so.

Will you tell me? Tell me about living with your Uncle in Sussex? Some of the best time in my life was spent there!"

It always astonished me when young mouselings talked about their brief lives as if they had lived for a hundred years and were ready for the end, and now I saw that human children were exactly the same. I stifled a laugh, knowing it would be misunderstood.

"You'll probably have many more summers at Sussex, and I would be happy to tell you more about Uncle Mak."

Wendy lay down on the bed and pulled the covers up around her, then pulled the blanket into a clever little seat shape, right next to her face. She set me down in the comfortable spot and looked very much like a mousette about to hear a bedtime story. So, I sat near her face in the little 'seat' and in my best bedtime story voice, I proceeded.

"Uncle Mak and Aunt Bibi live inside a beautiful old apple tree. He is an herbalist and a great healer, and Aunt Bibi is a copyist and a librarian."

Her eyes were wide as she listened, filled with wonder at the secrets she was hearing.

"I spent a summer as his apprentice and felt it was my calling to be a nanny and a healer. When I was thirteen, and my parents were eaten by a cat, I went to live with my aunt and uncle. After I recovered from the loss I was happier there than I had ever been before."

"Something good coming out of something bad?" she asked. She was a smart one.

"Yes, very good, exactly. I spent those happy years in the apple tree nest, learning and watching. Walking on the green hillsides of the South Downs, playing with the minnows in Babble Creek."

"Babble Creek?" she asked, surprised. "That's just where our country house is—on the South Downs near Babble Creek!"

"Really?" I said, now thinking about my family—and the end of summer reunion.

"We've been neighbors all these years—and now you're living right here in my house! What a remarkable coincidence," she stated.

"Wendy, I believe much more in providence than I do in coincidence," I said stroking her cheek. "Do you understand what providence is?"

"I think so. It's when God makes something happen that wouldn't have happened any other way—like causing two people, I mean creatures, to meet and become friends," she said, smiling at me warmly, and I couldn't help but smile back.

"Precisely! And I believe The Great Creator—or as you say, God, has providentially placed us all together for many sound reasons—some of which shall become clear in time, others we may never understand—but all of it working like a finely tuned watch for our greatest good," I said, looking closely to see if she understood.

"Yes! Yes, I see. Oh, Mrs. Chubbly, you have such a wonderful way of explaining things." Then she turned and kissed me—it was a great surprise considering her mouth was larger than my whole head. But I stood still for it knowing the child was naturally trying to show her affection for me.

"I see why Weency loves you so much, you're so wise and wonderful."

She had a lovely face and her eyes sparkled and smiled as much as her mouth did. What an open, refreshing face—what a beautiful soul this little human child had within her.

"Wendy, I came here tonight for a very specific reason," I said, trying not to frighten the child.

"Have I done something wrong, Mrs. Chubbly?" She asked, frightened in spite of my caution.

"Not at all, dear. Actually, it was Weency who did wrong, or so it seemed at first thought. Mice are not allowed to speak to humans," I said carefully.

"I can certainly understand why," she said, nodding in agreement. "I know what people are like, they can be very mean and I've seen people do terrible things to innocent animals— why, if people thought animals could talk and were smart like all of you secretly are, there's no telling what they might do..." She trailed off, thinking.

"That's correct. But Weency didn't know this. She innocently spoke to you and formed what seems to be a very strong friendship. I honestly came here tonight to make sure you were safe, to be sure you would cause us no harm, before I gave Weency my permission to continue her relationship with you." I paused, checking her reaction to my honest words.

"And?" She asked, nervously.

"And, I couldn't be happier that the whole thing took place. I'm delighted that Weency spoke to you, I'm delighted to know you myself, and I believe it was an act of providence by our Great Creator that we are now friends," I said, smiling.

"I'm so happy to hear you say that! I thought that was why you came, and I was frightened that you wouldn't like me and would forbid Weency to see me again."

"Oh, my dear, you think so little of yourself—you are truly a remarkable creature—the love just flows right out of you. You're beautiful, and intelligent, and very sensitive—I can't imagine any creature on this planet not wanting you as a friend." I reached out and kissed Wendy on her cheek and she blushed shyly.

"Thank you, Mrs. Chubbly—I wish I had a nanny just like you!"

"Actually, Wendy, you have one now. If at any time you need to talk things over, or you're lonely for your mother and you need a friend—just ask Chesterfield to come by the nest, and he'll bring me round to your room, simply ask for me."

"Wonderful! You are the kindest creature I have ever met, but must you go? You sound as if you're ready to leave!" she asked, pouting like any ten year old mousette.

"I can stay a bit longer."

"Will you tell me more about the apple tree nest?" she asked.

"Wendy, would you like to see the apple tree nest?" I asked, already knowing her answer.

"Oh, that would be just like a fairy tale—to see a mouse's nest in an apple tree!" she cried enthusiastically.

"I'd like to ask a favor of you," I stated.

"Anything! Ask away and I'll do it," she vowed.

"My family is having a reunion at Babble Creek. Providentially, it is to take place the last two weeks of summer," I began.

She interrupted excitedly, "Oh, I know just what you're going to ask—I'd love to bring you all up there. But how will I get so many mice into my father's automobile unseen?" We both sat there for a moment in silence, thinking and planning, when my eyes fell upon the Victorian dollhouse.

"Will they let you bring playthings with you?" I asked. She looked over at the dollhouse then and read my thoughts.

"Of course—the doll house. It's just perfect. I'll fill the cupboards with food, and you can all come up the night before, then I'll ask father if I may have it in the back of the automobile with me."

"And, " I added, "we'll all ride in luxurious comfort down to Sussex!"

We shook on it, both of us laughing at our clever plan. Chesterfield poked his head in to the room.

"I see you're all getting along well, but it is rather late. Mrs. Chubbly, your coach is waiting," he said, smiling at me broadly.

"Chesterfield is right, it is rather late. I must be going now, dear, but I will see you again very soon," I said, once again touching her cheek. "Now, you remember what I've said about you, for it's the complete truth—and if you ever need me..."

"I know, I'll just call Chesterfield and he'll fetch you," she said, sounding uncertain, and then she added, "Do you promise?"

"Of course I do. I give you my word of honour."

"And Mrs. Chubbly's word is as good as a done deed," Chesterfield added for good measure.

"Goodnight, Mrs. Chubbly—please say hello to Weency from me."

"I certainly will. Goodnight, dear child." I waved as Chesterfield scooped me up in his mouth and we rode off down the hall, down the stairs and back to the crackway. When he set me down in front of the nest, he stood there for a moment, waiting.

"Well?" he asked me.

"Your human is very special. Now, I understand why you love her so."

"Yes, she is very special," He paused, waiting for me to go on, and when I was silent, he added, "So, aren't you going to tell me?"

"Tell you what, Chesterfield?" I asked, playfully. "You mean you weren't listening?"

"Mrs. Chubbly!" he said, properly offended. "That would have been extremely rude. Do you really think…"

"Chesterfield," I broke in.

"Well," he said coyly, "perhaps I listened just a bit." Then we were both laughing. "You know, the whole trip to the country would be perfect, if I could come along to watch out for you," he said honestly. And I could hear the longing in his voice—to stay with his new family.

"Perhaps that could be arranged. Let me think about it," I answered.

"Do you really believe it would be possible?" he asked, as delighted as a child being promised a visit to the circus.

"Yes, Chesterfield, and I have a marvelous plan, I think it just might work!"

—THE SECOND LETTER HOME—

To: Mak and Bibi Chubbly

#1 Old Apple Tree Nest

Babble Creek, England

From: Mrs. Lacey Chubbly

℅ The Twingle Family

22 North Chelsea Lane

Chelsea, England

Spring, 1904,

Dear Uncle Mak and Aunt Bibi,

I am delighted to tell you that my new family and I will be accepting your invitation to The Chubbly Family Reunion!

The Great Creator has provided us passage to Babble Creek and we will be there for the last two weeks of summer. I will explain further, when I see you, the unusual way in which we shall travel.

I have a favor to request of you, and I'll explain my reasons for this as well when i see you this summer.

There is a house on the south downs near Babble Creek—not far from The Apple Tree Nest. Would you please ask Aunt Sandy to speak to twenty or thirty of her cousins and ask them to make a show of over running this house—I have included a map with directions, so it shouldn't be difficult to locate the house.

They don't need to set up nest keeping—simply to run through the walls for several nights or perhaps to appear once or twice in front of the humans (just to frighten them into believing they are under siege by mice).

I know it is a strange request, but absolutely necessary for the purpose of getting us to the reunion.

I love you all and am gratefully, and at long last, looking forward to seeing you soon. I will be marking the days until then,

All my love and devotion,

Lacey

21. Getting Ready

Summer was an endless flurry of preparation and planning. Wendy visited the nest daily and brought us wonderful gifts of food, handmade furniture that had been too much even for her large Victorian dollhouse, expensive fabric swatches of velvet and satin, and some fresh peppermint that she had collected herself from the garden. The child did everything she could to continually prove her loyalty, and apparently she had kept our meeting a secret from Mr. Lovely.

All of our carefully laid plans were falling into place, and as the end of the summer drew near, Chesterfield Cat came by to tell me that he too would be going to Sussex. It seemed that overnight the summerhouse had become infested with field mice, and he was to be brought up for the two week holiday to rid the house of its terrible invaders. I would have to remember to thank Sandy Fields and her cousins for a job well done.

We spent our days sewing presents for the numerous relatives we would be seeing at the reunion, and watching the mousekins blossom. The summer passed quickly in this manner and the night came at last when Chesterfield was to carry us up to Wendy's room. There we stood in the wallway, our many bags packed with presents and food for the journey to the country. At the appointed hour, when Mr. Lovely was sound asleep, Chesterfield came scratching at the entryhole.

"Mrs. Chubbly, are you ready?" he whispered.

"Yes, we are all present and waiting," I said, moving our baggage toward the opening.

"I'll bring the baggage first, and return for you shortly. Agreed?"

"That will be fine, Chesterfield." I began carrying bags out into the entry hall and lining them up against the wall, and like a fire brigade, Angel and the twins began passing the packages out to me.

The twins were chattering nervously, excited about the grand adventure that stood before them, and several times I had to put my pawtip to my lips, reminding them to be quiet. Chesterfield loaded his mouth with packages and dashed off to Wendy's room, then returned and did the whole thing over again three times before he was ready to take on passengers.

"It doesn't seem sensible to take you two at a time in my mouth," he said, scratching behind his ear with his hind paw.

"I suppose we could try climbing on your back, but I'm concerned about the little ones falling off," I answered.

"Oh yes! Let's ride on Chesterfield's back!" Eency said, excited by the idea. Angel didn't look too delighted, but Weency was nodding in agreement.

"Wait a moment, let me think," I said, surveying the traveling party. "Angel, you tie Lacey on your back, I'll tie Mop on mine—Eency, you and Weency can ride up front behind Chesterfield's ears, and Angel and I will sit behind you. How does that sound to you, Chesterfield?" I asked, fixing Mop in her sling on my back.

"I believe it will work, and I'll take it slow and easy— we should make it just fine."

Chesterfield lay down as flat as he could. Very gently, first Eency then Weency stepped upon his forepaw then up on to his haunch, then going paw over paw and holding on tightly to his thick black fur, they climbed upon his neck—Eency settling himself behind Chesterfield's ears and Weency sitting behind her brother with her paws tightly gripping his waist.

"You're sitting on my tail, sister," Eency whispered loudly.

"Oh dear, terribly sorry, Eence," she said as she pulled his tail out from beneath her and wound it round like a rope, carefully tucking it between them.

"You're next, Angel," I said, kneeling at Chesterfield's side. She got a boost from stepping on my knee and then, with great agility, she pulled herself up, paw over paw, and on to Chesterfield's back. She made it look quite easy, but it only served to remind me that I was getting on in years. I also had a large sleeping mousekin tied to my back and the further encumbrance of my black ratskin bag and my walking stick. When one gets to be an elder, one begins to find ways to use brains instead of brawn, and I couldn't imagine how I would pull myself and Mop up onto Chesterfield's back. Then Chesterfield flicked his tail impatiently and I saw my path clearly before me.

I slipped my black bag onto my arm and using my walking stick as a balance, I tightrope-walked straight up Chesterfield's tail and on to his back, then settled myself behind Angel.

"That was quite a trick, Mrs. Chubbly," Chesterfield chuckled.

"Thank you, Chesterfield. I believe we are ready to depart."

Chesterfield rose slowly to his full height, and all of us gasped in chorus. Mice are ground creatures—we live low and stay close to the earth, and our instincts were rattled when we saw how far from the safety of the ground we were. Then he began to move, gracefully padding down the long hallway toward the stairs.

"Marvelous! Can you go faster?" Eency cried out joyfully, holding on to Chesterfield's ears.

"Certainly not! Be quiet and behave yourself, Eency!" I scolded him. "You'll wake up Edmund Lovely and we'll all be finished."

"Yes, Eency—I can go lots faster, but we'll save the wild ride for a time when there aren't any female passengers," Chesterfield told him.

"Thank you, Chesterfield, that's very sensible of you," I added. As the large strong cat began to climb the stairs, the sensation was unnerving to all of us. We could feel his muscles ripple beneath us, pausing, then springing onto the next step. The climb was so steep that it forced all of us to lean forward and hold onto his fur with all fours—for dear life. His fur was slick and it looked as if Angel was going to faint.

"Mrs. Chubbly, I... I... Chesterfield, please!" was all she could manage to get out. But Chesterfield felt her losing her grip and stopped momentarily, bending his front legs down to level out his back and give Angel a rest from the strange sensations. I shook her from behind, just hard enough to get her attention.

"Angel, we're almost there, dear. I know this feels very strange to you, but you must hold on tightly to Chesterfield's fur, or you and Lacey will fall a dangerous distance."

"Yes, of course. I know, Mrs. Chubbly—but I feel so..." Then Weency turned herself around and put her arms around Angel.

"Strange, isn't it? But you were able to walk four days through the snow. You're one of the bravest mousettes I know." Weency said looking directly into her eyes.

"That was for Lacey," Angel told her.

"And so is this—for if you fall..." Weency reminded her.

"Right, Weency—she's on my back and we'll go together."

"Just don't look down. Here, hold onto me."

Weency let Angel hold on to her paws and lean forward against her as Chesterfield again began the long ascent. Then he pushed open the door to the nursery and Wendy reached down and placed us, one at a time, on to her bed.

"Thank goodness you're all safe—Father's still sleeping soundly but we must be very quiet," she whispered. Chesterfield rolled onto his back and gave himself a good rubbing against the floor. Then, trying to regain his feline dignity, he licked at his fur until it was once again neatly in place.

"There! That's better," he said, joining us on the bedcover.

The dollhouse was at the foot of the bed and Wendy opened it to show us around.

"I've taken out most of the furniture—I didn't want anything falling on you during the trip. I've left the beds, though, so you can get some sleep tonight—and the kitchen cupboards are full," she said, opening the tiny doors so we could see all of her preparations for her house guests.

"It's perfect!" Weency said, smiling at her friend.

"Do you really like it? Look! I've even put a rocking horse near the crib," she said, rocking the horse back and forth with her finger, to show that it really worked.

While the girls chatted, I helped Angel take Lacey off her back and she helped me with Mop.

"Do you want me to put the mousekins in the crib?" Weency asked.

"Yes, Weence." Angel carried Lacey and Weency carried Mop. "We might as well get them settled, they're still both asleep."

The two mousettes walked up the miniature flight of stairs and placed the mousekins head to foot in the white wooden crib, then covered them with Wendy's pocket handkerchief.

Angel looked around the room uncomfortably. Then she nudged Weency.

"Weency, where shall I sleep?" she whispered, not wanting to offend Wendy.

"Oh, you're right! There doesn't seem to be any bed here for you. I'll take care of it," Weency answered, also keeping her voice low. Wendy had been watching with delight as her new friends settled their little ones in the crib.

"What's the trouble, Weency?" Wendy asked, bringing her face close to the nursery on the second floor.

"Angel needs to sleep here, near the mousekins—she's nursing, you know," Weency said.

"I see. Well, this will take care of that," she said, reaching into one of the bedrooms and removing a single bed. "Where would you like it, Angel?" Wendy asked.

"Well, that was easy," Angel said, looking around the small room. "Over here, next to the crib, if you can just move this dresser."

Wendy was delighted to be of service. Playing in the dollhouse was one of her favorite things to do and she loved moving the furniture about and rearranging things. She moved the dresser over to the other wall and placed the bed next to the crib. Then she reached into her nightstand and pulled out a bright green woolen scarf, which she folded four times into a square. Then she tucked this onto the bed as a blanket.

"Playing doll house is much more fun with real live creatures." she said, adding a small pillow to the bedclothes. "Weency, you and Eency can share this bed," she said, lifting the twins into the upstairs bedroom and placing them beside a fine large bed with a real feather quilt.

"I'll get your things," Wendy told them, reaching into the large pile of baggage. "Can you tell me what you'll be needing?" she asked.

"I believe I packed our nightclothes in the red cloth sack," Weency told her, and Wendy plopped the tiny sack right down on the dresser near the bed. "What wonderful service, we'll have to stay here more often," Eency joked. Wendy and Weency were laughing.

"Anytime. It would be my pleasure," Wendy said loudly.

"Child and mouselings, I'm glad you're having such a wonderful time—but you must lower your voices. You'll wake Mr. Lovely and the game will come to a horrible end!" I reminded the young ones. "Chesterfield, I must speak with you. We've got a problem that must be resolved before we rest."

Chesterfield came over and lay down beside me.

"What is it, Mrs. Chubbly? " he asked.

"I believe we can ride on your back from the Lovely's summer home, to the apple tree nest, without a problem, but what are we going to do with all of our baggage?"

"Right. I certainly can't carry it in my mouth—there's just too much of it," he said. We sat thinking, looking at the large pile of baggage. Some of it was clothing, some was food, and the other bags had presents for the relatives. There really wasn't anything we could leave behind—and the trip would be too long, for Chesterfield to go back and get our things.

"I've got an idea," Wendy said brightly. She dashed from her bed and took down a hobby horse from her toy shelf. It was a real skin horse with a leather saddle, reins, and saddlebags. She untied the saddlebags and strung them across Chesterfield's neck. They were precisely the right size!

"Well? How does that feel, Chesterfield?" She asked him.

He stood up, shook himself around a bit, then leapt off the bed onto the floor. He raced around the nursery several times and finally leapt back up onto the bed and nodded.

"A perfect fit! Now just don't go trying to put that saddle on me, and we'll get along just fine."

He stood up on Wendy's pillow, and kneading it roughly with his front paws, dug himself a nice deep place to curl up. When it was fixed just right, he curled around and lay down, tucking his tail beneath him.

"Now, if you'll excuse me. Tomorrow is going to be a big day—and I need my rest." Then he shut his eyes and was asleep instantly. Wendy reached over and gently removed the saddlebags.

"He certainly is a remarkable cat," Wendy said to me, whispering.

"Yes, he is. How many cats do you know that would carry a family of mice on their back, all for the sake of bringing us home to be at my family reunion? For that matter, how many cats do you imagine have ever befriended a mouse at all?" I asked.

"Just one—Chesterfield," she answered, placing the saddlebags in front of our baggage.

"Let's pack, shall we?" I asked her. And together, Wendy Lovely and I began to stuff the saddlebags full of the things we wouldn't be needing in the morning. I set aside clean clothing for all, and then the saddlebags were tied shut and placed inside the doll house on the drawing room rug.

"You must be very tired, Mrs. Chubbly," Wendy said, stifling a yawn.

"Yes, dear, I am."

I gathered my bag and my walking stick and stood by her head.

"Here," she said lifting me carefully, "I'll show you to your room."

"This is the Nanny's room," she said, placing me next to the bed.

"Gracious! And who is this?" I asked, surprised to see a large rubber doll in the single bed.

"Oh, sorry. That's Mrs. Nose-in-the-Air. she's the Bendable's housekeeper. I must have forgotten her."

She removed the doll and turned down the bedcover.

"You know, we probably won't get a chance to speak to each other again, so let us go over our plan for tomorrow." I said, placing my bag and stick on the bedstead. "When we arrive at Sussex—you do have a front porch, don't you?"

"Certainly," she answered.

"Good. That will make things a bit easier. If you can leave the dollhouse on the porch and just unlatch it and swing it open far enough for us to slip out—but not far enough for any strange cats or humans to look in."

Wendy interrupted me.

"But Mrs. Chubbly, you can just go out the front door," she said, demonstrating that the mouse-size door on the dollhouse did indeed open and shut.

"Fine. Then you can just leave the dollhouse on the porch and we'll be safe from harm. When Chesterfield comes, we'll go out the front door and be on our way to the apple tree nest, before anyone is the wiser," I said. "Remember, we'll be back two weeks from the day we leave and the doll house must be on the porch for us to get in and safely home."

"I'll remember. Thank you, Mrs. Chubbly—this had been the greatest adventure of my entire life."

"But Wendy—this adventure has just begun." I said, smiling.

Above me I heard Weency and Eency saying their prayers. The twins were kneeling together, heads bowed and paws folded.

"Dear Creator, thank you for taking care of our daily needs, and thank you for keeping us and all the creatures we love safe from harm. Please do something especially nice for Chesterfield Cat since he's been so kind to us, and make sure we get to the apple tree nest safely. Oh, and please help Mrs. Lovely to be healed so she can come home and take care of Wendy," Weency said, and Eency added, "And please don't let Mr. Lovely find us in the back seat of his automobile—and please let this adventure be wild and exciting!"

"Eency!" Weency jabbed him with her elbow.

"Ouch! What?"

"You're not supposed to ask for things like that—just to be safe and have the people you love to be taken care of!" Weency said sharply.

"You can ask The Great Creator for anything your heart desires, but remember it is likely that you will get it. Now go to bed, you two!" I told them firmly, "And no more arguing."

"Who says you're not supposed to ask that way?" Eency whispered.

"Mother, that's who." Weency countered pensively. "Goodnight, Eence."

"Goodnight, Weence." Then they climbed into bed and all was quiet.

"Goodnight, Mrs. Chubbly," Wendy said, getting ready to close the front of the house.

"Goodnight, Wendy. Wendy—thank you, dear. Without your help I wouldn't be going home at all. This is a great gift you've given me, " and with that, the wall was shut and latched. I changed into my nightclothes and got into the comfortable bed and was soon fast asleep, dreaming about my younger days with Tailbit and young Lacey Chubbly, playing together in the fragrant herb garden by the apple tree nest. I was so happy then, and soon I would be home again.

22. The Trip to Sussex

It was a rude awakening. Mr. Lovely grabbed the doll house and must have swung it round and up into his arms, for we were all tossed violently from our beds and were scrambling to gather up the mousekins.

"I'll take it down, Father," I could hear Wendy's voice from beyond the walls of the dollhouse.

"No, I've got it, sweetheart. Hand me your bag and I'll pack the auto," he said gaily. I could hear the excitement in his voice, and thank goodness he was speaking loudly—he didn't hear the six of us scurrying around trying to keep the mousekins quiet.

The next thing I knew, the house was plopped down onto the seat of the auto, and as I peered out from behind the thin curtains, I could see Wendy smiling down at me, and Chesterfield Cat making himself at home in her lap.

"Perfect day for a trip to the country," Edmund said as he started the loud engine. Now both Mop and Lacey were crying and squealing so loudly that I was sure we would be discovered.

"What was that?" Edmund asked Wendy. "Did you hear that squeaking?"

"No, no, Father, I didn't hear any squeaking," Wendy answered nervously, and as Edmund drove the car down their long gravel drive she added, "How can you hear anything above the roar of the engine?"

"What's that you say? You think it's the engine? Perhaps, something's squeaking in the engine—I'll have a look at it when we stop for petrol."

We all sighed with relief. The little ones were quiet and we all walked upstairs to have a look out the window. The height of the house was just right and the nursery window gave us a beautiful view of the road and the scenery. The mouselings were mesmerized. Suddenly their world had grown incredibly large and they could barely take it all in.

Buildings so tall we could never see the top whizzed by. Humans walked holding furry little dogs with brightly painted nails. I saw a young boy peddling on a contraption that sat on three wheels, but it was strangely silent. We passed through the marketplace and all the voices of the sellers yelling and bargaining roared around us. Flowers and fish, pots and knives, the mouselings stood pressed against the window with eyes wide and mouths agape. Their heads filled with the cacophony of city life. Everything was a flash of colour and noise, and then we were crossing the London Bridge and the river Thames spread out beneath us like a bolt of shiny blue fabric unraveling and rippling in the sun.

"Oh! Ahhh!" the twins cried out, "What is it? What is it?"

"The River Thames," Angel answered sadly. "That was my home. Where I lost my family" She sighed.

And as fast as came, it was gone. Now, surrounded by trees, the flashing sunlight and dark shadows washed across Mr. Lovely's auto as we traveled down the long road. For a moment the air was cool and green. We were surrounded by nature and I felt my breath come more easily. The downs appeared quickly, purple with heather and golden with gorse, and the thick sweet smell of the blossoming flowers came heavily through the window and filled the air around us.

"Heavenly!" cried Weency, delirious from the experience.

I smiled, remembering back to my early days of running through fields of flowers like these. I wanted the mouslings to have that.

"You're going to love the country, mouselings—you'll certainly never forget it," I said, feeling the longing in my breast, tugging me home.

Chesterfield was acting just like a kitten, dashing back and forth from one side of the auto to the other, taking in the scent, sniffing at the summer air and then licking his thin lips as if he could taste it all.

Wendy sat and watched us all with a huge 'going on holiday' smile. Edmund sang happily to himself as he motored along, and it seemed to me that if one can predict how things will turn out, from the way they began—it was going to be a wonderful time for all of us.

The time passed quickly, and before we knew it we were pulling off the hard road and onto a dirt path through the thick green trees that led up to the Lovely's summerhouse. It looked like a small castle built from stone, grey and ruddy. It had a large front porch covered by a rose trellis that was in full bloom, with dozens and dozens of blood red roses, thick and velvety.

Annabelle Lovely stood on the porch in her pale green cotton summer dress, her auburn hair framing her beautiful face. And she was smiling! She looked so plainly happy standing there beneath the red canopy of roses. She was stunningly beautiful and joy radiated from her being. I turned to look at

Wendy. She was staring at her mother, surprised, as if she had never seen her mother smile, but the surprise melted into a warm smile of her own and tears came to her eyes.

Edmund, looking back over his shoulder, backed the automobile into its resting place. He hadn't seen Annabelle at all.

"Well, here we are," he said turning off the engine. But Wendy was already out of the auto door and running into her mother's open arms. The woman gathered her daughter to her and held her tightly, rocking her and crying. We were awestruck, and stood reverently watching the scene. Then Edmund was there, awkwardly standing by the steps, watching his wife and his daughter. Annabelle held out her hand to him and invited him in. He came to her, his heart racing. Edmund wrapped them both in his arms and the three of them stood there that way for a long time, just holding each other and crying, as if they had been apart for a decade and had just been reunited—and in a way, that was true.

Angel was crying, then Weency began and I couldn't help myself when I felt my tears began to flow.

"Thank you, Great Creator, for healing this family and bringing them back together in this bond of love," I whispered in prayer.

"Perrrfect," Chesterfield said, with a satisfied rumble. Then he looked away sadly, longing for the reunion that he would never have. "I do hope Wendy hasn't forgotten us," Chesterfield added.

She hadn't. When Annabelle and Edmund walked hand in hand into the summerhouse, Wendy came and brought the dollhouse to the porch and left it there by the front door, as we had arranged. Chesterfield followed her and sat down beside us on the porch. He made a great pretense of chasing a rose petal around with his paw, and when he was sure no humans were about he brought his face near the upstairs window.

"I'm going in to make a show of chasing away the field mice. As soon as I'm sure the humans aren't coming out, I'll be back for you, so be ready," he whispered.

"We will!" I answered, and I began to get the mousekins changed and fed for the long journey ahead of us. The mouselings went through the saddlebags and changed into clean clothing. Angel changed next and brought out some cheese and nuts for breakfast. I changed last, after everycreature was settled and eating I repacked the saddlebags on the drawing room rug with all of our treasures and gifts and clothing, Then I looked up at the small wooden front door of the Victorian doll house and a horrible thought struck me.

"Claws and fangs!" I shouted, bringing everycreature from the kitchen running into the living room.

"What is it Mrs. Chubbly?" Angel asked with great concern.

"We have a problem on our paws. When Wendy and I planned our exit from the house—we forgot entirely about the saddlebags, they're huge.!"

"Can't we just push open the front wall and drag them out?" Eency asked me.

"Well, that would be nice, but the wall is latched shut, and the saddlebags will never fit through that tiny front door," I answered.

"We can go without our things, if we must," Angel said. She was right, but there must be a way.

"I'm going to have a look," Weency stated authoritatively. And before I could stop her—she was out the door. She was only gone a moment and then she was back beside me, breathless.

"I can do it, Mrs. Chubbly! May I please borrow your walking stick?" she asked me.

"Wait a moment Weency—we're all in this together," Eency told her. "You're not going out there alone."

"And you're not going anywhere until I know precisely what it is that you intend to do. What's your plan?" I asked.

"The latches on the outside wall are metal hooks and metal loops-"

"They're called Hook and eye," I told her.

"Yes, there are only two of them—one of them I can reach from the ground, the other one is high up but I believe I can climb the house and with the aid of your stick, I can flip the hook out of the eye—"

"And then," I interrupted, "we'll have to push open the heavy wall to get the saddle bags out."

"We can do it, Mrs. Chubbly—we'll all work together," Angel stated.

"It seems it's our only chance. Chesterfield Cat will be back to get us at any time and we must be ready. All right, Weency," I said, handing her my stick.

"You're not going out there alone. I'm going with you!" Eency said, following his sister out the door.

We watched from the side window in the drawing room. Weency and Eency moved cautiously, staying close to the side of the dollhouse so they would not be seen. When they reached the first hook and eye, it took both of them together to press it from below and pry it free. The metal hook hit Eency hard in the forehead when it popped up, and I saw him fall to the porch, stunned. He was up again quickly, rubbing the spot but he didn't seem to be harmed as he and Weency began climbing up to the second hook. Weency had my stick tucked in the belt of her dress, and she was holding on to the siding of the dollhouse with her claws, pulling herself up. She had a look of fierce concentration on her face and for a moment in my imagination—she was a brave pirate, her sword dangling at her side as she scaled the wall. Eency was right behind her with a lump on his head as big as a green pea.

"Do you think he's all right, Mrs. Chubbly?" Angel asked. "Look at the size of that lump!"

"He's still climbing—he must be fine for now, and there's nothing we can do about it until he's back in—I can't see them, let's go up," I said, dashing off to the stairs with Angel and the mousekins following behind me. We reached the upstairs bedroom window in time to see the twins stop and step out onto the second floor ledge. It was a thin beam of wood that stuck out just below the hook and eye, but they were mice, and they were agile, so we held our breath and watched in silence as they balanced on the ledge, holding onto the wall. Very slowly they made their way across it, a hair at a time, until they had positioned themselves close enough to reach the hook.

"You'll have better leverage from the other end," Eency told his sister.

"I can't get around you, Eence. Can you climb up on the hook? I'll try and cross beneath you," she said.

He looked up at the hook and saw that it was an impossibly awkward thing to do, but he had no choice—he just nodded and got his back leg up and then he gripped the metal bar with his paw—and Weency began pushing him up from behind, the look on her face said she thought that it was not a good idea that they were doing this at all. Just as she looked like she was about to tell him to get down, he found purchase with both hind legs and was half hanging off the hook, his tail dangling in mid-air, but he was holding on securely.

"Someone's coming!" I warned, listening to the thumping sound of human footsteps. Angel looked at me, her eyes wide.

"Eence, someone's coming!" Weency told her brother in a harsh whisper.

"Great Creator, you're right!" Eency answered, hearing the thumping sound growing closer. The two mice pressed themselves tightly against the wall and held their breath.

"Weency, what shall we do?" Eency asked his sister in a terrified squeal.

"We'll never make it down in time. Just be still, don't move, don't even breathe. If we're still perhaps that won't notice us" Weency answered.

I recognized the familiar sound of the steps. It was Mrs. Hammond. She was a heavyset woman and always wore practical shoes—and she was always showing up at the wrong time. The loud thumping sound grew closer—I could feel the vibrations in the dollhouse floor. Then the screen door to the house flew open and out stepped Chesterfield Cat beside the large ugly black shoes of Mrs. Hammond. In his mouth he held Mildly Fields, a terrified look on the poor field mouse's face, though I knew Chesterfield was taking great care not to hurt him and it was all just for show, but Mildly didn't know that.

"What a good kitty you are, Chesterfield. I'll fix you a nice bowl of cream," Mrs. Hammond said sweetly.

Then Chesterfield turned and spotted Eency and Weency hanging from the side of the house, and just that fast he dropped Mildly (who scurried away as quickly as he could), and turned and bit Mrs. Hammond on the ankle.

"Owwww! Why, you filthy little beast!" she screamed. Then she swatted Chesterfield right off the porch with the back of her hand and ran into the house, slamming the screen door behind her, yelling all the way, "Mr. Lovely, I've got rabies!"

Chesterfield licked at his sore end, then came back up on the porch to the dollhouse.

"What are you two doing?" he asked angrily.

"The house is locked shut and our bags are stuck inside. We were trying to open the latch," Weency answered, sheepishly.

"Fine, but you could've gotten us all into hot water. Couldn't you have waited for me?" Chesterfield asked. Not standing on ceremony, he plucked Eency and Weency off the wall with his mouth and deposited them at the tiny door. Then he raised his paw and with one swift "whack", the hook was opened and swinging freely.

"Now, to open this wall," he said, talking to himself. He tried to wedge his claws between the wall and the house, but it was shut too tight. "You'll have to get it started from the inside," he ordered.

We were downstairs in a flash and all of us had our paws in at the edge of the wall.

"On the count of three—everycreature push. One. Two. Three!" I said, and we began with all our might, to push against the heavy wall. There was a great deal of grunting and groaning, but it didn't want to budge.

Then Angel switched positions and got down squatting near the base of the wall and I took the top.

"Again! One. Two. Three!" Angel pushed ferociously, and inspired, we all followed her lead. Then we heard the squeak of the old hinges and the wall began to move. Chesterfield had his claws in it from the outside, as soon as we had opened a large enough crack, and between us we managed to swing it wide enough.

"Let's move! Mrs. Hammond will be out here after my hide," Chesterfield said, laying down flat.

Angel and I dragged the saddlebags out through the crack and managed with great difficulty to pull them across Chesterfield's neck. He raised his chin and I dashed below it to tie the bags on.

"Up his tail!" I shouted to Eency and Weency. And in a mad dash, the twins ran up and across his back and held on to his ears as they had done the night before. Angel had Lacey in her sling, and ran up next behind Weency. Then I grabbed my medicine bag and adjusted Mop in her sling, and I was behind Angel.

"Hold on for dear life, I'm going to make a run for it." Chesterfield shouted. Behind us we heard footsteps and voices from the stone house.

"Wait a minute, Mrs. Hammond, are you sure it wasn't a weasel?" Mr. Lovely said, laughing and teasing her.

"No! It was Chesterfield Cat! He bit me right here, I tell you!"

"Chesterfield is such a gentle kitty, he's never bitten anyone," Wendy said, pleading with her father.

Then we all dug in and held his fur, and it was just like flying, when he leapt through the air, down from the porch and dashed off into the gorse bushes and down the lane.

My heart was beating like a drum and I felt breathless. Mop was bobbing up and down shouting, "Wheeeeeeeeeeeee!" and I would have been laughing but for the horror stricken look on Angel's face.

"You see, my prayers were answered!" Eency shouted, his voice coming back to us on the wind. And Weency was laughing and holding on tight to her twin.

"Be careful what you pray for," she told her brother, "not all of us were looking for a wild adventure!" she said, looking back at Angel, who was now gritting her teeth, eyes closed tight against the swiftly passing scenery.

23. Chesterfield and Uncle Mak

Bibi Chubbly stood beneath the Weeping Willow, her feet planted firmly on the slippery rock at the edge of Babble Creek. The summer air was hot and still and she felt the coolness of the water bubbling behind her as she watched the sky colour with the last pink rays of the setting sun. She turned at last, and dipped the water thimbles into the rushing creek, then hung them, full and dripping, on the carrying stick that sat upon her strong shoulders. Carefully, she turned with her heavy load and began to walk up the hill toward the apple tree nest. Before she had gone three steps, she heard a great rushing in the bushes. A terrifying tramping sound of a large creature hurrying through the underbrush at great speed—coming right toward her.

Before she could take cover, he was upon her—his huge black face and gleaming green eyes eerie in the near darkness of the trees at the creek's edge. She felt her heart pounding in her chest as she thought, "Who will take care of Mak?" Then, she heard a familiar voice calling to her.

"Aunt Bibi—Aunt Bibi, is that you?"

I watched her face, confused, then delighted, as she looked beyond the huge cat and saw us sitting upon Chesterfield's back.

"Lacey?" she asked in disbelief, as the buckets slid from her shoulders, spilling water everywhere. Chesterfield stopped and lay flat down on the grass, and I slid off his back haunch onto the wet ground. I ran to her and we held each other. I could still feel her heart pounding wildly as we hugged.

"It's all right, Aunt Bibi. This is Chesterfield Cat, and he comes in peace as our protector." then I turned back to Chesterfield and reminded him in a quiet whisper, "Aho-Maste Chesterfield."

"Delighted to meet you, Aho-Maste" he said, as a comfort to her, gracefully extending his paw, in spite of the heavy saddlebags. "I've heard so many wonderful things about you."

"This is my Aunt Bibi, Chesterfield, mouselings, " I said, my arm around her shoulder. She was stunned and silent for a moment, never having met a cat before, but she recovered quickly and took his paw in her own, with some trepidation.

"Aho-Maste, How do you do? Lacey has written us and told us about you as well." Then she turned to me and whispered, "You almost burst my heart, dear one! I was sure my life here was about to be over. It's a good thing your Uncle Mak is back at the nest and wasn't here to have a cat come up behind him!"

Everycreature dismounted, Angel with Lacey on her back and Mop holding her paw, then Eency and Weency coming next behind her.

Chesterfield was still and thoughtful, he couldn't help but overhear Aunt Bibi's whispering.

"I'd be happy to wait here with the baggage—while you explain things to your Uncle," he said, kindly.

Mop was pulling on Aunt Bibi's apron, shouting.

"Bibibibi bibibibi!"

"You must be Mousekin Mop," Aunt Bibi said as she bent down close to Mop. Mop reached her arms up and Bibi swung her up onto her hip. Mop made herself right at home and rested her tired head on Aunt Bibi's shoulder. That was the sweet medicine she needed, a mouskin in her arms.

"Yes, Chesterfield," I answered the cat. "If you'll just give me a few moments to talk to my Uncle Mak, I'd truly appreciate it."

"Certainly Mrs. Chubbly—no trouble at all."

Then he trotted down to the edge of the creek and had a long drink of water. After his long run, he sorely needed it.

Bibi reached for the empty water buckets.

"Let me get that for you, Auntie," Angel said, taking the water thimbles. She went down to the creek and dipped them next to where Chesterfield was drinking, careful to bend at the knees for Lacey was still sleeping soundly in her sling.

"I'll come back down to get you, Chesterfield, as soon as Mrs. Chubbly smoothes the way," she said quietly.

"Thanks, Angel," he said, sounding rather sad.

"Are you all right, Ches?" she asked.

"Sure—fine, I'm fine. It was a long run," he answered, shifting the heavy saddlebags around his neck.

"That's a dirty hand you were dealt, Ches," Angel said, "Having to wait down here in the dark like a common criminal—after hauling us all the way up the creek on your back." Chesterfield stared at her, shocked.

"Dear, sweet Angel—wherever did you learn to talk like that?"

"Oh, Midnight would have a poker game in the back room of the cafe after we closed for the night," she said, embarrassed by her past. "Mother hated it. If it wasn't for the way he played piano, she never would have allowed it at all. I would just sit and watch him—I could watch him all night. Father called him a no-good rambling gambler, but I knew better, he had a good heart" she answered, her voice growing wistful.

"The guards played every night down at the animal shelter, a wild bunch they were. You miss him, don't you?" Chesterfield asked. She just shrugged.

"Sometimes, yes, I miss him. I always will. It's the not knowing that gets to me. I've got to go," she said, suddenly grabbing up the buckets and hurrying up the hillside.

Eency came and met her at the crest of the hill. He placed the carrying stick on his own shoulders and hung the full buckets there, then the two of them followed behind as Aunt Bibi led the others up the path to the apple tree.

"Your Uncle Mak is going to pinch those chubby cheeks of yours, Mousekin Mop, so you better get ready. He just loves little mousekins," Bibi went on cheerily, giving Mop's cheek a squeeze. "How was the trip down? Did you really ride all the way here on the back of that cat?"

"Not all the way from London. We drove down in the back of an automobile, then we rode on Chesterfield from the South Downs at the bottom of Babble Creek," I answered.

"Next you're going to tell me that the cat drove the automobile!" she said, laughing with disbelief.

"No, actually—Chesterfield sat in the back with all of us. Mr. Lovely drove the auto—but I'm sure Chesterfield could drive if he put his mind to it, he's a very remarkable cat," I said, smiling.

"Yes, he certainly is remarkable. And all of these experiences you are having, so unusual- it's almost like the whole world is changing very quickly and you are in the center of it all, Lacey."

"More than you know," I began. But Angel broke in.

"He saved my life! Why if it wasn't for Chesterfield Cat—"

Then Eency added, "I wouldn't be alive right now either—he saved me from being eaten by a hawk!"

"Really?" Bibi looked at me, shocked. I just placed my paw over me heart, the way I had always done as a mousekin— to show a promise. The way I had seen Aunt Bibi do so many times when she swore the truth. "Well then, I'm sure your Uncle Mak will be delighted to meet such a courageous cat." She took my paw and walked me up ahead of the others for a moment and whispered."But wasn't he the cat that made the mouselings orphans?" Before I could reply, the apple tree came into view and there was Uncle Mak, nervously pacing the porch.

"Bibi Chubbly, where have you been for so long, I was worried!" he shouted to her, then he saw me. "For peace sake—Lacey! Did you wash up out of the creek? We weren't expecting you till the morning!"

I ran into his arms and felt like a young mousette again as he enfolded me in his big strong arms and hugged me tenderly.

"Holy Mother Mouse! How I've missed you, Uncle," I said, holding him tighter.

"Not as much as I've missed you, dear heart," he said, his eyes shining with love.

In a flash the mouselings were upon him. He sat on the porch step and Bibi sat beside him. Mop climbed right into his lap and was pulling at his whiskers, and the twins were on either side, Weency clamored for his attention, asking a million questions.

"Angelvoice, let me look at you—your Aunt Bibi and I haven't seen your pretty face since you were knee high."

Angel blushed shyly, then Mousekin Lacey began to stir in her sling.

"Give that sweet little darling over to her Aunt Bibi, and rest your back a while, Angel," Bibi said, taking Lacey out of her sling. Lacey's eyes grew wide, seeing this new face for the first time, but Bibi was an old hand at comforting little ones and in a moment she had Lacey chortling and gurgling happily.

"Uncle, I need to talk to you alone. Just a minute, mousekins—then you can have him back," I said, walking a distance from the porch.

"Well, let's walk out into the herb garden and we'll talk there, Dear Heart," he said, taking my arm and turning round to the back of the apple tree.

"What's the secret, something you can't say in front of little ears?" Mak asked, as we stopped by the tiny purple flowers of the tall lobelia plants. The garden was in full bloom from the hot summer day and the scent of all the flowering herbs rose to greet me like an old familiar friend.

"No, not at all. There was just too much going on, and I wanted you all to myself," I said, rubbing my paw fondly over the fuzz on a large comfrey leaf. I broke off a smaller leaf and began to nibble on it.

"You don't fool me for a second, I know that look on your face- I can read you just like a book—so what is it, Dear Heart?" he asked, touching my face.

"I've got a friend waiting down by the creek. Aunt Bibi thought it best for me to explain, before I brought him to the nest," I said, trying to put my words in order.

`"Lacey, I can't imagine you leaving a friend down at the creek in the dark—unless of course you've brought us a fire breathing dragon, or a cat," He said, fooling with me.

"Yes, Uncle Mak, Chesterfield Cat—" I answered.

"The one from the letter?" he asked, surprised. "You've brought a cat to the nest?"

"No, actually—Chesterfield brought us to the nest, he carried us here on his back," I said. Uncle Mak stood quiet for a long time, looking too serious. I held my breath, waiting. Then he turned to me.

"Well, you better bring your friend up to the nest and feed him before he gets so hungry, he forgets his manners."

He smiled, and I was breathing again.

Bibi had taken everycreature inside, and put them all to work setting the table, stirring the stew and whipping up some sweet cream for the fresh apple pies that were cooling on the counter. Uncle Mak and I were sitting on the porch steps talking, when out of the tall grass came Chesterfield Cat, and

Angelvoice in front, leading the way. Uncle Mak stood up and extended his paw.

"Aho-Maste, You must be Chesterfield Cat. I've heard a lot of nice things about you," he said. Chesterfield sat down under the apple tree and touched his paw to Uncle Mak's.

"Aho-Maste Mr. Chubbly, I've heard so many nice things about you as well. It's a pleasure to meet anycreature that means so much to Mrs. Chubbly." Chesterfield answered him, gallantly.

"Well, I'd sure like to invite you in for dinner, but you won't fit through the door," He said chuckling. " I suppose you ought to call me Uncle Mak, it seems like we are family now." Then we were all laughing and the ice was broken.

"Why don't we picnic out here, then we can eat together," Angel suggested.

"It is a lovely night," I added.

"Good idea! I'll go tell your Aunt and the others." And Mak was inside in a moment, gathering mouselings and bowls of food.

Dinner was a smashing success. Uncle Mak made a huge bonfire, and Aunt Bibi set out a delicious picnic of acorn stew, wild gooseberries and large curds of paw made cottage cheese, straight from old Farmer Laughlin's cows. There was a large pot of milk set out for Chesterfield, and of course I gave him samples of all the fare.

After we were all satiated, we sat around the fire and traded stories of days gone by, while the mouselings, now fat and sleepy, roasted chestnuts and grains of corn, popping and cracking in the flames of the fire.

Mak had dragged the saddlebags into the nest earlier. And now Aunt Bibi excused herself to unpack our things and get us all settled in our rooms for the night, which left Chesterfield, Mak, and I to say our goodnights.

"You have a fine family Mrs. Chubbly, an honour to have dinner with you all," Chesterfield said, stifling a yawn.

"Thank you Chesterfield. And it has become finer since you have become part of it," I said, touching his nose lovingly.

"You know, young Tom—you're a most extraordinary cat. It has given me great pleasure to get to know you, you have exposed some of my prejudices and limitations and opened my mind. For that I am grateful" Uncle Mak said reaching once again to shake Chesterfield's paw. "It gives me a good feeling to know that you are looking after my Lacey, and all the little ones, when I'm not around."

"Thank you so much, Mr. Chubbly," Chesterfield began.

"Please, call me Uncle Mak," Mak said, smiling.

"Well, thank you, Uncle Mak," Chesterfield said shyly.

"It's getting rather late and Chesterfield—you have such a long way to go. Wouldn't you prefer to spend the night?" I asked him.

"It would be nice, but I must be getting back. Mrs. Hammond should be over her hysteria by now, and I don't want to arouse anyone further." Chesterfield answered, smiling.

"That was a fine story," Uncle Mak added, laughing. "'Specially the part where you turned and bit her on the ankle," he said, slapping his knee. "I do believe cousin Weaver would like to have that for one of her story books, you don't mind, do you, Chesterfield?"

"Actually I would be delighted to be immortalized as the cat that bit Mrs. Hammond to save the twins—I think it's a nice reflection on felines and might improve cat and mouse relations," he said thoughtfully.

"True, true," Uncle Mak said, stopping to draw on his pipe. "Do you ever take chamomile? It's very good for the digestion and the nervous system," Mak told him.

"No, no. I don't know that Mother would have approved. I don't mean to be rude, but I must be off." He said, rising and fluffing up.

`"Sure, I understand—well, you remember, my nest is open to you—you just drop by anytime."

Mak stood to see him off.

"Thank you Uncle Mak. It's a fine feeling to have family again—after being an orphan for so long."

"Well, now you have it, Son. Don't be a stranger—you get home safe."

Chesterfield walked off slowly into the tall grass. We watched for a long time as he disappeared down by the creek. Then we listened to the rustling of the underbrush and the padding of his paws as he began his journey back to the Lovely's house.

Uncle Mak put his arm around my shoulder.

"Only you, Dear Heart, could have crossed that uncrossable gap. Never thought I'd live to hear myself say this but it sure is nice to have a cat in the family. A very uncommon cat."

"Yes, a very uncommon cat," I answered.

24. Edmund and Annabelle

The days passed pleasantly for the Lovely family. They strolled together on the South Downs, just the three of them, walking and talking, making up for the lost years, getting to know each other again. Annabelle met with Doctor Gustave every afternoon, and they would spend an hour together alone in the library, talking. Sometimes she would come out wiping her tears, but they were a different kind of tears than the ones she cried alone all those years in the sewing room. After Wendy had gone up to bed, Annabelle would sit and talk to Edmund for hours in front of their cozy fireplace. She hadn't talked to him this way, so openly, so passionately, since they were first courting. And Edmund fell in love, once again, with his beautiful wife. It seemed she was coming back to life Like an ember hiding its glow under the grey ash, Life was fanning the flames of Annabelle Lovely and she was glowing.

Edmund woke that morning with stirrings of love he hadn't felt in many years. With an unbridled longing in his breast, he dressed quickly and went down to the kitchen to talk to Mrs. Hammond.

"Today I would like you to entertain Wendy, and set a luxurious picnic, with our finest wine, in the wicker hamper— just leave it on the porch with a nice large blanket," he added, almost winking.

"Yes, Mr. Lovely," Mrs. Hammond said, smiling. She had seen the glow of love return to Edmund's smile. She had seen Annabelle respond to his gentle touch with a girlish blush—and vicariously she delighted as she prepared their picnic.

"Just the two of us—" he said half to himself. "We'll probably be back quite late, quite late! The weather is perfect and I'd like to make a day of it." His eyes were twinkling and there was a blush of colour on his cheeks.

"Certainly, Mr. Lovely. You can count on me," the housekeeper said, curtsying.

"Oh, and please let Mrs. Lovely know I will be taking her on a picnic so she will dress appropriately," he added.

"Yes, Mr. Lovely, I'll take care of everything," she said, winking at Edmund brazenly, forgetting her place for the moment. But Edmund was feeling so marvelous—he hugged the frightened woman and then kissed her right on the forehead as if she were his dear mother!

"Oh! Sir!" she exclaimed, as she dashed off to the kitchen, embarrassed by his show of affection. Edmund fairly danced down the hall singing, so full of himself.

Annabelle Lovely dressed in a long cotton print summer dress. It was white and cool with a pale print of black eyed susans—their bright yellow petals and long green leaves making splashes of colour here and there. She covered her bare shoulders with a yellow angora cardigan—just in case the air should grow cool. She twirled around like a young girl, then stood looking in the mirror for a long time, staring at herself with a half smile. Picking up a brush, she began stroking her long auburn hair till it gleamed—then she tucked it up on top of her head in a loose twist.

She turned this way, then that—looking at her profile, making sure her hair was in place. Then she smiled broadly and said aloud in a throaty whisper "Annabelle Lovely—you look like a young girl going on her first date." Her cheeks were flushed red, with thoughts of her handsome lover, waiting to take her off to the lake. In the brief time they had been together again, she had fallen in love with him once more and he had awakened feelings in her that she had given up as long dead.

She ran her hands down her arms and across her belly. She felt warm and tingly all over, so alive!

"My God! I haven't felt alive like this in years—I suppose one doesn't know what one isn't feeling, until one begins to feel again."

Then she heard Edmund's voice calling from the stairs.

"I'll be right down, darling," she called. She slipped on a pair of white leather sandals, grabbed her purse and was out the door.

Her heart beat like the wings of a hummingbird when she saw him waiting there. His warm deep brown eyes welcomed her and his open smile shone with admiration. She wanted to run to him, to fall into his arms, but something in her was still afraid.

"You look beautiful, darling!" he said, as he helped her to the door. He could feel the warmth of her hand in his, and he longed to hold her in his arms, to have her touch his face. It had been so many years since he had felt her loving caress—and even in his dreams, he thought of no one but Annabelle.

Mrs. Hammond put Wendy to sleep at her usual hour, but sat up herself—waiting for the return of Mr. and Mrs. Lovely, just in case they should be needing anything, she told herself. But in reality she knew it was more for the satisfaction of her curiosity. All day she was imagining the two lovers—running down the heather covered hillsides, laughing gaily. Edmund chasing Annabelle—her beautiful Auburn hair flying behind her, sparkling in the sun as she ran. She imagined them swimming together in the crystal blue waters of Clear Lake, splashing like children. And then she imagined Edmund gathering Annabelle in his arms and kissing her, the water dripping off the impassioned pair.

She sighed deeply, remembering her own younger days, the passion she had felt! She saw it written plainly on their faces as they left this morning, alone, for the picnic. And had answered, embarrassed, when Wendy asked her "Where have they gone off to? Alone together? But why, Mrs. Hammond, why couldn't I go too?" she told the child, "You'll understand when you are older."

The door to the darkened house swung open suddenly, startling the old housekeeper out of her daydream. She had been sitting in the corner of the dark drawing room in a wingback chair—not near enough to the fire to be seen at all. And she watched silently from that dark place, as the couple tumbled breathlessly into the house, from too much wine and their wild afternoon on the downs.

"Annie," Edmund whispered tenderly—then he closed her in his arms and leaned her against the banister, kissing her passionately.

Annabelle took his hand and Mrs. Hammond watched as Mrs. Lovely led Edmund up the stairs—not pausing to say goodnight—but leading him to her room.

The door closed behind them. And to the sound of the young lovers laughing together behind the closed door, Mrs. Hammond tamped down the fire and went off to bed, smiling.

25. The Family Reunion

The morning of reunion week, everymouse was up well before dawn. Aunt Bibi, Angelvoice, Weency and I had been cooking for days in preparation for the festivities. Uncle Mak and Eency had been gathering and chopping wood, digging the outdoor cooking pits, and setting up the outdoor sleeping space for the dozens of relatives that would be arriving that day. Creatures came from miles around, not only the mice on all sides of the family—the Chubblys, the Smoothstones, the Sharpeyes, the Surepaws, the Fields, and countless other mice that I had never met, much less heard about—but there was Clatter Woodpecker and some other birds he had invited for good measure, Wiley Weasel, a squirrel family that Uncle Mak had doctored long ago, a very fat hedgehog that kept the grass short around the Apple Tree Nest, a group of Lemmings that had wandered in (and Aunt Bibi couldn't help but invite them to stay for lunch) and a family of Voles that had been borrowing books from the Chubbly library for so long that Aunt Bibi just naturally considered them family, for they loved to read so.

Angel hadn't mentioned Silver or Lily to anycreature, and she was just biding her time, waiting for one relative or another to come to her with some news of her parents or Midnight—she just couldn't give them up for lost, not till she was sure.

I was hard at work setting out the huge bowls of fresh fruit, and keeping one eye on Mop, who was getting into everything, and the other eye on little Lacey who was crawling round and round the bowls of fruit, dipping her paw in now and then to sample some.

"You're a sight for sore eyes," a deep voice bellowed from behind me.

"Papa Woody!" I said, wiping my fruit covered paws on my apron.

"Come on over here and let me give you a squeeze!" Woody grabbed me up and spun me in his arms.

Woody Chubbly was the largest mouse I had ever seen. Not just fat, because he loved to eat Sandy's cooking—but big and tall and strong, from working with wood all his life. It wasn't light work and it called for a big mouse to do it, so underneath his great form, he was solid muscle.

"Put me down! Put me down, Papa Woody—I've got work to do here if you want to have lunch today," I said playfully.

"Well, that's reason enough to put you down. Lacey Chubbly, I can't remember the last time I looked at your sweet face!" Then he called loudly over his shoulder. "Sandy! Come on over here and see who I've found."

"Lacey! Thank goodness you've come—Cats and kittens, Lacey! We haven't seen you in the longest time!" Again I was hugged and squeezed in the finest fashion.

"Mama Sandy, you look younger every time I see you," I looked at the wooden heart shaped locket that hung around her neck and reached out and touched it.

"Aunt Bibi drew this likeness of Tailbot for me when he was a young mouse, and Woody carved the locket for me after Tailbit died so I could have him with me always, close to my heart. Would you like to have it?"

"Oh I couldn't. I won't. He may have been my husband, but he was your first young one." I felt tears come and I saw that Sandy was crying too. " When we first fell in love, he told me the story of how you and Uncle Woody took him in, adopted him when his birth mother died in childbirth, at one of your very first labors. I'm sure he told me the story so I would know that

we weren't actually cousins. He was a very practical creature. "
I said, smiling. and Sandy laughed.

"Yes, that was my Tailbit. Always making sure
everything was in good order." She said opening the locket, as
we both gazed at handsome young Tailbit.

"He told me you were a young midwife and had no
mousekins of your own to love. It was an act of generosity from
The Great Creator. You must have told him his birth story many
times. Tailbit was a great gift to all of us. You gave him a safe
haven and raised him with so much love, that he became the
Creature I most loved. I haven't thought about how much I miss
him." I said wistfully. And then she smiled the same crooked
way Tailbit smiled, the corner of her mouth turning up on one
side, her eyes sparkling at me, and I began to cry again.

"Oh how I miss him!" I said to her. And she surrounded
me with her arms and held me against her bosom.

"I know, Dear Heart, I know as only a mother can—I
miss him every day, but I can't know how it is to miss him as a
wife."

I pressed my face against her and the tears just came and
came. All the tears I hadn't cried when I saw the snake behind
him. I had watched stone faced as the long ugly thing unlatched
its jaw and sprang—devouring Tailbit. One moment we were

walking together by the creek—the next moment he was gone And I stood by helplessly watching as my husband, my love, was taken out of my life in an instant, devoured by the hungry serpent. But I didn't cry. For a long time I didn't do anything. I just sat and thought. We had been so in love, so happy, and married such a short time. Aunt Bibi watched me sit silently all those months and one morning she just pronounced "You need mouselings to care for, that's the answer." I was shocked. What did she mean? I knew I would never marry again, I knew I would never have a litter of my own, never—not without Tailbit. She packed my things and sent me to Nanny for a nice couple with a large litter, and she was right. I did come out of it. But I never cried for Tailbit, until now.

Woody seemed relieved to see me crying. He patted me on my back and gave me his handkerchief. It smelled like fresh cut cedar.

"I'm fine, Mama Sandy, just fine. For a minute there," I whispered, looking away. "You looked just like him. It's funny how our little ones come to act and look just like us - even if we don't actually birth them"

"I know it, Lacey, I see it every time I look at her smile," Woody said sadly. "But an ocean of tears won't bring him back—now don't you Elders have some work to do?" he asked us.

"I'm going off to help Mak get the fires going—you keep that hankie, it takes a lot of tears to mend a broken heart."

And then he was gone in the crowd. Sandy went in to get some fabric for the picnic area. And I turned and saw Angel watching me, while she nursed Lacey on the front porch. She tucked the sleeping mousekin into her sling and came over.

"You all right, cousin?" she asked, a paw on my shoulder.

"That was Woody and Sandy, Tailbit's parents. He was my husband," I said sadly, looking into the young mousette's eyes.

"I know, I heard. You must have loved each other very much."

"Yes, very much. And we were so young, only 18." I turned back to my work, then stopped. "You know Angel, after Tailbit died I vowed I would never marry again, never love like that again, but I was wrong. I'm old now, but you are very young and very beautiful—you have your whole life ahead of you." Angel shifted about uncomfortable, knowing what I was going to say next.

"Angel, I can see the hurt in your eyes, I know how you loved Midnight and how unresolved it is for you to not know what became of him—at least The Great Creator gave you his mousekin, that's something you will always have, a part of him. But she'll grow up and she'll go off and have a life of her own. You must never do what I have done—you must love again. Midnight would want that for you."

She shook her head and turned away silent, then she walked off.

As the day grew into afternoon the party was in full swing. The sky became overcast but it was warm and we all prayed that the sun would shine on us and not ruin our party with a storm. Our prayers were answered, and every time a huge thunderhead would appear in the sky, it would soon roll off into the distance without shedding a drop on us.

The sound of chattering was deafening. Elders and mousekins that hadn't seen each other in a good many years were making up for lost time. There was a lot of eating and drinking and Cat Tales told that even the tellers themselves found hard to believe. Tailbit's sister Weaver, stole the show.

She had every mouseling and mousekin that could walk or crawl surrounding her, and there were dozens of them! She kept them riveted in their seats all afternoon as she told them tales of adventure and love. They thronged about her and wouldn't let her go to eat, so I brought her some food. But they yelled, "more Auntie Weaver! Tell us about the pirate cats!" And between nibbles of cheese and nuts, she was captor and captive and went on with her stories in her beautiful clear voice. I hadn't seen Angel all day, then I noticed that Lacey was in her sling on Aunt Bibi's back. And I wondered if in my passion I had said the wrong thing to the young mousette.

Uncle Mak kept going up to the top of the nest, his paw keeping the sun out of his eyes as he searched the horizon, looking for Great-Great Grandfather Sage and Great-Great Grandmother Crystal. They had written that they would come, and the whole family had gathered, not just for the reunion— but for the opportunity to see the great patriarch of the Chubbly family on the event of his one hundred and twenty fifth birthday.

I was just going over to ask Aunt Bibi about Angel, when the sky split open. The rain came down suddenly, pelting everycreature with large warm drops. The younger mice began to scatter, running for cover, but the Aunts and Grandmothers first stopped to cover the food, always thinking practically. I scooped up Mop and had her on my hip, and called to the twins to follow me as I dashed into the apple tree nest.

"Where is Angel?" I asked them. "This is quite a downpour." But they just shook their heads. No one had seen her in hours.

26. Lancelot Goldentop

own at the creek, Angel was surprised by the sudden spring shower. She didn't flee, she didn't want to go back to the noisy crowd of creatures up on the hill. She waited, lost in her own thoughts, watching the sun pouring long filmy rays down through the dark clouds. She was certain the rain would end as suddenly as it had begun, and she was too relaxed, dipping her feet into the cold bubbling water of Babble Creek, to think about running for cover.

Behind the thick willow tree that hung over Angel like an umbrella of green lace, Lancelot Goldentop stood, silent. He was staring at the beautiful young mousette with the silver headlock and the gleaming white fur. Her eyes were dark and far away and he longed to know what she was thinking. He watched the way the sun streamed down on her from between the willow leaves, the way she smiled and sighed when the tumultuous water tickled her feet, the way her sad eyes shone bright when she looked up to catch a drop of warm rain in her open mouth. His heart was captured, and he gladly surrendered. She took his breath away.

Then the two, unbeknownst to each other, turned together and watched in awe as a huge rainbow spread its colours across the summer sky.

"Beautiful!" they gasped, together.

Shocked to hear another voice, Angel turned to see Lance, looking into the sky from behind the willow tree. She was about to shout at him angrily—after all—he was invading her privacy—spying on her, no less! But when she looked at him, her voice was frozen and she found she couldn't say a thing.

His handsome face glowed with such abandoned joyfulness, his smile so bright, so innocent, as he looked upon the vastness of the brilliant rainbow displayed before him. She had never before seen a mouse so gallant, so handsome—his eyes were a strange azure blue—the colour of twilight, she thought. Not green like her family, but strange and lovely. His fur was a pale tawny brown and smooth, and his headlock was a mass of golden curls, he was so different from Midnight— different like night and day.

"Oh, my," was all she could utter.

"Beautiful," he said to her, leaning forward from his hiding place. She blushed, knowing he didn't mean the rainbow.

His shyness melted away, as if it never existed—and then he was beside her on the slippery river rock. The rain had turned into a light drizzle and neither of the creatures noticed it at all.

Lance extended his paw in greeting. "Lancelot Goldentop." he said warmly.

"Angelvoice Smoothstone," she said, demurely extending her paw. Instead of shaking her paw, as he had always done—something in her eyes moved him. He raised her paw to his lips and kissed it lightly, holding it there a moment too long for propriety. Then his feet gave way on the slippery rock and he found himself up to his ears in Babble Creek, sputtering and thrashing about very unromantically.

Angel moved fast. She jumped in and grabbed a hold of him, pulling him back toward the bank, out of the furiously rushing current. They both stood unable to move, up to their knees in the cold rushing water, pressed tightly together, unable to breath—and their eyes were riveted for one fierce moment.

"Oh," she said again, breaking away from his arms and climbing out onto the rock. He was beside her and he wiped the water from her face and smoothed her headlock back away from her large green eyes.

"I believe you saved my life!" he said, softly, meaning more than she could imagine.

"Oh," she said again, breathing heavily from the adrenaline and from the accidental embrace.

"Is that all you can say?" he asked her, smiling "Cat got your tongue?" he said playfully. He felt a coolness of manner rise in him that he had long since forgotten. Suddenly, though he was dripping wet and she had just pulled him out of the creek, he felt quite in command.

"I've got to go," she said, feeling suddenly frightened. She was falling in love with a stranger! She didn't know who he was, she just knew that her heart was pounding wildly, she knew how she felt when he took her paw in his—and she knew that she was betraying Midnight—if he was even still alive. She rose to leave.

"Wait!" He grabbed her paw. "Don't go! Not yet."

She turned back to him and his clear blue eyes held her there. Then she was in his arms and he kissed her. There was nothing she could do, nothing she wanted to do. And she heard Mrs. Chubbly's words in her head "You must love again." And so she did.

27. The Great Prophecy

I spent the morning working with Papa Woody and Weency setting up a canopy to keep great-great-grandparents Sage and Crystal from having to sit all day out in the hot sun. Woody built the sturdy frame from WIllow branches. Weency and I hung it with scraps of flowing white chiffon.

"It's too plain," I said, standing back looking at the white form. "What colour did Bibi use on the cake?" I asked Weency.

"Purple rosettes and white frosting," she answered.

"Well let's get some heather and dress it up a bit It'll match the cake nicely when we're through."

We walked into the field and came back with more heather than we could possibly use. Weency tied sprigs of the purple heather into bundles, carefully making a bow out of each white satin ribbon strip. Then I hung them in place around the border of the canopy. The rest of the heather was spread around the two chairs that sat beneath the canopy. When we had finished, it looked breathtakingly beautiful and the whole area was scented with the heady smell of freshly cut heather.

The Grand Mousetriarchs sat under the canopy holding court. They were surrounded by young ones—and there was an endless line of family and friends ending in front of the dramatic canopy. Some waited to pay respects to Great-Great Grandfather Sage, on the occasion of his one hundred and twenty fifth birthday, others to ask him a question about family history. Some of the mice were waiting in that long line to ask Great-Great Grandmother Crystal to gaze into their future. It was common knowledge in the family that Mousetriarch Crystal had the gift of vision. She was a Seer. She could see the future clearly, and sometimes, when asked, she would tell all—but not always.

Angel and Lance stood together in line holding paws and talking animatedly. I had seen little of Angel during the last week, and Curly Goldentop had complained to me more than once that Lance was never around the nest when she needed him. It was easy enough to put one and one together and get two young mousekins, spending all their time together, getting to know each other, and falling in love. It was obvious to anycreature who looked at the pair and saw the way they looked at each other—I didn't need the gift of vision to see into their future.

Eency was next in line. He was fidgeting nervously and kept turning to his twin, who stood right behind him waiting her turn calmly, an earnest look of concentration on her face. Weency was so focused on her own thoughts that she didn't even notice Angel behind her.

"I am Eency Twingle," Eency said as he bowed formally, "I'd like to wish you a very happy birthday, Grand Patriarch Sage."

"Come closer young mousekin, let me have a look at you."

The elderly patriarch surprised Eency by reaching for him and pulling him into his lap. "You're a fine looking young mouse! You're my Granddaughter Lacey's charge, aren't you?" he asked, his widened eyes looking deep into Eency's.

"Yes sir, she's my Nanny," he answered, relaxing into Sage's arms. The elder mouse ran his paw through Eency's headlock. No mouse had done that since his mother was gone and Eency felt a strong feeling of affection rise in him for the old mouse.

"Crystal," he commanded, "Take a look at Eency Twingle. Do you see something in this fine mouseling's future?"

Crystal smiled at Eency and then her eyes grew clouded. She sat for a moment nodding her head as if in silent conversation. She looked dark and serious, and then she was smiling again. Sage knew her expressions well, well enough to know that she was indeed watching Eency's future unfold before her. But she did not speak. She would not tell him that he was to be a great inventor, she would not say that he would spend the next 10 years of his life sequestered in his father's workshop night and day working to hone his mechanical genius. She could not, because it was all precipitated by a tragic separation from his twin sister Weency. She knew that the agony of the separation would drive him inward in anger and pain to find his own way, to press him hard, like a lump of coal becoming a diamond, to hone him like a sword in the fires of pain and loneliness and would give him the courage and strength he needed to become a powerful leader. She knew that the immense gifts and strengths that would come out of his desolation would be exactly what he would need. And she knew that there were some things best left unsaid.

"I can tell you nothing specific, Mousekin, but be assured that you will have a great life, a good long life."

Then she was silent. Sage knew that she would not say, and he knew why. He looked at Eency sadly for a moment.

"You come and eat my birthday cake with me, Mouseling, I'll be waiting for you."

"It would be an honour, sir," Eency said, getting up to go. Eency came to me through the crowd, working his way around all the little ones, stepping over picnickers. Then he just looked at me, as if I would have the answer.

"It's all right, Eency. Sometimes it's best to just let the future unfold. A little knowledge is a dangerous thing," I told him putting my arm around his shoulder. I myself have never stood before Grandmother Crystal officially—I've never wanted to.

"Grand Patriarch Sage—I am Weency Twingle, and though we are not related—your Granddaughter Lacey Chubbly is my Nanny. I just wanted to tell you how happy I am to be able to be here for your birthday. Happy Birthday!"

He took her paw in his and pulled her toward him. offering his cheek.

"Give us a birthday kiss, Mousette," he said, his eyes wrinkling into a smile. "Best birthday present an old mouse like me can get!" he said, teasing her.

"You're wrong—" Crystal said to her, catching her by surprise. The great matriarch turned her head to one side, a strange expression on her face. "You are indeed our relation—

your Great Grandfather, Tick Tock Twingle ran off and married Matilda Golightly. Matilda is your nanny's Aunt Tillie, and that makes you our cousin—by marriage of course."

I was quite surprised to hear this, although I had an inkling about it when I found the book. So, that is how the manuscript came to be in the Twingle family library—and that's what happened to crazy Aunt Tillie! How appropriate.

"Oh, thank you Grand Mousetriarch. I'm very happy to know that. Thank you!" Weency turned to leave.

"Wait... Weency Twingle—I see your future very clearly—" Weency turned back and stood silent before Crystal, her paws folded in front of her, expectantly. Everycreature grew silent, waiting for the Grand Visionary to speak again. Crystal closed her eyes in concentration, she breathed a deep raspy breath and then opened her eyes suddenly.

"I see! Hmmm, but I don't quite understand this. Strange. Weency Twingle. Weency Twingle. Weency Twingle " she faltered, turning her head this way and that, searching with her eyes.

"What? What do you see? " Weency asked, now desperate to know.

"I see you flying through the air in a strange metal machine." the noise of the crowd came up in a long "Ohhhhhh" Everycreature said it in unison.

"It is a bird! A metal bird—shining silver in the sun, a copper crest on its head!" she continued.

"Ohhhh!" the crowd spoke again, in awe as she went on.

"No, no- that's Impossible! I am not even 11, you must be mistaken!" Weency shouted into the crowd. She interrupted Crystal out of sheer terror. She was so shocked to hear the vision that Crystal had of her future. And the crowd was silenced and in shock. No creature had ever interrupted Crystal before. It was an honour to just stand before her.

Grand Mousetriarch Crystal opened her eyes and smiled at Weency, kindly.

"Of course – a reluctant Messenger. Quite common in the history of all creatures. All Saviours and Messengers have shock or disbelief at first. Some times for many years, but The Great Creator has a path for each of us and the path always unfolds in the end. And the name Weency Twingle will be recorded in the sacred books. And the name Weency Twingle will be spoken aloud by creatures with great hope. They will await the arrival of Weency Twingle. " she said with a smile.

"Some creatures walk gracefully along their path, and others go kicking and screaming."

"Messenger?? Savior? Books? What are you even saying? I am a mousekin, just – me! I don't understand." Weency said, looking confused and frightened, her eyes began searching the crowd for Mrs. Chubbly.

Crystal reached out and took Weency's paws in her own. Something about the connection calmed the young mouse and she stood still looking into the eyes of the Seer, comforted by her touch.

Crystal began to breathe deeply again as she held Weency's paws.

"There are others with you. Others who are assisting you. Some who are in your care. But you! Weency Twingle! You are controlling the machine, guiding it through the sky! You are far, far away from here—traveling faster than you can now know, soaring through the air and through the barriers of space and time."

The crowd had gathered more tightly around the canopy. Every creature wanted to hear, for a revelation like this had not been spoken aloud in many years.

"In a far away land, over strange mountain peaks you will soar, beside you there is a bird of flesh and blood. He flies beside you like a guardian, a friend, a helper." Crystal grew silent for a moment. The crowd now lost its propriety and shouted:

"More! Tell us more!"

Crystal squinted her eyes, as if to get a better picture.

"Ahhh!" she exclaimed, her face shining with an ethereal glow. "You will save the lives of many, many creatures, a great healer!"

"Me?" Weency asked, badly shaken by all that she heard.

"Yes, Little One—you. You are a Messenger of The Great Creator and a great adventurer. You will travel through all of space and time in a way that we do not now understand – but that is what I see, and that is what you will do"

And then Crystal's eyes grew wide and excited. "You, Weency Twingle, are the one we have waited for, the one to find the Spring of Life and set things in order for all creatures and for all of creation!" she announced, ceremoniously.

The voice of the crowd rose in a thunderous cheer— "Hurrah!"

"Wonderful! Wonderful!" Grand Patriarch Sage exclaimed, delight showing in his ancient eyes. He reached for

Weency's paw and gave it an affectionate squeeze, "I am honoured to know you, Weency Twingle. " he said seriously. And with that she felt the power of the moment settle heavily on her.

"But I..." she started.

"Silence, Mousette!" Crystal said in a firm voice. "It is best to meditate on these things you have heard—before you speak your questions aloud. Our future rests in your paws. Meditate long and often, Little One. That is your greatest hope. And I pray this brings you the clarity and connection that this monumental future requires. However, you must remember, the things I see—the things I speak are merely a shadow of the future, a possibility that exists before you—and you must be thoughtful, you must always choose wisely, for if you falter— this will not come to pass."

"I will," Weency said quietly. "I will choose wisely and thoughtfully, and if The Great Creator is willing—I will find the Spring of Life!" She said, trying to sound self assured, but she was frightened and thought she might faint. All eyes were on her now. Every creature watched her in awe. Weency felt the immense weight of Crystal's prophecy on her tiny young body. She steadied herself. She wiggled her toes, took a deep breath and felt the grass and the solid earth beneath her feet, the way

Mrs. Chubbly had showed her, and thought to comfort herself, "In this moment all I have to do is breathe and trust The Great Creator, and not faint.The rest will unfold before me."

"I hope that I will live to see that day. We have all waited so long," Grand Patriarch Sage told her.

"You will, you will, my dear," Crystal said to him, with absolute assurance.

I knew that Weency would come to me. I knew what my role would be. In time, I would have to teach her all the ancient tales, the Rodent Mythology of the Spring of Life. I would show her the books, take her through Aunt Bibi's library. She would need to know all that has ever been told, all that has ever been recorded—and armed with this, I prayed that she would indeed choose wisely.

28. The Announcement

Ency and I moved closer, as Angel and Lance approached the Grand Mousetriarchs, paw in paw. Crystal looked at them and then looked over at Sage who smiled at her—a knowing smile. Then she stared at the couple, gathering her words. She began to speak before either of them could utter a word of greeting.

"Congratulations!" Crystal said, brightly. Then she turned back to Sage. "These two are to be married—here—today!"

Once again the crowd rose up in a cheer. "Hurrah!" They shouted and there were many creatures offering congratulations to the pair, whose love was quite apparent.

"It will be a good marriage, a bond of love and trust—you two will have a happy long life together—and many, many mouselings."

Angel looked at Lance and he smiled at her. Then they turned to the crowd and he kissed her cheek.

"Hurrah!" The crowd roared.

"Happy long life!" They screamed.

"And many mouselings," I thought to myself, "How nice for them! Angel is a wonderful mother and I know that Lancelot will be an excellent provider."

"Will they come live in our nest?" Eency asked me in a whisper.

"I certainly hope so, Eency. We'll have to invite them."

Grand Patriarch Sage stood between the pair and took Angel and Lance by their paws. He raised their paws in the air and then he joined them together.

"I will perform the ceremony," Sage announced to the crowd. "This will be a very special birthday celebration indeed!"

Crystal rose from her seat and stood beside Angel, her paw on the mousettes shoulder. The crowd grew quiet.

"In the great tradition of our family, and of all rodents from the time that rodent history has been recorded by our foremothers—Angelvoice Smoothstone and Lancelot Goldentop will become one at the moment that the sun is setting upon the horizon, here beneath this white canopy—to signify the purity and innocence of their love. Beneath these heather flowers—to signify the sweetness of their life to come," Crystal continued, smiling broadly at the couple. "Yes, at the hour the sun sets—to signify the ending of the lives they knew and the beginning of their new life together, and by the paw of our Grand Patriarch, who will officiate the ceremony. It is the law—as I have spoken it."

Crystal and Sage nodded together in agreement. And the crowd rose once more in a thundering cheer so loud that Eency covered his ears with his paws. Then the female elders and the mousettes took Angelvoice away to prepare her for her forthcoming wedding, and the males took Lancelot off in another direction—for the two must not see each other until the moment the sun is setting.

Weency stood aside, watching in silence, her mind on more weighty matters. I went to her then, knowing she needed an elder to guide her.

"Why aren't you preparing Angel for the wedding?" She asked.

"There are many here who can do that for Angel. Bibi is an old paw at it—and her Grandmother Myra will take the place of Lily. This is my time to be with you, Weency, it is my calling, and from all the things that Grandma Crystal spoke—you must begin your work right away." Then I took her paw and led her to the apple tree nest, and she followed behind me up the winding stairs, to the library.

29. The Wedding

T he sun moved slowly toward the horizon, filling the sky above the endless green cornfield with splashes of rose and amber.

Angelvoice sat as still as she could, nervous as she was, while the elders stitched the last bit of paw-made lace to the end of her bridal train. Once again she began fidgeting in her seat.

"Be still, Dear—you must be still!" Bibi told her as she fixed a sprig of heather behind Angel's ear.

"I'm trying, Aunt Bibi," she said, moving about to adjust the heavy lace dress. "But this dress weighs at least ten stones."

"Hush, Dear!" Bibi whispered, embarrassed. "This dress belongs to Grand Matriarch Crystal—you should be honoured."

"Oh, I am," Angel answered politely. Then she sighed heavily. She was hot and nervous, and weighed down by the layers upon layers of heavy cotton lace.

"There!" Aunt Myra said, as she tied a knot in her thread and tore off the loose end. "All done."

Bibi helped Angel to her feet and spun her around for all to see. There was a chorus of "Ohhh's" and "Ahhh's". She did look breathtaking—with her gleaming white fur and the floor length lace layered gown, with her white lace train held out behind her by Lancelot's pretty little sister Gwenavere.

Lancelot wouldn't let the elders dress him.

"I always dress myself," he stated flatly.

"But Lancelot—it is an age old custom! After today you can dress yourself for the rest of your life." Grandpa Chip tried to convince him. Lance had just finished tying up the collar of his white lace shirt, himself.

"Oh, all right," he said pulling out the string. "There, you do it."

Grandpa Chip retied it, expertly. All the males ignored his mood, each of them remembering how nervous they were on their wedding day. Lance stood still while Uncle Mak slipped the black silk jacket on to his waiting arms. Then Woody tied on the white lace cuffs and even got so personal as to adjust Lancelot's tail into its proper place between the back flaps of the long black coat.

Crystal Chubbly stood behind the canopy watching the sun.

"Now!" she said. Sage rose from his seat beneath the canopy and in a booming voice he announced:

"All creatures far and wide

Free yourselves from whence you hide,

Gather all before me, now,

To hear the sacred marriage vow.

The sun is falling ever fast,

The wedding time has come at last!"

Hearing the call, all of the waiting creatures appeared from every corner. From the cornfield, from the farm, from the orchard and from the creek they came. Dozens and dozens of mice and moles, squirrels and voles, lemmings and birds, walking slowly toward the canopy. Then as the crowd settled down to the right and to the left, each finding a seat in the grass, Lancelot emerged being led by Eency and Angelvoice being led by Weency. They were brought forth at opposite ends of the crowd. There they stood still, majestic in their finery and their eyes were covered by sashes of rose coloured silk, lest they should see each other before they were joined as one. Crystal took her place beside Sage, as witness to the vows.

"Come forward, two to be made one,

And stand before the setting sun."

Sage spoke the ancient words, his voice strong and sure. Weency and Eency led the bride and groom toward the center of the seated crowd, and as they passed, the multitude of creatures tossed heather blossoms at their feet and the sweet smell filled the dusk air.

I sat in the front row at the base of the canopy—for it was my place to present Angel's paw to Lancelot at the appropriate moment, and as I waited, I felt as if I was truly giving away my daughter—we had grown so close in our short time together.

Curly Goldentop sat near me, softly weeping from joy and sadness. How long she had waited for this moment—never thinking what it might mean.

"Who gives this bachelor mouse away

On this sublime, auspicious day?"

Sage called out, dramatically looking over the crowd in mimicked searching.

Curly stood, wiping her eyes and raised her right paw above her head.

"Tis I, the Birthgiver, I the one,

Do now release my eldest son."

Her voice broke as she recited. She walked up to the canopy and stood in front of the Great Patriarch, as he continued,

"Who gives this mousette's paw away,

On this sublime, auspicious day?"

Once again Sage dramatically searched the crowd.

I rose from my place and stood tall, raising my right paw above my head.

" Wait! " Crystal shouted. The crowd began a murmuring. "What is this? " they whispered. " What is happening? ", "This isn't part of the ancient ceremony."

"Silence," Crystal commanded, and the multitude obeyed and fell silent. Sage turned to his wife, but said nothing. She stood there, her eyes burning with unspoken knowledge, searching over the heads of all the creatures.

"We must wait—some creature is coming," she announced, raising her paws high above her head to keep the crowd locked into silence.

Scores of creatures began turning their heads, this way and that, craning their necks, searching, waiting. Then—in the distance—they all heard it.

Everycreature grew still and perked up their ears.

The August wind blew warm and gentle over the crowd, and it carried a high sweet lilting song. It became louder, it grew near, then it was just behind them, floating over the crowd, lulling all the listeners peacefully, with its mournful sweetness.

The blood drained from Angel's face as she heard the ghostly song.

"Lily!" she cried out, as she fell faint into Weency's arms. I broke protocol and went running through the crowd to Angel. As she came to, I turned her toward the tall river grass and pulled the sash from her eyes.

Out of the tall waving river grass, Lily appeared like an apparition, pale and wan. Her long blue dress now torn into flowing shreds from traveling hungry, tired and alone on foot and paw, so many miles to reach the apple tree nest and her family—her silver headlock was blowing around her in the wind. She saw the crowd and stopped singing mid-note, her mouth agape in a silent scream of shock when her eyes fell upon her daughter, Angelvoice, alive and beautiful.

They ran toward each other, unbridled—and wrapped in each other's arms, laughing and crying, they turned and turned in a strange dance of love—for each believed the other long dead.

"Cover the mousette's eyes!" Crystal commanded calmly.

Lily looked around, and realized she had arrived at her daughters wedding. I handed her the silk sash, as it was truly her place. As Lily tied the sash over Angel's eyes, she looked over at the handsome bachelor mouse, who had respectfully turned his head away—though his eyes were still covered.

"Do you love him, Angel?" she asked her daughter.

"Yes, Mother—more than I ever believed possible."

"And does he love you?" she asked again.

"I believe he does. I can feel it in my heart." And although the two creatures had only just met, she knew he was her destiny and she answered with certainty. Lily walked Angel back to her place beside Weency.

"You look lovely, darling—thank The Great Creator he spared your life." Then I took Lily by the arm and together we walked the long aisle down to the canopy.

"Now." Crystal told Sage, as she looked at the sun—its last rays bursting across the sky, illuminating the underside of the purple clouds with a silver glow. The crowd sat in a slowly darkening shadow. One by one, they began to light the candles that they held in their paws and their talons. And the darkness came to life, filled with the tiny sparkling candle-flames, like a thousand fireflies flickering and hovering before the sacred canopy.

"Who gives this mousette's paw away,

on this sublime, auspicious day?"

Sage intoned once again. Lily raised her right paw above her head, as she had seen her own mother do on her wedding day, then she looked back at Angel one last time—and her heart filled with hope for the young mouse's future. Grandmousekins—she thought, and then she spoke the ancient words.

"Tis I, the Birthgiver, by the law,

do now release my daughter's paw."

Crystal began the chant, and slowly the voices of the multitude joined in, gathering momentum—then all were swaying in time to the rhythmic chant.

"Peace within, and love enough,

to fill each waiting heart.

Together forever, two be one.

And they shall never part."

Over and over, they chanted, some in high voices, others in deep warm voices. And in the swelling harmony of good wishes—Eency and Weency led the betrothed couple down the long aisle. Step by step, moving in time to the rising and falling chant, Angel and Lancelot approached their destiny. When they reached the canopy, Sage raised his paws as a sign, and the crowd grew suddenly still.

Weency and Eency came over and sat beside me, both of them enthralled by the ceremonious rite of passage. Lily stepped forward and took her place, then Curly and Lily each held the left paw of their offspring as Sage asked the long awaited question.

"Do you, Lancelot Goldentop, love Angelvoice Smoothstone, with the fullness of your heart?

"Do you promise to respect her dreams and her visions, protect her from harm, gather for her offspring, and give yourself in this bond of love, completely?"

"I do," Lancelot answered quickly.

"Do you, Angelvoice Smoothstone, love Lancelot Goldentop, with the fullness of your heart?

"Do you promise to respect his dreams and visions, to nurture and care for him and his offspring, and give yourself in this bond of love, completely?"

There was a moment of silence. Angel's mind raced—to the cafe—to Midnight, her dark renegade lover—to Lacey, sleeping silently in Aunt Bibi's lap, then to Lancelot hiding behind the willow tree in the rain. Her silence caused a palpable tremor to move through the crowd as each creature waited, with great apprehension. Lancelot held his breath, a look of anguish on his face.

"I do," she spoke, at last.

Sage motioned to Curly and Lily. The two mothers joined Angel and Lance's left paws together. Then Lancelot reached out and took Angel's other paw, tenderly. As Sage began to speak, Lily and Curly untied the silken eye covers and let them fall away, and the two lovers gazed undaunted, into each other's eyes.

"By the power of The Great Creator,

"As the Mousetriarch of all the generations which stand before me—as witness to this holy act—I now commit that these two hearts are joined as one.

"In gladness and sadness,

In times of plenty and times of hardships,

Through all the lessons of life The Great Creator provides—

Till death do you part,

And your spirits become one again with All.

What The Great Creator has bound in love,

Let no creature tear asunder.

I now pronounce you Husband and Wife."

The crowd stood with a mighty cheer, candles raised high above their heads. Many were openly crying with great joy—as Lancelot Goldentop kissed Angelvoice Smoothstone Goldentop, his wife.

I was watching Lily. Her eyes sparkled with the swelling happiness she felt, and I thanked The Great Creator for the timeliness of their reunion. Then a curious thing happened—

Angel pulled the sprig of heather from her headlock, and as was the custom, she tossed it high into the air.

Every mousette reached out her paw to catch the falling flowers, longing to be the next to stand before the canopy with their right mate. But the wind caught the sprig of heather up and up. It sailed through the air and landed neatly on the collar of my dress. Every head turned, every face filled with surprise, as all witnessed this strange act of providence. My thoughts flew to my own wedding, held on this very same spot—and I saw the handsome face of Tailbit Chubbly as he moved to kiss me. Then

I was once again looking at Angel and Lancelot. The words I had spoken to her just two weeks earlier came back to me unbidden, "You must love again!" I told her, that day. And now she had become the teacher and I the student.

I turned my head to smell the sweet heather, caught magically in the lace. Perhaps someday, I will love again.

30. Wendy's Surprise

The second Winter came hard with a freezing snow that transformed the Lovely's garden into a gleaming fairyland of ice-covered trees and snow drifts frozen into curling waves.

By then, my growing family was long settled into the warm, safe Chelsea nest. Lily was always singing happily to herself as she puttered around the kitchen, and cared for Angelvoice, who was now mid-way along carrying Lancelot's first litter. And from the looks of her, it was going to be a large brood!

Angel and Lance, by family vote, took over the Twingle's master bedroom. Lily moved into Angel's bed in the nursery and had taken charge of the mousekins.

I found myself with plenty of time on my paws and I spent every free moment preparing Weency for the years of study to come, teaching her herbal healing and meditation, readying her for the future foretold in Crystal's revelation.

Wendy had begun her lessons again, as soon as we had returned from Sussex, and her new tutor kept the child hard at her books. We rarely saw her, though we always found food and presents in the entryhole, and always before anything was needed.

Lily had just finished washing the dinner dishes, and I had dried the last red clay bowl and placed it on the stack in the dish cupboard. The water was hissing and boiling in the thimble pot hanging over the fire.

"Ahhh, tea water's ready. This is my favorite time for a cup of tea," I said, filling the red clay pot with chamomile leaves. " The mouselings are asleep, Angel and Lance are off in their room—probably thinking of names for the mousekins to come." I said, ladling the steaming water into the pot and setting it to steep on the table.

"Well, they still have lots of time to go, plenty of time to think of new names—how many do you think they'll have?" Lily asked, drying her paws on her apron.

"I examined her yesterday... it's still quite early to be sure, but it feels like she'll have at least four—maybe five—and they're all large for only a few months along." I said, happy that Angel was doing so well. I remembered how difficult her last birth had been—and how tiny Lacey was when I pulled her out of the sack. I knew this time it would be an easy birth—and the mousekins would probably be healthy. I had kept Angel on a strict regimen of daily exercise, healthy food, regular naps and meditation, and plenty of herbal drinks to get her back to perfect health before the big event. And this time, her mother and her husband would be with her. Every midwife knows that the outcome of the birth depends more on the thoughts and feelings of the birthing mother than on anything else, but—I wasn't taking any chances.

"Would you like a nice hot cup of tea? It will help you sleep," I said.

"Cousin Lacey, I'm so exhausted from chasing Mop and Mousekin Lacey all day—nothing could keep me from sleeping. No, not tonight. I'm too tired to sit up at the table," she said, hanging her damp apron on a hook near the fire.

"Very well," I went to hug her. "Sleep well, Lily. I'll see you in the morning."

I put some chips on the fire and stirred it back to life, then I sat alone at the table, listening to the crackling of the burning wood and warming myself. Just as I was about to pour the tea into my white cup, there was a scratching at the crackway.

"I don't believe I ever had a cup of tea from top to bottom without interruption and I probably never will," I said to myself as I scurried over to the entryway.

"It's Wendy," Chesterfield said, as I poked my head out of the hole.

"Is she all right?" I asked.

"She won't talk to me about it, she just said 'Please Ches, bring Mrs. Chubbly—she promised to come if I needed her.' and I promised I would fetch you right away. So, here I am."

He lay down low and whipped his tail around in my direction.

"A promise is a promise. Unfortunately I never think about how exhausted I might be when the time comes to keep the promise," I said as I dashed up his tail and sat down sideways on his back just behind his head, "I can't imagine what could be troubling the child. Since we've been back from Sussex, I thought the Lovely family was just fine. Annabelle's been working in the garden again, Edmund's been taking them all on weekend outings."

"I don't know," Chesterfield answered thoughtfully, "Since we've been back, Annabelle spends all of her time with Wendy and Edmund—I haven't had a good scratching in months, she hardly notices me anymore, much less talks to me. All for the best, I suppose."

I held tight to his thick fur as he trotted up the stairs and came to a jolting stop on the landing.

"I'll let you off here," he said, flattening himself to the floor just outside Wendy's bedroom door. It was open just a crack and I walked right in.

"Mrs. Chubbly! You came!" Wendy exclaimed, jumping down from the bed and scooping me up in her warm hand. She raised me up to her face.

"Of course I came, I always come when you ask me to," I said, smiling.

"I know you do, but I suppose I was feeling afraid that this time you wouldn't. It's so late."

Wendy placed me on her pillow, then she lay down with her face near mine.

"It is very late. Can't you sleep?" I asked, stroking her hair with my paw.

"No, no I can't. I'm very worried about Mother," she whispered.

"But why? Your mother seems to be doing so well. I saw her going out to work in the garden many times before the snow came. You told me yourself, she's even begun sewing again," I said.

"Something is happening—I'm afraid she's getting sick again." She said looking at me with large sad eyes.

"What makes you think so?"

"When we first came home—she would get up early in the morning and eat breakfast with Father and me, before my tutor arrived. She would even make lunch herself and we would eat together in the schoolroom. I would tell her about my lessons and she would really listen to me." She stopped talking and looked to me for reassurance.

"Go on, dear," I nodded.

"She was reading me bedtime stories, every night— tucking me in and kissing me, and she looked so healthy, so happy." She finished, silent tears wetting her cheeks.

"Wendy, why are you crying?" I asked, wiping a tear from her cheek.

"She's been keeping to her room again. Sleeping late in the morning—having Mrs. Hammond bring a tray up to her room—and only tea and toast! She leaves the dinner table suddenly with a horrible look on her face—as if she is going to be ill, she hardly eats anything at all." Wendy's voice began growing more and more agitated.

"When Father takes us to Kensington Gardens, and I go off to play, the two of them will be sitting there talking—and she'll suddenly burst into tears, and most of the time she's still smiling—even when she's crying! She's acting so strange. She's even stopped reading to me at night, and that was our special time together. Now, when I ask her to read me a story, she says she's just too tired right now."

I listened attentively to Wendy's words, but even as I listened, my years as a midwife and healer had me automatically categorizing Annabelle Lovely's symptoms. "Wendy, Does she still seem happy when she sees you? Does she still hold you and kiss you?—and how is she with Edmund? Is she still affectionate?" I asked her.

"Yes—yes to all of that—but she's acting strangely again. I'm afraid she's going to go back to keeping to her room— I'm afraid it will get worse and worse, and then it will be like it was before the cure!" she said, crying now. I brushed her hair away from her eyes and touched her cheek gently.

"It's going to be all right. Listen to me, dear child. Everything is going to be fine, in fact, things are going to get better than ever. From all you've told me, I believe your mother is going to have a baby."

She looked at me as if I had told her that brown cows give chocolate milk.

"A baby—but how is that possible? I've heard her tell Father for years that she could never have a another baby!"

"Wendy, I believe in her state of grief, what she really meant was she never wanted to have another baby—after what she had been through, losing your brother."

She thought about this for a moment, her brow furrowing into deep creases, and then her face lit up.

"A baby? Then I am going to be a big sister, like Weency," she said, delighted.

"Absolutely, my dear—and if my calculations are correct, your parents had their reunion in August, it seems your mother is having extreme morning sickness now, which means she should be having the baby around..." I stopped to count off the months in my head, "May. Early May."

"Wonderful, perhaps we'll have him on my birthday." she said, with a far away smile.

"Him? Do you think you'll have a brother?" I asked.

"I don't know why I said that. It would be nice to have a brother—it would be right, don't you think?"

"Yes, dear child, I do think it would be just right—but as long as your new baby is healthy. I'm sure The Great Creator will provide you and your family with just the right baby— whether it's a brother or a sister."

"I know." she said, yawning.

"Well, that was a nice yawn, maybe now you can rest easy."

"Bedtime!" Chesterfield broke in, cheerily, "Your carriage is waiting."

He was smiling and I knew he had spent his time with his ear pressed to Wendy's bedroom door.

"It's rather late, do you think you can sleep now?" I asked, standing to leave.

"No—I mean yes—Oh, I'm just too excited to sleep!" she said, picking me up in her hand. "Thank you, Mrs. Chubbly. I'll come to visit the nest and let you know."

"Yes, do come. Weency's been missing you—and we haven't seen much of you these last few months."

"I will, I'll come tomorrow. Good night Mrs. Chubbly." Then she kissed me and placed me carefully on Chesterfield's back. I'm sure she went right to sleep.

"So, you were listening again," I scolded, as we arrived at the nest. "Why don't you just come in next time," I said as I climbed down off his back.

"It is wonderful news, isn't it. Perhaps I will come in next time, but only if I'm invited—I may press my ear against the door now and then, but I'm not rude enough to be an uninvited guest." he said, looking very prim.

"Hi Ches," Eency said, from the crackway.

"What are you doing up at this hour?" I asked him sharply, "It's way past your bedtime."

He rubbed at his tired eyes, then just stood there in his rumpled bedclothes, looking at me.

"Are you ill, Eence?" Chesterfield asked, looking him over, "You look terrible."

"I don't know—I just can't seem to get back to sleep," Eency said miserably. I took him by the paw.

"What a night! Come along young mouseling, I'll fix you some tea. Good night Chesterfield, see you tomorrow."

"Good night Mrs. Chubbly—good night Eence, you're in good paws. I'm sure whatever concoction she gives you will knock you out in a flash."

I walked Eency to the kitchen and got him a cup. The teapot was covered, thank goodness, and still hot. I filled my white cup, then the red clay cup for Eency.

He straddled a stool, his face in his paws, looking very tired and miserable indeed.

"What's disturbing you Eency? What's keeping you awake so late?"

"I fell asleep for a bit, earlier—and then I had a horrible dream. I can't remember it exactly—just bits and pieces," he said, blowing on his tea.

"What do you remember of it?" I asked.

"I was in a big dark room, surrounded by machines that looked like wild beasts made of metal. I felt sick and aching inside like there was no one to turn to, like I was alone in the world—trapped in this huge dark room."

He closed his eyes trying to bring back the dream, grasping at the pictures that floated through his foggy mind.

"I called out to you—nothing. I called out to Weency—my voice echoed back to me. No one answered."

He looked frightened as he spoke, but he wouldn't cry. I saw him holding it back. I heard it in his voice, tight and choked as he went on.

"Then I was crying—scared. The room was so cold, I felt the wind blowing on me—howling. I was shivering and crying, it seemed like I was crying forever."

As he spoke I remembered Crystal's silence about his future—and I thought about Weency and me talking in the kitchen at night, about her training, about her studying with Uncle Mak. Had he overheard us? Had she told him? But they were twins, most times words weren't necessary.

"You know how sometimes in a dream you're in one place and then you're someplace else? Well, I think that's what happened—because I was crying in the dark room with my face in my paws and when I looked up—I was sitting in a cave. I was sitting at the edge of a stream of water, running right out of the floor of the cave—it was so clear and it was bubbling up high, out of a hole in the rock floor. It sounded like it was singing! It was just beautiful—and the smell!" He closed his eyes and breathed deep. "The cave smelled wonderful—like the moss and the wet earth by Babble Creek, like newborn mousekins. In a way," he said tenderly, "It smelled like Mother."

"How wonderful for you," I commented, thinking of my dreams of Tailbit—how real they are, the senses come alive and everything is more real than reality itself.

"I knew it was a magical place—all my sadness was gone and I was filled with such an incredible feeling of being alive—bursting with life. Outside the cave, I heard voices, laughing. It sounded like you and Weency, and others. There were other voices, talking and laughing. Then I reached to touch the sparkling water and there was a flash of light. I found myself in the cold dark room, again—the wind was blowing through a long black curtain hanging on the wall. I went running toward it, trying to get through it—but the wind was whipping it at me. I was yelling 'Weency! Weency—wait for me!' and I heard her voice from far away calling back to me 'Time waits for no creature, Eency. You must be ready—be ready'. Then I woke up crying out. I went to your room and you were gone."

I finished my tea and refilled our empty cups. Eency gulped the warm tea down; he drank as if the tea would make his bad feelings go away.

"I'm here now, Eency. You must have been frightened to find my bed empty in the middle of the night. I'm sorry I had to leave without telling you." I touched his paw.

"What does it all mean, Mrs. Chubbly?" he asked, "Is it a true dream? I feel as if something wonderful has been taken away from me—" he said, sadly.

"I'm not sure," I told him.

In my heart I understood the dream clearly. But Crystal was right. There are some things best left unsaid. "It sounds as if it was a true dream—a glimpse of the future." Eency looked perplexed.

"True? Like that's what is going to happen to me? It doesn't look promising..." His voice trailed off.

"Eency, it was just a glimpse, like looking at the tail of a cat and thinking that you know what the whole cat must look like. You can't tell anything really just from the tail. That dream was part truth mixed with a large dose of your greatest fears. The future has a way of working itself out nicely. The pieces of the puzzle will fall into their proper places—have a little faith, Eency." He looked into my eyes, searching.

"You know something—don't you," he said, sure of it.

"I know that we are each given many opportunities, we take them - or not. I know that we are each cooperative components of this universe and partners with The Great Creator. I know that if we are open and listening and centered, that we are given a knowing, you might call it a sense about things to come.   And I know that everything is going to be fine... in time. But now it's time to sleep. Remember, tomorrow will take care of itself Eency, it always does, thank The Great Creator."

31. The Truth Revealed

The very next night, after the little ones were asleep, Weency and I sat in the kitchen going through the herbs in my medicine bag for the thousandth time.

"You must set up your own code. Although I learned the basis of mine from Uncle Mak, in time I had to find my own way, a system for remembering the hundreds of different combinations I created myself," I said, absently lining up the small cloth sacks on the table.

"Um hmmm," she nodded.

"Many of the simple herbs are colour-coded with Mak's colour ribbons, but the more complicated recipes I discovered in time, I've designated with several colours braided together." I picked up a sack of healing herbs and placed it into her paws opening the braided ribbon.

"This healing potion is comfrey leaf, calendula blossom and plantain leaf. The dark green ribbon shows the comfrey, the light green shows the plantain and the orange shows the calendula." I opened the pouch and placed it under her nose. "Smell. In time you'll be able to distinguish the ingredients just by smelling and tasting." I said, placing a pinch of the course green mixture on her tongue.

"Yes. I can taste it, but what happens if I get confused, if I use the wrong herb – make a terrible mistake?" She looked tired, struggling with herself to stay alert, to be thoughtful.

"Most herbs are healing and gentle, very few of the plant medicines you'll be working with for the first year are toxic enough to cause damage. Of course, you must always start your work in meditation and connection with the Great Spirit. Great Spirit will always guide your paw, you can trust that ultimate truth. Healers are vessels of light – channels connected to The Great Creator of All. You are never alone and always guided. You know the feeling you get when you are sitting and meditating and you feel your connection with Spirit and with all things?" I looked into Weency's eyes to see if she was getting this fully.

"Yes Mrs. Chubbly- it's my favorite feeling—of being safely held in the arms of something so big. And I feel part of all things and all creatures. Then I just understand and know whatever I need to know," she finished, softly.

"Precisely!" I said. "There are no mistakes – only events which awaken us to our highest selves, one lesson after another."

We were both tired, and I knew we were cramming, but we had so little time and Weency was already eleven years—she had quite a bit of catching up to do.

"Now, what kind of tea would you make for us, to refresh us, so we may continue our studies?" I asked. Before Weency could answer, we heard a soft knocking at the entryhole.

"Wendy!" Weency shouted, glad to be pulled away from her studies at last. She knew I was relentless, and would keep her at it until her eyes began to close and she could no longer fight sleep.

"Yes, it sounds like Wendy. Answer the question, then we'll stop and go visit with her together."

"Energy," she said aloud, "Ummm. Anise seed, ginger root, and ginseng root—in combination or any one of these alone, ground into a fine powder and steeped in boiling water for five minutes. Can we go now?" she asked, impatiently.

"Perfect answer, Weency, but don't forget Indian tea, the active ingredient is caffeine, a very powerful stimulant when one is tired and a sedative when one is agitated, also a good painkiller. " I told her as I placed each sack carefully in my ratskin bag.

"Please, Mrs. Chubbly, my head hurts."

"Peppermint, brewed double strength, wonderful for headaches." I said smiling.

"Mrs. Chubbly!" Weency exclaimed, exasperated.

"Enough, enough—let's go see Wendy, I think she has some good news for us."

Together we hurried to the crackway and when I poked my head out I was surprised to see Chesterfield Cat sitting beside Wendy. They rarely visited together, for Wendy came only in the night and Chesterfield almost always refused to give up sleep for anything. He had grown fat and lazy in the last few months—with no mice to chase, and Wendy secretly tending to all our needs.

"Mrs. Chubbly, you were right!" Wendy said, dropping flat down on the hall rug with her face close to mine.

"About what?" Weency asked, forgetting how tired she had been a moment before. Chesterfield butted right in.

"About the baby, of course," He said as if it was already common knowledge in the nest.

"Chessie, I wanted to tell, that's why I wanted us all to be here together. Where are Eency and the others?" Wendy asked me.

"It's very late, dear. They're all sleeping." I told her.

"Yes, and I was sleeping too. Having a marvelous dream." Chesterfield stifled a yawn with his paw, "I was just about to drop out of a tree onto Mrs. Feniwig's schnauzer, when you woke me," he added, rubbing the sleep from his eyes.

"I talked to Mother this morning. As soon as I got up I went straight to her room, and there she was looking very green. So I asked her what the matter was and she seemed afraid to tell me," Wendy brought her voice back down to a whisper. "So I told her, Mother I am not a baby anymore. You've got to stop hiding things from me, we don't need to have any secrets from each other. After all, we are a family."

"Brave, Wendy. That was wonderful," I told her.

"So? What ever did she say to that?" Weency asked.

"Well, I was sitting on her bed, and first she took my face into her hands and looked at me for a long time. Then she began crying terribly saying, 'You're right, you're right—you're not a baby anymore'," Wendy told us mimicking her mother's teary voice perfectly. "Then she looked very brave and said, 'Wendy—we are going to have a baby.' I said, 'That's wonderful

Mother', then she said 'I'm so relieved you're happy, I was worried that you'd be upset.' then I gave her a nice reassuring hug and said 'Mother, I'm delighted we're going to have a baby—that's just the medicine you need.' And then she looked at me strangely and said 'Dear me, you have grown up.'" Wendy looked at me proudly, "So that's the news—I'm going to be a big sister. And Mrs. Chubbly, you were even right about May— Mother said, Doctor Hartley says the baby will come end of May, but Mother said that Doctors are always off, and only the mother herself can tell for certain. Mother says first week of May—I do hope she has the baby on my birthday. Wouldn't that be perfect!"

"Perfect!" Weency chimed in. "That's when Angel and Lance are going to have their mousekins."

"Perfect!" Wendy said again.

"Speaking of perfect—how is Lacey Chesterfield doing these days, I haven't seen my little mousekin since August." Chesterfield asked, acting the proud father as always.

"Your little mousekin is scurrying about like the nest's on fire and chattering incessantly. I'm sure she'd love to see you," I told him, "Whenever she hears you scratching at the entryhole, she shouts, 'Chessie, Chessie!' and it's all we can do to keep her from running right out into the hall!" He puffed up right away and smiled his most lovely smile.

"I knew she'd be sharp as a pin—after all—she does have my name."

"Careful, Chessie—pride cometh before," Wendy started,

"Pride cometh before a new litter—perhaps Angel will have a black and white male and name him Chesterfield—that would be perfectly fine for a human baby as well, you know—you might want to suggest that," he told Wendy seriously

We all broke into laughter, just looking at him all puffed up so.

"Well, on that fine note—I'm off to bed. Thank you for letting me take part in the good news and for serving as the night's entertainment. Now, I've got a Schnauzer to finish off," he said as he slunk down the hallway toward the fireplace.

"Sometimes I think he'll puff up too large and explode," Weency said, and then the two of them were laughing wildly again.

"He certainly is a charmer, even when he's being silly," I added, thinking how close Chesterfield and I had grown during the short year I had been at the nest. "I never thought I could love a cat, I'll certainly miss him," I said aloud, feeling wistful, as we do when we know in our hearts what the future will bring—even before we know it in our heads.

"Miss him? Why? Where are you going, Mrs. Chubbly?" Wendy asked, looking surprised. Weency turned to me and watched my face without speaking. She had learned a lot in the past five months, and she knew when to be silent, to watch and wait before she spoke too soon.

"It's all right, Wendy—I'm not going anywhere just yet. I meant eventually—when I must move on—and one must always move on at some point in time. When that time comes, I shall miss him very much. And I shall miss you too." I said tenderly, looking into Wendy's eyes. "You've taught me a great lesson about prejudice and closed-mindedness. And reminded me that we are one. You've reaffirmed my belief that there are good creatures in every species, no matter what a group may do as a whole—we must never judge or jump to conclusions. If we remain open minded, and open hearted—we will all have more love in our lives than we can ever imagine. The love of a cat? The love of a human? It doesn't matter does it, for there are no degrees of love. Love is the one thing that is unchanging—the one thing that can cross all barriers, all boundaries.—For when it truly is love, undiluted by fear or gain, not seeking to be loved in return, just plain love for the sake of love itself, it's perfectly understandable in any language—and it does the same great good when it fills your heart," I told her.

"Oh, Mrs. Chubbly—you're frightening me, you do sound as if you are going. Please don't leave—who will help me with the new baby? And the mousekins? And who will I come to talk to, when I just don't understand anything, and I'm frightened and confused? Like now."

Then Wendy was crying, and Weency just looked at me, waiting and watching. "And besides all that," she said through her tears, "I love you, Mrs. Chubbly!"

"Dear, dear Wendy, I love you too, very much, dear child. You know, sometimes when you love someone you must let them go, perhaps to go on to do some greater good. But when you love someone truly, they become a part of you, they live on in a special place in your heart. If you close your eyes, I know you can see your mother standing on the porch, smiling as she was on that day she first took you in her arms and held you and loved you openly. Though she's not beside you, you have her there inside you. And when I'm gone, I will see your face shining at me, whenever I need to be near you. I'll just close my eyes, and there you will be, and the truth is—we will never be far apart and we will never be apart forever. When you love someone, there will always come a time when you will be with them again. The Great Creator wouldn't have it any other way."

"It just wouldn't be fair, would it?" she asked, pensively.

"No, of course not—it just wouldn't be fair," I answered.

"All right then, I will always have you here." she said, touching her heart, "And you will always be sitting on my pillow, like the night we first met, sitting beside me," she said, closing her eyes, "stroking my face with your soft furry paw," she said.

"Trust me, Wendy, it will really be alright, everything will. And if you ever feel doubtful, remember, we are all in the powerful hands of our Great Creator. Rest safe in the knowledge that The Great Creator will provide for the mouselings and The Great Creator will take good care of your new baby. If you meditate silently on what troubles your heart, The Great Creator will fill your heart with the answer. You only need to practice listening to that voice within, trust it, then follow it steadfastly."

We parted sadly, all of us disturbed by my words about leaving. Though I scarcely knew what I had said, I knew the time would soon be upon me to move on- after the baby came, after the litter was born, and Angel was well and strong again. There were many things I knew I had to do and one of them was to go home. I felt the Apple Tree Nest calling me, Babble Creek crying out to me, the wind across the heather covered downs whispering 'come home' and I knew that I had to bring Weency home to Uncle Mac. It was time for the next part of her training to begin in earnest . There was nothing else that could be done, it had to be, and when I looked into her bright eyes, I knew she knew it too.

32. The Terrible Argument

Weency woke with a start. The nursery was pitch dark and she could barely make out the sleeping figures of Mop and Mousekin Lacey in their trundle bed. She thought for a moment about going back to sleep, about willing herself back into the marvelous dream, but she felt such an urgency to share it.

She turned back to Eency, asleep next to her and shook him gently.

"Wake up Eence. Wake up!" she whispered, trying not to disturb the little ones. She had shared everything with him as long as she could remember, and even though he had been quite grumpy and standoffish since they returned from the reunion, her heart had to share with her twin.

"What? What is it?" he asked, groggily pulling the bedclothes up around his chin. "It's still dark—I'm sleepy," his voice drifted.

"I dreamt I was a midwife," Weency whispered, containing her excitement. "I was assisting Angel—helping her birth her mousekins. Eency? Are you listening?" she asked, agitated.

"Wait—what did you say?" he asked, coming back up out of a heavy sleep. He pulled himself up and supported his head with his paw.

"I said, I was helping Angel birth her mousekins. It was wonderful! I knew exactly what to do and Mrs. Chubbly was smiling at me, nodding her approval as I caught each mousekin. She had two sets of twins, two females with golden fur like Lance, and two males—white and silver like Angel. They were so tiny and so beautiful."

"Weency, it was just a dream." Eency stated flatly, annoyed at being woken up suddenly, in the middle of the night.

"No Eency, this felt different. It was so—real. I'm sure it was a true dream, a vision," she said, disappointed that her twin wasn't sharing her joy.

Eency thought about his cave dream and felt embarrassed at how harshly he was disregarding his sister's feelings.

Lately he had been dreaming every night. For the past five months, since the night he dreamed about the magical water flowing from the cave, he'd had odd and confusing dreams, each with a hint of something to come, or so it seemed. Shocking and revealing dreams about the future filled his nights. Crystalline, sharp-edged dreams, so real they had to be true. And now he brushed aside Weency's dream as nonsense. But Weency was so busy with Mrs. Chubbly since they returned from the reunion, they never had time for him anymore, so he kept his dreams to himself. He felt a festering anger at his twin that he never felt before, and although his heart wanted desperately to heal it, to reconnect with his best friend, something in him kept shutting down and pulling away into a deep dark protective coldness.

"Well, maybe it was a true dream, but do you really think that because of some dream you're going to be midwife to Angel?" he asked. His voice had an ugly edge to it that Weency had never heard before.

"No, Eency. I don't think that at all. Besides, dreams aren't like that," she answered softly, trying to draw him into a kinder mood. "Some of it was true, I'm sure, and some of it was wishful thinking, mixed pictures of the truth and some fantasies about what I want."

"You've gotten so smart about dreams! About everything!" he shouted, his voice rising with disturbing passion.

"Hush! You're going to wake Lily and the mousekins!" she whispered loudly. She looked over at Lily's bed and saw it was empty, but the mousekins were indeed beginning to fuss from the noise. And she wondered where the elder could be at this late hour.

"You're so smart, Sister, I'm sure you'll figure out what to do about that too!" he yelled just as loudly, "It's no wonder you never talk to me anymore. I guess you've just gotten too smart to talk to anymouse except Mrs. Chubbly." He spat the name at her with a crooked sneer.

Weency's lip quivered. She sat in shocked silence trying hard not to cry. Eency had never, ever, behaved this way before.

He watched her. He heard her breathing change in the darkness, and knew his words had shocked her, hurt her. Instead of ending his raving, Weency's reaction only served to make him feel guilty and miserable. He knew he was being wretched and ugly, but he was fueled by the dark feelings and in a strange way it made him feel better to treat his twin in such a nasty manner, to pour out his anger upon her.

"Sure, you don't have time for me anymore," he was shouting again and waving his arms about wildly now. Though it was too dark to see him, she could imagine his face contorted in anger, from the bitterness in his voice. "But you don't mind waking me up in the middle of the night to tell me some crazy dream about you! You're just selfish! You think of no creature but yourself! This whole new world you've discovered since Grand Matriarch Crystal revealed your exciting future is ALL about you!" He lay down hard on the very edge of his side of their large bed, and turned his back to his sister. Mop was sitting up whimpering in fear from all of Eency's yelling.

"Cat's Claws! Eency, you're terrifying Mop," She said, as she went to her sister. She tucked Mop back in and rubbed her headlock.

"Well, Weency, why don't you go wake up Mrs. Chubbly? I'm sure she'll listen to anything you have to say, even in the middle of the night!" Then he pulled up the cover with a violent tug, and was still.

"Mrs. Chubbly is already up," Lily's voice came from the entry hole of the nursery. Eency flushed red in the darkness, and wondered how long Lily had been listening to his fury. "Weency, Mrs. Chubbly asked me to come wake you. She'll be needing your help in the kitchen, with Angel." Then Lily turned and left as suddenly as she'd come.

Weency sat there, stunned. Angel must be having her litter, and she was frozen with anger. Her head was aching. Her throat was tight, and her face was hot and burning from holding back her tears. In eleven years, though she and her twin had sometimes disagreed, they never fought, not like this. Eency had never acted so cruel before.

She wanted to hit him, to scream at him angrily and shake him hard till he came to his senses. She felt him there in the darkness, cold and seething with his own self-loathing.

A soft grey light sifted through the nursery window. She heard the trill of a morning lark far away in some distant happier place. As the sky lightened, she tucked the covers higher on the sleeping mousekins and walked back to her own bed.

She looked at her twin, lying there in brooding silence, in the bed they had shared for eleven years. They were born here, in this bed. Inseparable. Never apart. Even at opposite ends of the nest, she could sense his thoughts, feel his feelings.

She thought about Angel, getting ready to bring forth new life. How wonderful it had been when Lacey was born. She and Eence had worked together, helping Mrs. Chubbly, soothing Angel, and then watching in awe and great joy as the tiny white mousekin finally took her first breath. Why was he so furious, so unlike himself? Didn't he know how much they all loved him?

Weency took a long slow deep breath, as she did when she sat in meditation with Mrs. Chubbly. When she exhaled for the third time, she felt her anger rushing out of her. Out with the bad air and the bad feelings, she thought to herself. She repeated this exercise twice more. Stay open and relaxed, she told herself. My emotions can keep me from seeing things clearly, she repeated to herself, as Mrs. Chubbly had taught her.

Her body did feel open. She breathed again, calming herself for she had to be centered at the birth. When she exhaled, she shuddered hard, felt empty and still, and then filled with a white light. She felt it seeping into every part and every cell of her being, filling her with a healing peace. And she heard a familiar soothing voice that seemed to emanate from within her heart, say "All is unfolding as it should, Precious One. You are all held in the same arms."

She looked over at Eency, beneath the bedcovers, and thought she saw his back heave as if he were crying silently. Then she was filled with the magnitude of his pain. She knew she would soon be leaving. He must know it too and her heart went out to him.

"Eence," she whispered softly, reaching out to touch his shoulder. He flicked her paw away, tightly. She reached out and touched him again.

"Eency, I love you – I love you so much. Please come, we should all be together." She implored.

"Just leave me alone."

—THE LAST LETTER HOME—

June 8th, 1905

Dear uncle Mak and aunt Bibi,

I received your letter and it filled me with boundless joy!

Our bags are packed and ready. Weency and I will be leaving here in the morning before sunrise. She and I are delighted, but all the others in the Chelsea Nest and the Chelsea house are mourning us, as if we were dead and buried.

Angel's four new mousekins will be monthlings this week. Both sets of twins are doing well—fat and happy, hungry all of the time. Grandmother Lily is in her glory and has assumed her natural place as wet nurse, so Angel can catch her breath between feedings.

Chesterfield Cat can't do enough for them—of course he's especially fond of Chesterfield mousekin jr.

Mr. And Mrs. Lovely had a healthy baby boy—James George lovely—Annabelle named him for her father, needless to say the lovely family is happier than ever before. Providence had all of the new creatures born on the same day—May 8th.

Angel struts about, glowing. She's a natural mother. Tell Curly she should be glad she's not here to watch Lancelot. Lance is insufferable. He is so full of his accomplishment—he sincerely believes he's the first mouse in the history of rodents, to sire such a beautiful, intelligent litter!

Weency has been sketching and we'll bring along some pictures of everycreature.

I'm certain you'll receive this letter long before we arrive. I am taking Weency on an herb gathering tour of the countryside, so we'll be on foot all the way to Babble Creek.

I pray The Great Creator will make our lessons easy, and painless on the way down. I'm sure Weency's heart will be heavy—leaving her twin behind for the very first time.

I've informed Clatter Woodpecker of our intended route and he has promised mail delivery, so we shall be able to correspond during the journey.

I would be ever so grateful if you would ask papa woody to build a second desk for my study, as i will be sharing it with Weency.

I have already spoken with Wendy regarding her bringing the entire nesthold down for a visit, and she was delighted to be able to help. I do believe we should wait until the new mousekins are yearlings—so, we may all look forward to a visit—next summer.

I can't begin to express how difficult it is for me to leave the Chelsea Nest. Eency, Angel and Lance, Lily and all of the mousekins—and strangely, most of all, Chesterfield Cat. My sadness is balanced by the joy I feel when I think that I'm finally coming home after all these many years away. And I find enormous satisfaction that not only will I be in the bosom of my family—but at long last I have found a true apprentice to The Great Healing Arts. The calling burns within Weency's breast. She soaks up her lessons like a parched sponge. I know, Uncle Mak, you will be rejuvenated by her endless enthusiasm and startling intelligence.

And now, I must go and say these most difficult farewells. I love you all and know that I will be sustained by your love—as each step of this arduous journey brings me closer to my heart nest. Then I shall indeed unpack my bag, at last.

With great longing,

Lacey

33. Until We Meet Again

Lily assured me repeatedly that she had matters well in paw, and everycreature would be loved and cared for.

Angel was in perfect health and all the new mousekins were growing more beautiful with each passing day. The only creature I felt true concern for, was Eency... but I knew what had to be and I knew it would be kill or cure. I was hoping The Great Creator would speedily provide the appropriate reunion for Eency and his twin sister, but of course the matter was out of my paws.

One never knows what painful events in our past can shape us into the amazing creatures we are to become. And as I am fond of saying, "There is no event that is not awakening us to our highest self." When The Great Creator took a knife to Eency—to reshape him into a jewel, what could anycreature do but stand by, silent and wait for Eency's day of enlightenment. Then he would be shaped to perfection and ready to take his proper place in the grand adventure to come.

Eency was cool in manner when I hugged him goodbye for the last time, and Weency was with him now—trying desperately to reach his heart, to get past his anger—one last time before she had to leave him. But that was not to be. He went off silently, somewhere in the nest where he would not be found. Weency walked through the nest forlornly. She placed her bags in the wallway and sat down at the kitchen table one last time, looking over the familiar things of her mousekinhood. She looked at the white porcelain tub where she and her twin had been bathed lovingly by Mother Twingle. She saw it plainly, young twins splashing in the soap bubbles, as her mother laughed and splashed them gleefully, in the warm soapy bathwater. She saw Father Twingle placing the hot water stopper in the hole in the pipe and showing Mother how she could pull it out and have hot running water. Mother gasped in amazement and ran to him, throwing her arms around him. There was so much love and sweetness, now gone. She would take it all in. Remember every hand painted flower and every hand sewn leaf, every family meal and every story time in mother's lap, she told herself. She felt old. "I'm only eleven. But now I must be grown up. I have things to learn and the future is looming before me. It's time. I just thought Eency would always be right here by my side." She whispered aloud. Then she took a long deep sad breath, and let herself feel the depth of the sadness in her heart as she let it go, knowing it was time to surrender to something bigger than herself. And so she did.

My bags were packed and sitting in the hallway. I walked slowly around the Twingle's nest, one last time, absorbing every detail, committing it to memory with great intention. In a brief time I had come to love this wonderful nest dearly. If a time ever came when I could no longer go to Babble Creek, in my heart I knew I would be happy in the Chelsea Nest. After many years of being here and being there, and always moving on, it was the first place, the first family that truly worked its way into my bones and I was dreadfully sorry to leave it behind.

I walked to the crackway, and before I stepped out, I straightened my cap and apron, and placed my black bag and my trusty cane against the wall, just inside the hole.

"Is it you, Mrs. Chubbly?" Chesterfield asked.

"Yes, Chesterfield," I said, stepping into the dark hallway. "It is I." I looked down at my feet and noticed his grey felt catnip mouse and a wave of nostalgia overcame me as I sat down upon it.

"For old times sake," he whispered, coming close to me.

"Yes, Chesterfield," I agreed, looking up into the beautiful green eyes of my dear friend.

"There's so much I haven't said," his voice broke, "I don't know how to say goodbye, Mrs. Chubbly."

"Let us not, then, Chesterfield. I've said far too many goodbyes in my lifetime."

We sat quietly for some time. It was well before sunrise and the summer night was warm and silent. The only sounds we could hear came from beyond the wall. Hungry mousekins cried out for their four o'clock feeding, and elders scurried to reach them. Chesterfield cocked his head and listened to his little ones. A sweet glow filled his eyes.

"This is the hardest one, Chesterfield. All those new lives beginning," I said sadly, "There's so much I will be missing, my friend."

"But, I'm here, Mrs. Chubbly, I'll be your eyes and ears, a surrogate nanny!" he said, trying hard to sound chipper. "I'll memorize every first word, every first step, all the trouble they get into. Every hair in their furry headlocks, and when you return," he stopped and looked at me. I had to turn away.

"But, you are coming back, aren't you Mrs. Chubbly?" His voice sounding desperate with fear.

"Oh, Chesterfield—I wish I could say. I can't predict the future. Weency and I have a formidable task before us." I said, sighing. Heartache, I thought. Every goodbye is a splinter of glass piercing my heart.

"I see," he said, icily.

"Chesterfield Cat, don't you dare do that!" I said softly. He was so wounded. When I saw the sadness in his eyes, I felt my heart would break.

"Mrs. Chubbly, you've been a mother to me, a friend—everything! My teacher, my sister..." The tears began to pour from his eyes. I touched his warm nose very gently.

"Chesterfield Cat, you have been all of those things to me, as well. I love you dearly, Chesterfield, dearly."

"How can you go?" he cried. "What will become of us without you?" I had to laugh at this.

"Chesterfield, it is you, who has carried the burden of our care for all these many months. You, who rescued us over and over, and dragged us out of harm's way like a guardian angel, more times than I can count. You're wonderful, Chesterfield. You're a hero, filled with love and courage." Then I kissed his pink nose and he began purring a long loud satisfied purr. "You just needed some creature to remind you," I said looking up at him earnestly. "So, if you believe that I've been running our universe, then I believe I'm leaving it in good paws. And you and I both know we are in the arms of The Great Creator."

He smiled his most charming smile at me, and his green eyes flashed.

"I love you, Mrs. Chubbly. Imagine that. Me, loving a mouse."

"Imagine loving a pile of mice. Obviously, you do." And we both laughed.

"I don't want to even think about how much I'm going to miss you," he said softly.

"You know Chesterfield, I believe this universe is woven together quite neatly—there's not a thread out of place, and we are all woven into this magical fabric. We are always connected." He looked at me quizzically. "Can't you feel it? If you let go of all your fears for just a moment, don't you see it? Of course we'll be together again, it's woven into the fabric of things. Mrs. Chubbly and Chesterfield Cat, it's just a matter of time." I said, reassuring him. "Someday, somewhere, we'll be together again and just think of the stories we shall tell each other when next we meet!"

"Oh yes, I brought you something!" He turned around and picked something up in his mouth, then delicately laid it down in my lap.

"It's a book of sorts," he said. "A going-away present."

It was an amazing book. The cover seemed to be made of thick paper that smelled of birch trees, and so were the pages. I opened it gently, as it was very old and in fragile condition. My eyes ran over the strange drawings and symbols on every page as I turned them, searching for something recognizable. I had the strangest feeling that I had seen this book before, though I believed that I hadn't. Like a language that I once knew as a child, and had forgotten long ago. There was something that I felt when I held it in my paws and opened it, something familiar. And although I didn't understand any of the symbols, or language in the book, it somehow felt like it was mine. So odd. Like when you find an old journal that you wrote in when you were very young, and tucked it away on the back of an old bookshelf to be forgotten, and then discovered it years later when you grew up, and it was like a different creature had written it. Something in me thought, "I know this book- and it's important."

"I know how fond you are of books."

"Thank you, Chesterfield, it's quite fantastic. Wherever did you find it?" I asked

"In the wine cellar—I dug out an old nest while chasing some pack rats. It looked like a mouse's nest, very civilized, much too tidy for a rat. What does it say?" he asked, craning to look at the open pages.

"I really don't know. It seems to be in another language. I'm sure Bibi will be able to decipher it."

I closed the ancient book, felt a kind of strange electric current vibrating through the book into my paw, and I slipped it carefully into the pocket of my apron. I will attend to this later with Aunt Bibi. Then I stood up.

Chesterfield rose and extended his paw, graciously. I looked at him for a moment and smiled, "Very nice, Chesterfield—but that's for acquaintances," then I pushed his paw aside and threw my arms around his furry neck, hugging him tightly.

"Don't say goodbye, Chesterfield. Goodbye is too permanent. Fare thee well, my dear friend. Until we meet again."

END

About The Author

Cindy Le Bow has written fiction, non-fiction, screenplays and Comic Books in the 1980's including Vampirella, Creepy, Eerie and Popeye. She studied Theatre at NYU, and performed Musical comedy on tour in the US and Canada. She is the mother of 6 extraordinary, talented Adults who were home educated. She mostly taught them to follow their hearts and to love life, everything else they learned on their own. She was born and raised in New York City and currently lives on a remote mountaintop farm in Northern Alabama, where she writes amazing tales, teaches writing workshops, grows Organic Vegetables and Healing Herbs, and creates stories for her grandchildren.

Books in this Series:

The Secret Tales of Mrs. Chubbly is a trilogy in 4 parts:

Book 1, "The Secret Tales of Mrs. Chubbly " introduces our characters at their home and nest in Chelsea, England, and reveals the secrets that will make you part of the Greatest Adventure of Creature Kind! There is birth and death, and grief and tragedy and falling in love! How do we hold the beauty of our innocence sacred while we grow into our true wisdom and personal power? Will Crystal Seer's prophecy come true? Or will all be lost? Only Mrs. Chubbly and our brave mice know the answer.

Book 2, "The Ten Year Journey"

Book 3, "The Flying Machine"

Book 4, "The Spring of Life"

Follow us at: Mrschubbly.com to find out more!